CYPHER

Robert Thomas

HATCHBACK Publishing LLC
Genesee, MI 48437

Cypher
©2018 Robert Thomas

HATCHBACK Publishing, LLC.
P.O. Box 494
Genesee, Michigan 48437
Since 2005
www.hatchbackpublishing.com

ISBN: 978-1-948708-30-2
11 10 9 8 7 6 5 4 3 2
Second Edition
Printed in the United States of America

First Printed Edition 2016
Page Publishing Inc.
ISBN 978-1-68348-920-7 (Paperback)
ISBN 978-1-68348-921-4 (Digital)

For Worldwide Distribution
Printed in the United States of America

CONTENT

CHAPTER 1

Losing My Hero

It was an early Monday morning. Sara was always the first to wake up. She got things prepared for her family before waking them up to get ready for their day. She always got the coffee pot going before waking up her husband, Mark. Sara was a beautiful, thin, natural blonde. She had long, flowing hair and a great smile, with muscular legs that were perfect for high heels. Her sweet, soft voice was always comforting. Sara often would lay out by the pool out back, giving her a gorgeous, golden tan that complimented her look. Mark was a strong medium sized man with dark hair and a sexy voice that made listening to him even more interesting.

It's no wonder Johnnie was a nice looking boy. The older ladies always liked to talk about how cute he was which always made him feel uncomfortable and usually embarrassed.

It was time for Sara to wake up Mark, so she walked into the bedroom.

"Honey, wake up. You're going to be late for work."

Mark, waking up slowly, opened his eyes and groggily asked, "Already? I feel like I barely slept."

"You're going to be late for work if you don't get up. You've been working so much and I know you're exhausted. I wish you didn't work every weekend," responded Sara.

Mark, was trying to focus on Sara, squinting his eyes to get a better look at her. "Bills don't pay themselves, honey."

Sara looked lovingly at him. "Well, I guess you better get up then. Oh, and wake up Johnnie also."

Mark stretched his body, groaning as he got up. "Okay, dear." Walking over to the stairs, Mark yelled up to Johnnie, "Johnnie! Wake up, son. It's time to get ready for school."

"I'm getting up, Dad." *I hate getting up for school. What shall I wear today?*

After getting dressed, Johnnie ran downstairs and joined his parents for breakfast.

"Hmm, pancakes are my favorite," said Johnnie with his mouth full. "Dad, are we going to watch the ball game later?" He was excited.

Mark looked at him with hope. "I will try, son, it all depends when I get home from work."

Johnnie grimaced shaking his head. "Work, work, work, you always say that, Dad."

"I'm sorry, son, I will do my best to be here. Okay, honey. I am off to work." He kissed Sara

6

goodbye as he got his things together.

"I love you, honey." Sara held him tightly as they kissed.

"I love you too, honey, see you when you get home. See you tonight, son, I love you." Mark said, looking back at Johnnie.

"I love you too, Dad."

"Mark, be careful at work," Sara whispered as she grabbed him hard and hugged him again as he went to the door. Her eyes were full of worries as she lovingly looked deep into his eyes.

"I will, honey," Mark said, smiling to ease her worry. He always downplayed how dangerous his job really was knowing how much Sara worried about him.

Turning her attention to Johnnie as Mark left, she forced her worry aside. "Hurry up, Johnnie, or you will miss the bus."

Johnnie finished his last pancake and being rushed, he ran up the stairs fast to finish getting ready for school.

"Johnnie, Johnnie! You need to get to the bus stop!" Sara yelled up the stairs to her son. Johnnie flew down the stairs, trying to get to the door.

"Bye, Mom," he shouted as he tried to dash past her. Sara slowed him down.

"Wait! Where is my kiss, young man?"

"Mom!" shouted Johnnie, "I am too big for kisses now," explained Johnnie to no avail as Sara grabbed him.

"At least give me a hug, young man," she said sneaking a kiss on Johnnie's cheek before he could get away.

Johnnie hugged Sara. "I love you, Mom."

Sara smiled as she responded, "I love you too, Johnnie. Be good at school.

"I will, Mom!" Johnnie shouted as he ran to the bus stop making it in time before it left. He got on the bus and looked around to find someone to sit next to.

"Hey, Johnnie, sit next to me!" George, Johnnie's friend, shouted as he entered the bus.

"Hi, George."

"Dude, you want to come over after school?" George asked.

"I can't today. I'm going to watch the game with my dad," Johnnie said hopefully. "It's a big game for the Yankees."

"Oh, you and your baseball," George responded.

*****

On his way to work, Mark got a call from his boss on his cell phone.

"Hello."

"Mark, we have a situation at the old bridge. I need you there right away," said Tom, his boss.

"Is everything Okay?" Mark asked.

"Nothing you can't handle, but those guys need your help Mark."

"No problem, boss, I can go right there after I get my gear. Anyone going with me?"

"I don't have anyone I can spare, and I really hate sending you there as it is, but you're my best

8

worker, and they need your experience," explained Tom.

"Okay, boss, I am almost there."

When Mark pulled up at work, he went in to look for Tom.

"Hey, Tom, you got any paperwork for me?"

Tom handed Mark some papers, "Go there and assist them in this project. These repairs are major."

Mark took the paperwork from Tom and headed for his locker. "Let me grab my gear, and I am on my way."

"Be careful, Mark, this bridge is old and is in very poor shape. I don't need anything happening to my best worker."

Mark laughed. "Nothing's gonna happen to me, boss. I will see you when I get back."

When Mark went into the locker room, Tony was in there sitting on the bench.
Mark sat down next to him.

"Good morning, Mark, ready to finish the basement repairs today?" asked Tony.

"No, I can't. Tom is sending me out to the old bridge to assist with some major repairs," Tom explained as he grabbed his gear and put it in his bag. He changed into his work outfit and put on his boots.

"Oh, well, looks like you got some serious work ahead of you then. Hey, no problem, man, just be careful out there."

"Thank you, Tony, looks like it's going to be a long day. I was hoping to get to watch the game with Johnnie. I hate missing these games with him.

I know he is gonna be disappointed."

"Hey, man, you're a great father, and Johnnie knows you love him. Shoot, bro, you work so hard to provide for them," Tony said, trying to reassure Mark.

"Yes, well, money isn't everything. I need more time with my family."

"Yeah, I hear ya', man, and you have a nice family, too."

Mark nodded in agreement as he looked at the clock. "Well, I better get going, see you later, Tony."

"Hey, don't forget these!" Tony shouted while throwing Mark his gloves. "And be careful out there."

"Thanks, man, you be careful also."

Driving to the site, Mark called Sara on his cell phone. "Hey, honey, looks like I might not get home in time for the game. They need me to go out and help with some major repairs on the old bridge."

"Mark, be careful, that old bridge is in bad shape." Sara held back the sound of worry in her voice.

"I will, honey. Can you let Johnnie know I will make it up to him?"

"Yes, I will explain to Johnnie when he gets home from school, but he is gonna be disappointed. He misses you, Mark"

"I know, honey. I'm very sorry. Baby, I have to go now, I am almost there to the job site. I love you, honey."

"I love you too, Mark," Sara said in a soft sweet

voice.

"See you when I get home, love."

"Bye, honey."

"Bye, my sweet love." Hanging up, Sara began to work on the laundry that was starting to pile up.

Pulling up to the job site, Mark hopped out of the truck and asked for the supervisor. "Hi, I am Mark. Tony sent me over here to help out, is your supervisor around?"

"Hi, Mark, I'm Richard, follow me." Richard walked toward a tall man holding some papers up looking at them while talking to some workers.

"Gary, this is Mark. He was sent over by Tom."

"Good morning, Mark. Thank you for coming," Gary said as he reached out to shake Mark's hand.

"Thank you, Gary. What do you need me to do this morning?" Mark asked him.

"Well, we were just talking about the repairs and going over the paperwork, but it looks like it's going to be extensive. I hope you're everything Tom said you were because I'm going to need you on this one."

Mark looked at Gary intently, "I'm sure I can do whatever you need. I've been doing this for years."

"Great! Let's go over this real fast, so we can get to work."

Gary laid out the paperwork on the hood of his truck, pointing out all the areas that were in need of repairs. After the brief meeting, Mark put on his gear, and was getting ready to go down to the worst parts underneath the bridge.

"Hey, Mark, you will be working with Richard. He is pretty good at repelling," Gary told him.

11

"Cool, no problem, boss." Mark said as he had walked over to Richard. "Looks like we will be partners for this job."

"Right on, how long have you been doing this for, Mark?" Richard asked as he strapped up for his decline.

"I've been doing this for over twenty years now," responded Mark as he strapped himself in also.

"Good deal, see you underneath," Richard said as he began his decline.

Mark watched him before he had stepped off the ledge right after Richard got to his spot.

*****

At the school, Johnnie and George were hanging out at recess on the playground, racing each other toward the monkey bars. They both jumped up and grabbed a bar opposite of each other, swinging back and forth trying to knock each other off. They were laughing very loud as they struggled to try to get each other to drop off first. Johnnie had wrapped his legs around George as he tried to pull him down.

"I got you this time, George."

Both laughed as they struggled hard against one another. George had held on so tight to the bar that his knuckles became white.

"That's what you think, Johnnie, you can't pull me down."

Finally losing his grip, George fell to the ground and was looking up at Johnnie. Then Johnnie dropped down next to him, both laughing together as they laid on the ground.

"I didn't think you could pull me off," George said while laughing and trying to catch his breath. "I will get you the next time though."

Johnnie chuckled and responded. "I'm the champ."

The bell rang signaling that recess was officially over and Johnnie looked at George. "There's the bell, let's race to the line."

George got up off of the ground and stood up. "Okay, Johnnie, you want a race? I bet I can beat you."

Johnnie got up as well and got into race position. "Okay, we go on three. One, two, three!"

Both boys ran as fast as they could to get in line to go back to class. George and Johnnie both ran past the other kids, but George got there first.

"Whoop, I won!" George said with a huge smile on his face.

Johnnie was breathing heavy as he was almost out of breath again. "You're fast, George, but next time, it won't be so easy."

George was still laughing while holding his stomach. "Oh, you want a next time? Okay, next recess we race again."

*****

Back at home, Sara continued to work on laundry when she got a call from George's mother.

"Hello."

"Hi, Sara, are you busy?"

"Hi, Monica. Not too busy, just doing some laundry, you have to keep up on this stuff when you have a husband who works hard and a boy who plays even harder. How are you?" Sara continued folding the laundry as she talked to Monica.

"I am doing very well, Sara. I know what you mean. Tim and George keep me so busy also. But the reason I called is because I was wondering if you wanted to go get some lunch this afternoon. I am free today, and well, I didn't want to eat alone. George is at school, and Tim is working, and to be honest, I could use some company."

"Sure, Monica, lunch sounds good. I could use a break anyways, and it would be so nice to get out of the house with a good friend." Sara stopped folding laundry and looked at the clock on the wall.

"Okay, great, let's meet at that nice Italian place by the theater."

Sara happily accepted the invitation, "Oh, I love Italian. Let's meet up at noon then. That will give me time to get these clothes folded."

"Sounds great, Sara, maybe afterwards, we can do some shopping?" Monica wanted to spend more time out then just lunch.

"Hmm, shopping, huh? Well, I guess it wouldn't hurt. I really could use a few things." Sara was thinking about a nice outfit she saw the other day.

"Sounds great. I will see you at noon then."

"Perfect, see you at noon, Monica." Sara went back to folding her laundry and trying to get one more load done before she had to leave to meet

14

Monica.

Meanwhile Mark was not sure how long he would be on this job site. Taking their lunch break, Mark used the opportunity to talk to Gary to find out if he would need him for the rest of the week.

"Hey, Gary, you got a minute?" Gary sat down on the back of his work truck.

"Sure, Mark, what's up?"

"Well, this job is much bigger than Tom expected I think. Will you be needing my help tomorrow?"

Gary looked around for a minute at his crew. "Yeah, I probably will need you out here for the rest of the week. This job is pretty extensive. I will call Tom tonight and go over things with him and see if I can use you for the rest of the week."

"Sounds good, Gary, this bridge still gets used a lot, so it really needs to be done."

Finishing their lunch, Gary yelled to the crew, "Let's get back to work, guys." Mark and Richard strapping in for their descent back down underneath the bridge where they had previously been working.

As they got back to work, it was now lunch time for Johnnie and George at the school. Sitting next to each other as usual, they saw Wayne Jones walking towards them.

"Johnnie, here comes Wayne. I wonder what he wants."

Johnnie, looking very concerned, responded, "I don't know, George, but he is always up to trouble."

Wayne stood in front of Johnnie looking at him intensely as he told him, "Give me your snack cake, Johnnie boy."

Johnnie put his hand over it. "No, Wayne, why don't you go back to your own table and leave me alone."

Wayne started reaching over to grab Johnnie's arm when George told Wayne to get lost.

"Oh, your girlfriend has something to say, huh?"

Johnnie responded in anger. "He's not my girlfriend, Wayne, so why don't you go back to your table and get a life?"

"I will see you on the playground, fruitcake." Wayne said laughing. He turned and walked away, as he headed back to his table.

After eating their lunch, Johnnie and George went outside to play. George saw Wayne walking toward them.

"Here he comes, Johnnie, what are you going to do?"

"I don't know, George. I don't want to get in trouble." Johnnie looked nervous as Wayne walked up to him.

"Well, well, well, if it isn't Johnnie fruitcake. I didn't think you would even come outside." He pushed Johnnie down to the ground and stood over him. "Now you don't talk so tough, do you, Johnnie fruitcake?"

George, seeing Johnnie not wanting to defend himself, grabbed Wayne and pulled him back and then pushed him.

"How about you try me, Wayne?"

Looking with amazement, Wayne punched George in his eye. He turned as if that one punch would end the fight, laughing while he started to

16

walk away.

George fell down, but got back to his feet and turned toward Wayne. "That's all you have, Wayne?"

Wayne turned and saw George back on his feet and ready for more, as he walked back over to him. "No, I got plenty more for you, George."

Wayne tried to grab George, but he punched Wayne back and knocked him down. "Get up, Wayne!"

All the kids saw the fight and ran over to cheer them on, as they formed a circle around the two boys. Wayne got up and tried to tackle George, but he grabbed him and started punching him. Finally, Wayne pushed George back as they squared off to one another. Grabbing each other, George landed a hard punch on Wayne's face knocking him down. Getting on top of him, he started beating Wayne hard with his fist. Johnnie, seeing a teacher running over to them, grabbed George off Wayne.

"George, you're going to be in trouble. Mrs. Smith is coming."

Mrs. Smith grabbed George and Wayne. You two come with me to the principal's office.

*****

Monica pulled up to the restaurant in her sleek black Lincoln Continental. She walked up the walkway looking at the flowers that were on both sides. Sara just finished folding the laundry from the last load that she had been working on and was on her way to go meet Monica. Taking the long way so she could enjoy the wonderful scenery, she enjoyed the view, which was riddled with trees from the forest along the way. Pulling up to the restaurant, she walked in and found Monica waiting to be seated. While they waited they had a short conversation about how nice the weather had been and how they were both needing to get away for a vacation.

After being seated, Sara and Monica both ordered a cup of coffee. Sara took hers black; however, Monica got cream with hers. Sara and Monica began to talk about their boys. Both were so proud of their little guys, telling each other stories and laughing.

"I am so glad you called me, Monica. I really have been needing to just get out and have some girl time."

Monica nodded in agreement. "Girl, I have too. I've missed our chats, but lately, we both seem so busy. We need to start making time for each other like we used to."

"I so agree," said Sara as she sipped her coffee. "Maybe we can meet once a week?"

"Oh, Sara, that's a great idea. Let's plan something for next Friday."

"Sure, I can do that. But I can't stay out long. Fridays are busy after Mark gets out of work, so I need to have things done. He hates it when I'm not ready for him."

Monica grinned a little. "Sounds like Tim, maybe all men are like that." She laughed as she took another bite of her food.

"Perhaps, but it's just a busy day for us."

Monica, thinking about that, said to Sara, "Well, we can do it on a Thursday if you would like?"

"That would probably be much better for me, Monica. I will have a little extra time and won't be so hurried."

"Good, then we can relax and talk a little longer."

Sara agreed as she finished her coffee.

$$*****$$

At school, George and Wayne both went into the principal's office. Principal Hardwell began to ask the boys about the fight.

"So, boys, what seems to be the problem?"

Wayne tried to blame George for starting it. George disputed his story with what really happened. Principal Hardwell heard both sides and decided to suspend them both for three days.

"Boys, you both know better than to be fighting. I don't know what started it, but you're both suspended for three days, and I better not have any more problems out of you two when you come back."

Walking out of the office, George warned Wayne. "If you ever mess with us again, I will finish this fight."

Wayne responded as he tried to not look scared, "This fight isn't over, George. I will see you two again on the playground real soon."

George looked very angrily at Wayne. "I am warning you, Wayne, you better leave us alone."

Both kids had to sit in the office and wait for their parents to come to pick them up. Neither was talking to the other, they just sat there and waited to go home.

*****

After eating, Sara and Monica stopped off at the local clothing store to do a little after lunch shopping. Monica found a nice dress on sale she really liked.

"Sara, look at this one."

Sara slowly walked over while browsing on her way. "Oh, that would look so nice on you, Monica."

"I know right, girl, and its half off. I am buying this one."

Monica and Sara continued to look around the store to see what else was on sale.

"Sara, you should get that black dress, it would look so cute on you."

"Oh, Mark would love this, but it's a bit pricey. I don't know if I should."

Monica looked at the price. "Well, I think it would look so good on you. Why don't you try it on?"

"Nope, if I try it on, I will buy it for sure." Sara really thought about it though.

Monica looked at the dress in Sara's hand. "Girl, you know you want to buy it."

"Ugh, yes I do. Should I?" Sara knew that Monica would tell her to do it.

"Girl, you better buy it. Mark's going to love that

dress on you."

"Well, it has been a little while since I have bought anything expensive. Maybe just this once." Both ladies laughed as they walked to the checkout line.

*****

Back on the job, Mark and Richard had been working steadily on the repairs, trying to get as much done as they could on the first day. Richard climbed over to Mark to help him get these last few boards secured before they took their last break.

"Looks like it might be a long week, Mark."

"Yeah, I am sure it will be, and this deadline is a bit of a stretch considering there are so many repairs needed on this bridge, and they all are very severe. I am almost out of nails, do you have more on you?"

"Sure do, but I don't know how many I have Mark. I have had to use some extra to reinforce the beam where I was strapped into."

"Well, hopefully, it will be enough to get us through the next hour. I hate to climb back up when we are so close to our break time."

"Yeah, me too. I should have enough though."

Richard looked in his nail bag that was hanging from his side. "I have a few more strips of nails still also. Hey, give me hand with this board."

Mark reached out to hold the board in place with one hand and shoot the nails in with the other hand, while Richard held up the other end, so Mark could keep from having to readjust.

*****

Sara and Monica had stopped off for an ice cream on their way back to Sara's house.

"I can't wait to wear this dress this weekend. I am going to talk Mark into taking me out for a nice evening. We haven't been out in so long, and I really need it, you know."

Monica nodded her head in agreement. "Tim and I go out every few weeks at the least, and I have to tell you, Sara, it does make our marriage so much better."

Both ladies ordered a hot fudge Sunday and sat and talked as they slowly enjoyed their ice cream.

"Well, this has been so nice, Monica, but I really need to get back to the laundry that I was working on. And I am hoping Mark will be home soon."

Finishing their ice cream, Monica and Sara left together, while talking along the way to their cars about the boys and how much the two of them loved hanging out together all the time.

*****

George was still sitting in the office waiting for the receptionist to be able to get a hold of his mother to come to pick him up. However, because she had spent the day with Sara, they were not able to get a hold of her, so George sat there until school was out and had to take the bus home. Walking home with Johnnie from the bus stop, they discussed the event of the day. George seemed a bit concerned as to whether or not he would be in trouble. George, only living a few houses down the street, walked home with Johnnie every day. Upon getting closer to the house, they saw Monica was at Johnnie's house who had stopped by to talk some more.

The two boys walked in and were greeted by their mothers. Sitting down on the couch, George began to explain to his mother about the fight in the schoolyard and the suspension he received. Monica, being very upset as well as Sara, began to talk to the two young boys. Sara asked Johnnie why he didn't stand up to the bully.

"Johnnie, why didn't you stand up for yourself? Were you afraid of him?"

Johnnie looked down at the ground. "No, Momma, I wasn't afraid of him. I just didn't want you and Dad to be mad at me."

Sara looked at Johnnie compassionately. "Johnnie, we will never be mad at you for standing up for yourself."

"I'm sorry, Momma, but I really wasn't afraid of him. And next time he tries to pick on me, I will fight him." Johnnie smiled now that he realized he didn't have to take being bullied by Wayne anymore.

Monica commended George for sticking up for his friend but also made sure the two boys understood that it's not okay to fight unless it's for the right reasons, like being bullied. Or fighting for someone who couldn't fight for themselves. After a lengthy conversation with the boys, Monica and George went back to their house and waited for Tim to get home to discuss the event with him.

Later that evening, Mark was on his way home from working on the bridge. When Mark was pulling in the driveway, Johnnie got excited knowing his dad made it home in time for game night. Running to open the door, Johnnie was all smiles.

"Dad, you made it home just in time for the game." Mark patted Johnnie on the head, as he walked into the house.

"Hi, honey," Mark said to Sara then kissed her gently.

"How was your day, baby?" Sara asked Mark.

"Well, it was very interesting. This old bridge is worse than I thought. They are hoping I can work the rest of the week with them."

Sara was not looking too happy about it, and asked Mark, "Do you think Tom will let you go back out there for the rest of the week?"

"I don't know, honey. Gary, the foreman out at the old bridge, is supposed to call him tonight, then Tom is gonna call me right after."

Sara really did not like this idea of Mark working out there all week. "Do you want to go back out there, honey?"

Mark nodded. "Yeah, I don't mind. I mean I have done this for so long, that it's no big deal to me and I would prefer to make it safer."

Sara kissed Mark. "Well, just be careful out there, honey." Sara was trying not to look worried.

Mark smiled at her. "I am always careful, honey. Please don't worry okay?"

Sara kissed Mark on his cheek. "Good, because if you're not, I am gonna hurt you when you get home."

Mark grinned. "Oh? What do you plan on doing?"

Sara squinted her eyes and curled her lip. "You just get hurt out there, and you will find out, Mister."

Mark laughed. "Okay, okay. No worries, dear. I promise I will be safe."

Mark, sitting next to Johnnie, asked him about his day at school. "Son, how was school today?"

Johnnie looked at his dad with somewhat of a sad face. Taking a deep breath, Johnnie began to tell his dad what happened. "Well, Dad, there was a fight on the playground today."

Mark had a more serious look on his face. "Oh? What happened, son?"

Johnnie began to explain, "Well, see, Dad, there is this bully at school named Wayne and well, he came over and was trying to pick a fight with me. But I didn't want to fight him because I was afraid if I did, I would get into trouble."

"So what happened, did you get into a fight, son?" Mark questioned.

"No, Dad. George stood up and told Wayne to leave us alone, and they got into a fight." Johnnie was kind of ashamed that he didn't fight Wayne.

"Son, next time someone tries to bully you, don't be afraid to stand up for yourself. You will never get into trouble, son, if you are defending yourself."

"Yeah, that's what Mom said also." Johnnie looked back at Mom who was in the kitchen. Mark also looked back at Sara and smiled, then returned his focus back to Johnnie. Putting his arm around him, he began to finish the conversation.

"Sometimes, the hardest thing to do, son, is to face your fears and overcome them. But you have to be courageous to overcome fear and do what is right even if it means you have to stand on your own. The greatest thing a man will ever have to overcome is fear. And having courage doesn't mean you don't have fear, it just means you dig deep down inside and overcome that fear. Fear will always be there, son, but being courageous means you acknowledge that fear and face it, not allowing it to stop you, but rather pushing through to do what is right no matter what the cost is." Mark had hugged Johnnie. "Do you understand, son?"

"Yes, I understand, Dad. Do you think I have courage?" Johnnie asked.

"Yes, you do, son, and I have confidence you will do the right thing. I really believe in you, son."

Johnnie looked at the time. "Dad, the game is on."

Mark smiled very big. "Yes, son, but I think dinner is ready. By the way, honey, what is for dinner?" Mark looked into the kitchen at Sara.

"Fried chicken and potatoes tonight, and it's just about done, so tell Johnnie to come set the table," Sara responded.

Mark hugged Johnnie and told him, "Son, you

heard your mother. Go get the table set for dinner." Johnnie got up and yelled to Sara, "Coming, Mom!"

Running into the kitchen, Johnnie grabbed the plates and put them on the table, along with the silverware. Then ran back to the living room, and slid across the floor trying to stop in front of the couch, before he sat down and began to watch television until dinner was done.

The house filled up with the wonderful smell of fried chicken, making Mark even hungrier. Mark walked into the kitchen and kissed Sara.

"Smells so good, honey."

"It will be done soon, baby," she said as she kissed Mark back.

"You did a great job talking to Johnnie about that stupid bully." Sara looked disgusted about the situation.

"Johnnie is a good kid. He will do the right thing," Mark said looking back into the living room at Johnnie. "And I never want him to be afraid to stand up for himself or others."

Sara agreed, focusing back on the stove as dinner was just about done. Mark turned and walked back into the living room, sat down next to Johnnie and watched television with him. Johnnie sat almost on top of Mark as he was so happy to be with his dad watching television together. Sara yelled into the living room for Mark and Johnnie to come eat. Both got up and walked into the kitchen together. As they sat down to eat.

*****

George at his home explained to his dad what happened at school as well. Tim understood why George stepped up and took on this bully. He didn't give George any real punishment for the suspension. However, Tim did give George some chores to do while he was off as to not let him think it was okay to get suspended from school. Tim had always taught George to stand up for what was right and to do the right thing no matter what the cost, to punish him for it would seem hypocritical.

Tim knew how good a kid his son was. He had always been proud of George for not backing down. This fight seemed to be one necessary to have. George had learned from his dad how to determine when to fight and when not to fight. Tim was a fan of boxing and would often let George watch boxing with him. He would talk to him about things during the fight. As long as George wasn't fighting out of mere anger, then Tim was fine with him getting into a scrape or two, especially if it was to protect someone else or himself. It actually made Tim proud to have a son who could help others out like that.

George was no weakling, he built up muscles from working with his father most summers, carrying and stacking wood. One of Tim's ways to make money was to sell firewood along with his regular job in the factory.

Wayne, his parents didn't even care if he went to school or not, so it was no wonder why he bullied other kids. Wayne's parents were barely even involved with his life. His dad was an alcoholic and his mom was a prostitute hooked on drugs. Wayne didn't get much attention from either one unless it was bad attention. His dad and mother were abusive toward him and didn't care what happened to him just as long as it didn't cause them any real problems.

*****

After eating dinner, Mark and Johnnie returned to the couch for the baseball game they had been planning on watching together. Johnnie was excited to be able to watch this game with his dad, for he had been waiting all day for this moment with Mark. Even though the game had already started it was good to just spend time with his father. Mark sat next to Johnnie, putting his arm around his son. They relaxed on the couch and enjoyed the game together. The game kept both on the edge. The score stayed scoreless for most of the game. Finally, New York got a solo home run in the seventh inning, which would eventually be the final score, one to zero.

Johnnie looked at his dad. "That was a great game, Dad."

"Yes, it was, son. But for you, it's bedtime now." Mark looked at the clock on the wall. "You have school tomorrow, young man."

Johnnie did not want to go to bed, still excited about the win. "Can I stay up just for a little while longer, Dad?"

Mark looked back at the clock on the wall. "No,

son. You need your rest for school tomorrow."

Johnnie was not happy about going to bed, he loved every minute that he could get with his dad. "Okay, Dad." He hugged Mark and Sara. "Good night, Mom and Dad."

Both parents said good night to Johnnie as he went up the stairs to his bedroom.
Mark sat back on the couch, as Sara come over and sat next to him.

"Been waiting for this all day, honey. I missed you so much today." Sara looked deep into Mark's eyes.

"I missed you too, baby, been waiting for our alone time together since I got home."

"How was the game tonight?" Sara asked Mark.

"It was a great game, very close. But New York won," Mark answered.

"Awe, that is so good, honey." Sara kissed Mark as they embraced one another on the couch and began to ignore what they were watching together. Alone time for Mark and Sara had become scarce these days. There hadn't been much time alone with Mark's work schedule, especially since he had become one of the best in his field. It seemed like they always needed him to do the harder jobs that took the longest to complete. To actually be able to sit down and watch a baseball game with Johnnie was very rare, so this night had been exceptionally well for Mark. Some alone time with Sara was the icing on the cake for him. They had begun to miss each other's company.

This was the perfect opportunity for Sara to ask Mark for a date night, so she could wear her new dress for him.

"Mark, honey. Are you working this weekend?" Sara was hoping Mark would say no.

"I don't think I am, honey, this job will take a few weeks easily, but they don't seem too likely to work past Friday. You know these companies don't like to pay too much over time. Why? Did you have something in mind?" Mark asked Sara.

"Well, actually, I was wanting to have a date night with you, you know, just the two of us. We could send Johnnie to stay the night over at George's house."

Sara knew she could always get Monica to let Johnnie come stay the night and even sometimes the weekend.

"I will put in for the weekend off just to make sure I am able to have it off." Mark knew he was able to get it off if he really wanted it.

"Oh, baby, that would be great. We need this time together. I have missed you like crazy." Sara smiled so big and was so very excited to be able to go out with it just being the two of them.

"I have missed you also, honey, and I am so ready to have some time with you, just the two of us. I love you so much, honey." Mark leaned in and kissed Sara.

"I love you too, baby."

Mark turned off the television and grabbed Sara's hand and the two went into the bedroom for the night. Just getting settled into bed, and the phone rang. It was Tom calling him about the work schedule for the rest of the week.

"Hello," Mark answered.

31

"Hello, Mark, this is Tom. Go ahead and finish the week out at the old bridge."

"No problem, boss. But I was wondering about the weekend schedule?"

Tom responded, "They won't be working this weekend, Mark. They're union workers, so they only work Monday through Friday."

"Oh, great, then I can make plans with Sara for this weekend." Mark was excited about this good news.

"Yes, okay, Mark, have a good night and enjoy your weekend out with Sara when it gets here." Tom knew Mark worked long hours for him and usually most weekends, so he didn't give him any extra work.

"Thank you, Tom. I will see you in the morning. Good night."

"Good night, Mark." Mark hung up and returned his focus back to Sara.

He looked at Sara with excitement. "Guess what, honey, I got the weekend off."

Sara sat up. "Are you serious?"

"Yes, I am. So you better figure out what you want to do this weekend because we are gonna do more than just go out."

Sara was so happy she started to think already what all she wanted to do this weekend with Mark. Mark and Sara had talked for a little while before Sara finally fell asleep in Mark's arms.

Waking up early the next morning, Sara got dressed and headed into the kitchen to get a pot of coffee started. She went back into the bedroom to wake up Mark for work. After which, Sara returned back to the kitchen to begin preparing breakfast whistling as she gets things out, so she can start cooking. Sara was in a very joyful and playful mood after hearing the wonderful news Mark gave her concerning the weekend coming up.

Mark, getting up and getting dressed, made sure Johnnie got up. Then going into the kitchen to get a cup of coffee, he smiled at Sara, saying, "Good morning, honey."

Mark had poured himself a cup of coffee then walked over to Sara and gave her a nice kiss on the cheek.

"Sara smiling said, "Good morning, baby." Then kissed Mark back. She returned her focus to her cooking. Mark took in a deep breath of the aroma that was in the air.

"Mmmm, smells so good, honey."

"Why, thank you, baby. It will be done soon."

Mark looked around. "Is there anything I can help you with?"

"Sure, baby, can you make the toast and set the table for me please?" Sara asked Mark while cooking some bacon and mixing up some eggs for scrambled eggs.

Mark went over to the cupboard and grabbed the bread. "Sure thing, honey."

Mark began to make the toast. While it is in the toaster, Mark got the plates out and set the table for his family. Sara knew what a gem Mark was. For he always helped out around the house even though he worked so hard and put in long hours most of the time. Yet Mark always found time to help Sara out at home also. Never wanting to neglect his family, Mark always made it a priority to pitch in when he could. Sara always appreciated Mark and never took him for granted and always did her best to satisfy Mark's needs as well as Mark for Sara. This was the perfect marriage if there ever had been one. Mark and Sara never let the other go without the others' needs being met. Maybe this is why they had made it through the past ten years together with minimal arguments or fights. No marriage is without trials at some point, but Mark and Sara had found a way to work together and find a common ground to stand on which had allowed these two to keep their fights minimal and also from getting out of control.

As Johnnie came walking slowly into the kitchen, looking extremely tired, he had sat down at the table. He seemed a little more tired than usual.

"Good morning," Sara and Mark said to Johnnie.

"Good morning, Mom and Dad," Johnnie replied."

"Are you okay, son?" Mark asked Johnnie.

"Yes, well, I don't know, Dad, it's going to seem weird with George not being there for the next three days," Johnnie said with a very sad face.

"Yes, I understand, son, but everything will be okay, and it's only for three days. That will go fast," said Mark as he tried to encourage Johnnie.

Sara had brought Mark and Johnnie their breakfast, and they all sat down and ate together. Sara got Mark some fresh coffee. After eating his breakfast, Mark got ready to leave for work. Kissing Sara goodbye, Mark hurried to get out the door. Johnnie got up and went to the bathroom to brush his teeth and then got his book bag and slowly walked outside and headed down to the bus stop to wait for the bus.

Johnnie was not too excited about today knowing that George wouldn't be there. He sat on the bench and waited for the bus.

Mark was on his way to work to meet up with the crew at the old bridge. Along the way, he found it hard to keep his mind from drifting off as he drove, knowing he had a great night planned this Friday with Sara. Not sure yet as to their plans, but one thing he knew for sure was, they were going out. It had been forever since they had been able to.

Back at the Steele home, Sara was already planning this weekend for her and Mark. Both were so excited. This time together was much needed. Mark had been working long hours and had been so tired, but the money had been good, and they had been able to stay ahead of their bills and save money at the same time.

Sara made some phone calls and began to set up a night away with Mark at a very nice hotel with a package that comes with dinner and some dancing. Just the kind of romantic weekend she had been wanting for some time now. After making the reservations, she called Monica to see if she wouldn't mind letting Johnnie stay for the weekend while they go out. This shouldn't be a problem since they both often stayed the weekend at each other's house. These two boys were almost inseparable. It was like they were real brothers.

Even after spending the day together at school, they always tried to hang out together for a while after they got their homework done.

At lunchtime, Johnnie was playing a good game of chase with Darrell and Randy. These two brothers often hung out with Johnnie and George. These two boys were known for being tough kids that you don't fool with. Kind of makes you wonder why Wayne would try to mix it up with these guys. After all, the four boys were very popular and known for handling their business, except Johnnie, however, he was more reserved. Some would say he was more diplomatic out of the four.

*****

Mark was about to take his lunch break when he saw Richard struggling to get his rope untangled. Yelling over to him, Mark asked if he was okay.

Richard responded, "Yeah, I just got my rope tangled up somehow."

"Do you need help?" Mark yelled over to him.

"Well, I think I can get it," responded Richard.

All of a sudden, the beam broke where Richard was tied in. Falling, he hit another beam that broke his fall, hanging there only by his body being bent over it backward.

Mark untied himself and began to climb over to him. Still tied in by another rope, Mark was able to stay somewhat safe. After reaching Richard, Mark realized the severity of the situation. Mark began to try to make sure Richard was coherent.

"Richard, look at me, are you okay?" Mark asked.

Richard looked up at Mark. "I can't feel my legs," Richard responded while breathing very hard almost gasping for breath.

Mark, knowing he will need some assistance, radioed to the top to alert them of their situation. Gary grabbed one of the workers and had him get the wench ready, so they can pull the men up. Finally getting the rope down to them, Mark began to tie Richard in. When the beam they were both on began to give way, Mark hurried and got Richard all set. Mark radioed to Gary to let them know they were ready. Before they could pull him up, the beam that Richard landed on gave way from the pressure of Richard landing on it and now the weight of the two men as well. Mark's rope almost snapped from the force of falling, having to also grab the rope Richard was tied into. Gary radioed to Mark, asking if they were okay. Mark responded to them to hurry.

Gary could see the situation developing from the top, and knew he better get the two back up to the top as soon as possible. Mark radioed Gary to also get an ambulance and told him that Richard was severely injured. Gary signaled for his worker Tim to start pulling them up, but it seemed from the force of being pulled when the beam broke, it had now become jammed. The two men hung there waiting, while all the workers tried to get it unjammed. Tim was trying to hurry and get it unjammed and tried to let some rope out, but nothing was moving.

Finally after several tries, it did move out a little. Gary let Mark know they had to let out some rope. Mark prepared for the two to be lowered just a bit. Not being able to see where it was jammed, they tried to pull them back up a little, and again, the wench stopped.

Not sure how to get it free without taking it apart, they tried to lower them again a little more to see if they could find the jammed spot. Mark radioed to Gary explaining they need to hurry. Richard was now disoriented. Mark was trying to keep him focused while the rest were working to get them up. Gary explained the situation as he tried to keep Mark and Richard calm. Mark gained Richard's focus and began to tell him that everything was going to be alright.

"They will get us back up to the top, just hang in there, Richard."

Mark tried to reassure Richard that everything was under control. Richard, barely able to speak at this point, just nodded that he understood. After letting them down a little farther this time, they tried to bring them back up, but this time when the wench jammed, it jerked the rope causing it to fray. Gary was't by the machine for he had to walk away and called for an ambulance. Upon his return back to the wench, seeing the fray he began to be even more in a rush to get them to the top. He and a few other workers got prepared to descend. However, while they were getting ready to prepare to climb down, the rope broke, and the two men Mark and Richard fell to the ground.

Gary and the others watched in horror, as they seen both men fell to their deaths. There was nothing they could do but watch. Everyone was frozen, no one even moved a muscle. The only sound heard was the sound of the wench running. All were shocked at what they just witnessed.

Finally after a few minutes, Gary's focus returned when he heard in the background a faint siren, signaling the ambulance was almost there. The others were still standing in place, as Gary turned off the wench. As the rest looked back at Gary as he turned off the wench, the ambulance pulled up. Gary walked over to them and began to explain the current situation. After about thirty minutes of talking to the two men from the ambulance, Gary sat down and called Tom to let him know what had just happened.

Gary took a deep breath as he waited for Tom to answer. Tom picked up the phone.

"Reynolds Construction, this is Tom speaking."

"Tom, this is Gary. We had a problem at the old bridge."

Gary told Tom everything that happened. Tom was in shock and couldn't believe what he was hearing. After hanging up, Tom sat at his desk with his head down, not knowing what he was going say to Sara, but he knew it was a phone call he had to make. This was the kind of phone call a boss never wanted to make, especially since Tom and Mark had become such great friends. Tom and his wife Annabel, had been out to eat many times with Mark and Sara making this phone call even harder. Mark had been working for Tom now for almost

39

fifteen years. Five years before him Sara got married. Tom and Annabel were even at the wedding.

After gathering his thoughts, he picked up the phone and called Sara.

"Hello," Sara answered as her phone rang.

"Sara, this is Tom. Um, there was a problem today at the old bridge."

Sara interrupted and began to panic asking Tom what kind of problem and how was Mark.

Tom tried to speak. "Sara, I need you to come the hospital right away." Tom paused for a second until he heard Sara break the silence.

"Tom, what has happened to Mark?"

Tom, trying to regroup, said, "I am sorry, Sara. I need you to meet me at the hospital."

Sara began to cry. "What happened to Mark? Tell me what happened to Mark." Sara's crying could barely get out her words.

Tom tried to explain to Sara what happened, how Mark was trying to rescue a coworker, and how they both fell. "Sara, please just meet me at the hospital. I am on my way there right now."

Sara demanded some answers. "Tell me what happened to Mark."

Tom, not wanting to do this over the phone, gave in to Sara's demand. "There was an accident, and Mark tried to rescue one of their workers, and they both fell."

Sara began to really panic. "How bad is it, Tom? Tell me if Mark is okay."

"They didn't make it, Sara, I'm sorry," Tom said in a lowly voice.

Sara dropped the phone as she slumped down to the floor, putting her head in her lap. She sat and cried out loud, almost screaming. Tom tried to get Sara's attention by yelling on the phone, but Sara did not hear anything as she had tuned out everything and just sat there sobbing.

Her heart was crushed. Mark was her true love. He was her whole world and now he was gone, taken away from her in a moment's time. Sara, gathering her strength, hung up the phone and sat on the couch. Sitting there she felt as if everything has been stripped from her. Her dreams, her love, even her very life. After a few minutes of sitting in silence, Sara gathered her strength and headed to the hospital.

Going into the hospital, she saw Tom and Gary both sitting there waiting for her. Sara went up to Tom and asked what happened. Tom and Gary explained the situation and how Mark tried to save him before the beam gave out. Gary explained to Sara how they had tried to get them both up but ran into problems with the machine. After filling out some forms of which Tom helped her with, Gary assured Sara that they would take care of everything. After getting everything done at the hospital, Sara decided to go to the school to get Johnnie. This was something he needed to hear from her.

Driving to the school, she was struggling to stay focused, still wiping away her tears. She finally made it to the school after what seemed like an hour's drive, which actually only took twenty minutes. She went in to talk to the principal and got Johnnie out of class. After getting Johnnie, they drove home. Johnnie asked his mom what was wrong, but all Sara told him was, "I will tell you when we get home."

Pulling into the driveway, Sara stared at the house for a minute. Johnnie waited for his mom to open her car door, as he looked at her, wondering what had happened. Finally, Sara got out of the car and walked into the house. Johnnie following behind her. After going in, Sara and Johnnie sat on the couch. Sara began to tell Johnnie about the tragic event that had happened to their family. Johnnie not knowing how to handle this screamed out loud and cried as he was in disbelief. Sara tried to be strong in front of Johnnie and held him tight, but she couldn't, as she broke down again. They both sat there crying together.

Sara held Johnnie in her arms not wanting to let go. As the evening came to a close, Sara tried to finally fix Johnnie some dinner, but Johnnie didn't want to eat. He went upstairs to his bedroom and laid on the bed until he fell asleep. Sara did not know what to do. She just sat and stared at their pictures on the wall until she finally fell asleep on the couch. Neither of them was able to eat any dinner. For both of their worlds had been turned upside down. This would have been almost considered the perfect family if there had ever been one. Mark and Sara were so in love with one another. Mark had been a great husband and father and Sara had been the perfect wife and mother. One accident, one day, and now, everything had changed forever for this family.

CHAPTER 2

The Grief

The sorrow of waking in the middle of the night, Sara had sat up on the couch that she had fallen asleep on. Leaning down, she wiped her face with her hands and shed a few more tears. Being very sick to her stomach, she felt as if she was going to vomit. Getting up and making her way to the bathroom, she lifted the toilet seat and leaned over and began to puke. Still weeping as she heaved up the little bit of food she had consumed before yesterday's phone call bearing the horrible news of her late husband. After finishing, Sara wiped her mouth and washed her hands, splashing some of the cold water on her face. Sara turned off the light as she walked out of the bathroom, and slowly walked down the hallway to where the stairs were.

Looking up the stairs, she began to slowly climb up each step till reaching the top. Taking her time, she walked down the barely lit hallway to

Johnnie's room. As she very quietly opened the door to his bedroom and peeked inside to make sure he was still safely asleep in his bed. Sound asleep, Johnnie never heard a sound, as Sara closed the door and walked back down the stairs as she walked back into the living room, where Sara once again sat back on the couch of which she was once sleeping. Laying her head down on a cushion, she once again cried herself to sleep.

After waking back up around 6:00 a.m. as it was Sara's custom, she put on a pot of coffee and went back to the living room, this time sitting in her chair. She looked over at the shelf that laid out a few frames with her family pictures. Getting up, she walked over and stared at them, trying to understand how this could have happened. Looking intensely at the pictures, she turned to the couch and picked up the one picture she had fell asleep with. It was a picture of Mark by himself from a vacation they had taken together before Johnnie was born. She had fallen asleep with it in her arms. Returning it to the shelf, she went into the kitchen and grabbed a cup of coffee. Not bothering to wake Johnnie up for school this morning, she decided to let him sleep. It had been a rough day followed by a rough night and she wasn't going to bother him. Sitting down in the kitchen, Sara began to think of all the family members she needed to call.

Walking back into the livingroom, she got her personal phone book from the stand by the phone and took the cordless phone with the phone book and sat back in her chair and began to make the phone calls to Mark's parents to explain in detail to them of the accident, which was something she was not looking forward to. After spending a lengthy amount of time on the phone with them, Sara went down the list of people she needed to contact, calling Mark's sister and two brothers as well. They all helped Sara by contacting the rest of the family, so she didn't have to, but Sara, however, felt she needed to talk to Mark's immediate family herself.

After which she also called her own parents. Both sides of the family offered to help with all the details of the funeral. Mark's sister Tammy who, for whatever reason, never decided to get married and have a family of her own had offered to come spend the day with Sara and assisted her with the preparations. Sara felt so overwhelmed by all that happened and all that had to be done, accepted Tammy's offer and invited her to come over around noon.

Hearing Johnnie moving around upstairs, Sara walked back into the kitchen and prepared some breakfast for them both. Pulling out a package of bacon and some eggs, she got out a few pans and got the bacon cooking while scrambling some eggs.

Usually, Mark would make the toast, so Sara, looking over at the bread box and began to cry once again. Feeling the deep sorrow of her lost loved one, she walked over and pulled out the bread and began to make toast for her and Johnnie.

Returning to the stove, Sara started cooking the eggs while tending to the bacon. Johnnie finally came walking into the kitchen very slowly and sat down at the table, laying his head down where he normally would have put his plate. Sara, at this point, would have already said something to him about sitting down before the table is set. However, today wasn't a normal day, and Sara didn't want to upset Johnnie anymore than he already was.

Johnnie finally looked up at his mom and said, "I love you, Mom."

Sara smiled for the first time since she received the news about Mark and responded, "I love you too."

She finally asked him if he could set the table. Johnnie getting up went to the cabinet and pulled out three plates as it was his custom to do and not realizing he had one too many and began to set the table, even setting a place for Mark. He did not realize what he did until he saw Sara looking at the spot that Mark used to sit at and she started crying again. Johnnie realized what he had done and apologized to his mother and quietly put the plate back in the cabinet. Feeling bad about what he had just done, he went over to Sara and gave her a hug, telling her again that he was sorry. Sara hugged him back as she had understood it was a simple mistake. After drying her eyes, she finished cooking breakfast, and they both sat at the table and ate together. Usually, breakfast time was fast paced as Mark and Johnnie both had to get ready to go shortly after, but today, they both took their time and just ate in silence.

Johnnie looked at his mother, intensely and asked Sara, "Mom, am I going to school today?"

"No," replied Sara as she continued to eat her breakfast. Johnnie finished his breakfast and went back upstairs to his bedroom leaving Sara alone to her thoughts.

Sara cleared the table and cleaned the dishes before going to take a much needed hot bath, where she could relax for a little while before Tammy arrived. Sara sat on the side of the tub, letting her mind drift off while the water ran to fill the bathtub. Sara regained her focus on the water, for it would have run over had she not done so. Stepping into the tub, Sara sunk down into the hot water taking a deep breath. She laid back and closed her eyes.

She was almost in a state of meditation as she enjoyed the feel of the hot water on her soft skin. She finally relaxed for the first time in what was only one day but had felt as if it had been a week. She could almost feel her body releasing the tension as the steam from the hot bath had filled the room. Had someone walked in, they would have thought it was a sauna. Allowing herself this little time of silence was something she normally used as an escape from the stress of being a mother and a wife. Not to mention how active she had been in the community. But this was a time to forget, a time to just relax and let herself try to recover from all the hardships from a long day and night. However, this was an unusual time for her to get an escape this early in the morning. For her hot bath escape was usually an evening thing. But for this saddened mother and widow, it was much needed just to start her day off and mentally prepare for all that awaited her. Perhaps this short vacation from all that she had to face over the past twenty-four hours would get her through until evening time, when she would return for another nice relaxing visit from reality.

After taking a nice long hot thirty-minute bath, Sara stepped out of the tub and dried off, grabbing her housecoat and putting it on her hot steamy body. Sara went into her bedroom and began to pick out clothes for the day. Sara always dressed according to her mood, unless there was something she needed to attend. Then she would dress accordingly. So it was no surprise that Sara picked out some black slacks and a black blouse to wear today, seeing how her mood was one of depression and sorrow. After getting dressed, Sara returned back to the chair she had been sitting in before Johnnie had awoken.

*****

Tim, hearing the news at work, had taken time to call Monica to let her know about the tragic accident. In utter disbelief and shock, Monica hung up from Tim and cried for a few minutes before gathering herself together, so she could call Sara who was more than her best friend, for these two had become like sisters. After gaining her composure, Monica made the phone call to Sara to see what she could do to help her in her time of grieving.

Sara answered the phone in a quiet voice, "Hello." Hearing the comforting sound of her best friend's voice on the other end, Sara felt the love Monica had for her.

"Sara, it's Monica. Tim called me this morning with the terrible news. I am so sorry, hun, is there anything I can do?"

Sara responded, "Well, actually, yes, there is, if you don't mind taking Johnnie for the day. Mark's sister Tammy is coming over to help me get things in order."

Monica agreed to take Johnnie for the day. "Yes, of course, Sara, it would be good for Johnnie to get out anyways, besides George is home from school anyways and already being bored so at least those two can be together. And perhaps that will be comforting to Johnnie," explained Monica.

"Yes, that will be great for Johnnie. When do you want to pick him up?" asked Sara.

"I can come now if you would like."

Monica, who was already up and ready for the day, didn't waste any time trying to come get Johnnie. Monica loved Johnnie almost as her own son, for Johnnie and George had been friends from birth. They practically spent all their time together.

Sara agreeing hung up and went to talk with Johnnie. She knocked on his door.

"Johnnie, may I come in?" Johnnie still in his pajamas and was laying on his bed.

"Yes, Momma, come in." Sara walked into the bedroom and sat on the bed next to Johnnie.

"Honey, get dressed. Monica is coming to pick you up so you can spend the day with George."

For the first time this morning, Johnnie halfway smiled. "Okay Momma. I will get ready, when will

50

I be going there?" asked Johnnie.

Sara responded, "Monica is on her way, so hurry and get ready."

Sara, getting up and turning to walk out of the bedroom, was stopped by Johnnie calling her name. "I love you, Momma," Johnnie said as he got up and hugged Sara. Both were in tears while they hugged.

"I love you too, honey." Sara held Johnnie as tight as she could before going back downstairs.

Monica and George were on their way to pick up Johnnie. As Monica was driving them to Sara's house, she took the time to explain to George what had happened so that he was prepared for it in case Johnnie happened to break down while they were together playing. George, not really knowing how to take all of this in, just listened to what Monica was telling him. She explained also how it might be difficult for Johnnie for a while, and he will need his friends to help him get through this. George, being the faithful friend to Johnnie, reassured his mom that he will do anything for him.

Pulling up at the house, Monica had parked in the driveway. They both got out of the car and walked up the walkway to the front door. Sara greeted them both and told George that Johnnie was upstairs in his bedroom. George of course wasted no time running up the stairs to see his friend. Sara, turning her focus back to Monica, offered her some coffee. Monica accepted as they walked into the kitchen together. Monica sat down at the table while Sara got them both a cup of coffee before joining her at the table as well. Monica began to tell Sara how sorry she was for her loss, and that she was here for her if she needed anything. Sara, being very appreciative, thanked Monica for her offer.

And said, "I really just need a good friend right now." Monica nodded in agreement.

"I am here for you always, Sara, you are my best friend." Sara smiled as she sipped her coffee.

"That means everything to me, Monica." Sara looked at her with sadness in her eyes.

Monica, staring back, told her, "Anything you need me to do just ask."

Then she took a sip of her coffee as well. Sara then explained to her that after Tammy and she were done, she would come over. Monica smiled and told Sara,

"That would be great." After finishing their coffee and having some small chitchat, Monica prepared to get ready to go.

"Well, Sara, Tammy should be here soon, so I should get the boys together and get out of the way, so you and Tammy can get this done." Sara got up and hugged Monica.

"You don't know how much I appreciate you, Monica, you mean the world to me." Monica hugged her back.

"It's no problem, Sara, you would do this for me if anything ever happened to Tim."

Letting Sara go, Monica walked over the stairs and yelled up for the two boys to come down. Sara walked over to her and put her hand on her shoulder.

"Thank you so much, Monica."

"No problem, girly, just call me if you need me, okay?" Monica said with a soft voice.

"I will, Mon, I promise." Sara had grabbed Johnnie's shoes for him as he comes flying down the stairs with George behind him.

Sitting down and putting on his shoes, he looked over at his mother and said, "Mom, will you be okay?"

Sara smiled and nodded yes as she hugged Johnnie very tight.

"Be good over at Monica's, I don't want you two getting into any trouble today."

"Okay, Mom," Johnnie said as they all walked out the door.

Getting in the car, they pulled out of the driveway and headed down the street. Monica had decided to take the two boys shopping with her before returning back to her house.

Sara did a little bit of light cleaning while waiting for Tammy to come over. She was dusting off the stands and wiping off the counters, when Tammy knocked loudly on the door. Sara stopped what she was doing and went to answer the door.

"Hello, Tammy, come on in," Sara said after opening the door. Tammy walked in and immediately noticed how clean everything was.

"Wow, Sara, you really keep this place kept up." Sara looked around, and said thank you to Tammy.

"Shall we go sit in the kitchen? I have some coffee made if you would like some?" Sara asked Tammy.

"Sure, that would be very nice, Sara, I would

love some coffee. Thank you."

Sara led Tammy into the kitchen, having only been here a few times every year, she was always amazed at how well Sara kept the house so clean. Especially noticing the clean smell of lemon in the air from Sara, dusting and cleaning all the stands and end tables as well as the coffee table in the living room. As they sat and went over all that needed to be done, they began to make a list. Sara notified the insurance company of the accident and death of her husband after a long ordeal with them which still didn't get resolved due to not being able to send them the actual statements which she had not received as of yet. She and Tammy went over a list of people still needed to be contacted as well as contacting the funeral home and making arrangements. Mark had everything set up for him and his family a few years ago with the funeral home. It was really just a matter of making them aware of her policy with them. The rest they would take care of with the exception of flower arrangements. Mark had everything picked out, even right down to the suit he would be buried in. This made it to where all Sara and Tammy had to do was make arrangements as far as family participation things like pallbearers and food.

Suddenly, the phone rang. Tom called Sara to let her know that they would help out with whatever funeral expenses that she may have. Sara felt a little more relieved, and had thanked Tom for helping them out. Mark had a great policy written up already though, so Sara really didn't need any assistance from Mark's work, but it was good to know that the help was there if needed. Sara let Tom know that she would notify him when the funeral will be, so he can pass it on to Mark's coworkers.

After hanging up with Tom, Sara and Tammy began to make more phone calls to both sides of the family going down a long list that they had compiled together while drinking some hot coffee. Sara made several from her phone, while Tammy using her cell phone made several calls as well. After finally finishing all of these phone calls, Sara and Tammy began to discuss what they will do for lunch. Both agreed that they wanted to go out for lunch as they tried to decide on what they would like to eat. After finally settling on some Mexican food, Sara mentioned this place called Mexicana Cove. They both grabbed their purses and took a much needed break from this depressing work and headed out to town to eat.

While driving, they just chitchat about random stuff to try and keep their minds off Mark. Taking in the scenery as Tammy drove along the winding road, which was surrounded by the lush forest on both sides, giving opportunity for another conversation about the beauty of the landscape where Sara lived, for it was a very beautiful place surrounded with so many trees and forest. A great place to go for walks as well as picnics. With many little roadside parks to stop off at and just take in the beauty of this place. Many couples had used it for romantic walks and picnics. It was such a great place for lovers to live, especially for true romantics such as Sara and Mark. It was a timeless place for sure. A place that would take your breath away. Many small rivers running through the wooded forest, had given the wonderful place even more added beauty and sound. Many small paths that led to various little spots that would make a very romantic little area for couples who were full of love and passion. Just to drive through there would make you feel the warmth of a lover's heart. Some would say it was the kind of place that would conceive children with its many small private areas that one could find. But today, it was meant for a distraction for these two ladies, and it would have even lifted the depression itself off these two had it not been a place that Mark and Sara had visited often when they first married and moved here together. Sara had picked out this house a year after they were married, and Mark fell in love with it as soon as he saw it. This place would inspire the kind of passion that lovers were made of. Even behind the house where Sara and Mark lived was a nice little forest with a running brook. With trails that went farther than the eye could see. Johnnie and George would make camps out there and even had a secret club for them and with a few friends in the neighborhood as well.

Sara and Mark would often hold hands and go for a walk in the forest and just enjoyed each other's company. Sara always talked about everything to Mark, probably because Mark was such a good listener, and he obviously loved to listen to everything that Sara had to talk about. So many wonderful memories with Mark in this place. Not just with the house and the woods out back, but the whole area as well. After drifting off for a while on the thoughts of all the wonderful things, Sara was brought back by the sound of Tammy saying her name.

Now realizing that for the past few miles, she wasn't even aware of anything that Tammy had been saying to her. Coming around the bend they had entered into town. Tammy asked Sara if she was okay, it was obvious that she hadn't been paying attention to her as she was talking to her while driving.

Sara responded, "Yes, yes, everything is fine. I was just thinking about some things that me and Mark had done as we drove past the forest. Mark and I used to go there a lot when we were first married. Before he started working all the time."

Tammy understood and began to comfort Sara before changing the conversation.
Finally pulling up to the restaurant, they both went inside and waited to be seated.

"Mmmm, smells so good in here, I always love the smell of Mexican food," Sara said to Tammy as they stood and waited to be seated.

Tammy agreed, "I love the smell of Mexican food as well."

Being seated, they both ordered some iced tea. Tammy, having not seen Sara in quite a while, was talking her ear off. Sara really found it hard to focus at times to all Tammy was saying. Sara would rather be home laying down on the couch again, as she was feeling so exhausted as if she never even slept at all. But she knew she needed to get out, and Tammy was after all a very nice lady.

Sara was just finding herself distracted with so many thoughts. Even at times being frustrated with Tammy's constant conversations that seemed endless. Most conversations with Tammy never ended, they just went into a new direction. Sara, needing a small break from it, excused herself and went to the restroom. Not really needing to go, but needed to splash some cold water on her face which did make her feel better. And a few moments of silence was good for her also. Kind of made her feel somewhat relieved for a few minutes. Taking in a few deep breaths before returning back to the table where Tammy was waiting for her. Tammy, welcoming Sara back to the table and began to finish what she was saying, and then they both had sat quietly for a few minutes but shortly after, she started talking again. Until she was interrupted by the waiter who came to take their order. Both ladies had barely even glanced at the menu and started fumbling through the pages hoping for something that would catch their eyes real fast.

Tammy was fond of burritos and ordered a few with beans and rice, while Sara settled on a taco salad. Sara had been here many times and would rarely order anything other than taco salad or the combination plate, which came with a taco and a tostada as well as a burrito with beans and rice on the side. For Sara, Mexican food was a real treat, she absolutely loved Mexican food and would eat it as often as she could. After placing their order, the waiter returned with a basket of chips that was made fresh that morning and some salsa which was only mild spicy, which the two ladies enjoyed as they continued their conversation. Tammy only took a moment's break from talking to snack on some chips as they waited on their food to come. Sara tried to remain focused as Tammy got her all caught up on what she had been doing since their last meeting, which had been a little while, so it seemed that there was much to discuss. Tammy was always busy doing so many things. She loved to stay active and be busy doing lots of different activities in the neighborhood. Perhaps one would think as active as she was that by now, she would have met someone to settle down with.

One thing which Tammy enjoyed was being a freelance photographer. She has had many of her photos published for magazines. She also wrote poetry and even had a few books published. But her real passion was helping out at the homeless shelter, where she would stop in every few days and volunteer her time. After a few brief stories and some chips, the waiter arrived with their food. Sara, feeling the need to get back home, wasted no time digging in.

Tammy, on the other hand, seemed to enjoy taking her time as she continued to talk to Sara about everything she could possibly think of. Sara every so often acknowledged Tammy as if to appear to be fully paying attention. It's not that Sara did not enjoy Tammy's company. As a matter of fact, Sara loved Tammy and would normally interact quite a bit. But of course, Sara was not her usual self and Tammy, being aware of it, excused Sara's lack of involvement. Knowing how difficult this must be for her to be going through this.

And poor Johnnie. He loved his father and looked up to him as if he was his hero. Johnnie always admired his father for the kind of man and father that he was. Johnnie and Mark's relationship was amazing. It's hard to understand why such a thing could even happen to Sara and Johnnie.

Sara and Tammy finished their meal, and sat for a few while they drank their tea and was waiting for their bill. Tammy grabbed the bill as it was set down on the table, not allowing Sara to pay even one cent.

"This is my treat, Sara." Pulling out her credit card and handing it to the waiter.

As he walked off, Sara responded, "Well, thank you very much, Tammy, that is very kind of you. However, I am very sorry that I am not good company today, just so hard to stay focused, you know. My mind is racing everywhere. So many memories, and seems like everywhere you go or drive past reminds me of Mark and something we have done together. Just so very hard right now to keep my thoughts gathered."

Tammy was being so understandable. "I really understand, Sara, I couldn't imagine what you're going through, I mean, I know how I feel and how much I hurt having lost Mark also. He was so good at what he does, that this kind of accident should have never happened to him. He didn't deserve to have his life taken away so early. He was a good person and a very good brother."

Sara was almost in tears again. "Yes, he was, Tammy. He was a good husband and a good father as well. These kind of things you know can happen, but you never think it will happen to you. I mean not to us, not with Mark being such a good man."

Both almost in tears now, they decided that it was time to go. Leaving the restaurant, they both hugged before getting into the car, trying to comfort one another. For these two, it was a surprise that they hadn't broke down already. Tammy may not have had her own family and all, but she did love her immediate family. She was always there for her brothers as well as her mom and dad. So it was no surprise that Tammy was taking this very hard as well, she loved Mark.

Tammy had always been a strong woman and able to handle things much better than most. Sara also being able to hold it together for the most part, perhaps yes because she was strong also, but even so, it appeared the shock had not worn off yet either.

As they made their way back to Sara's, this drive was much quieter than the drive into town had been. Tammy, realizing now that Sara just needed to be alone with her thoughts, let her be as she just drove them back to her house. The drive itself in a way was soothing, had it not been for the breathtaking scenery perhaps this trip would have been much harder. After getting Sara back to her home, Tammy decided to just drop her off.

"Sara, there is nothing more for us to do right now. I am going to go unless you need me. I feel you need to be alone for a while."

Sara thanked Tammy for a nice lunch. "Well,

yes, I do feel that also. I just need to maybe lay down for a few. I still feel so exhausted. But thank you so much for a nice lunch out. Please forgive me, Tammy, I really appreciate you coming over and helping me with everything. You have been a huge help today."

"It's no problem at all, Sara," Tammy responded. "Please don't hesitate to call me if you need anything, okay? I am always here to help you." Grabbing Sara's hand. "I love you and Johnnie."

Sara smiled and gripped Tammy's hand tighter. "We love you as well, Tammy. Again, thank you so much for everything you did today. Please take care and be safe driving home." Sara had stepped out of the car.

"Thank you, Sara, call me soon, okay?"

Sara nodded yes as she shut the door and walked to the front door. After going in the she had pulled off her shoes before she laid on the couch again, where she will spend the next several hours crying and sleeping. Sara, not wanting to be bothered, got up and unplugged the phone as it rang. Feeling so depressed, she laid back down and drifted back off to sleep.

*****

Johnnie and George were at the park playing together on the many different toys that they have there for young kids to play on. These two would seem to have endless energy, I mean with all the running around they do. It would make one exhausted just to watch them in action. They played on every piece of equipment at the playground. The most fun was with the monkey bars. But this one was round with all kinds of different levels, where they could swing and chase each other. Johnnie and George often had battles in this round cage of death as they liked to call it. Both swing at each other and tried to grab one another with their legs as they try to either pull the other one down or knock the other one off. This was their favorite game to play and did so quite often. For these two young boys, roughhousing was an everyday occurrence. Often wondered how these two never seemed to get hurt by it. Most of the time, it was a tag team effort for these two, as they would pair up against the two brothers Darrell and Randy who in their own right was about as tough as they come. These four boys together were a usual terror to anyone who wanted to cause any problems, especially George who always seemed to find his way into something mischievous. One thing was for sure, you never want to leave George and Darrell together on their own for any length of time. For these two, it wouldn't take long before something bad happened. Darrell had a reputation for being one who finds trouble out of nowhere, and some could even say the same for George at times.

As for Johnnie, he was a thinker first and a fighter second. And Randy, for his age, he was very bright and could always talk his way out of something, or at least most of the time, but on the occasions that didn't work, Randy was always one who could back it up. Johnnie and Randy always seemed to have their hands full with George and Darrell. Trying to keep these two out of trouble was a full-time job. Nevertheless, when trouble did come their way, one thing was for sure was that these four boys would stick together till the end. One would be amazed at how nice these four boys could be, helping out around the community and always assisting those who had needs, such as opening doors for elderly women and such. However, these four boys could also have quite the ill temper.

George and Johnnie played together all morning until it was time to go have lunch. Monica gathered these two boys up, which was by far not an easy task. But she finally got them in the car to go have lunch at a little diner that was on the way home. One of which both boys was very fond of. It was a small place along the road which led back home and had the kind of menu that any youngster would enjoy.

Monica tried to focus on driving found it hard to not get irritated with George and Johnnie who both sat in the backseat as Monica now appeared to have become their chauffeur have yet to settle down. Monica spoke to them very loudly in a tone that would set any young person back in their seat, and informed them that it is now time to settle down and relax. Both looking intensely at her knew better than to keep on. For Monica was a kind-hearted woman, but she knew how to handle these two in a way as to keep control of her sanity. Making them settle down, Monica could now

focus much easier on the task at hand, which was
to get these two safely to the next destination
without anymore roughhousing in the backseat.
You would have thought that Johnnie and George
had brought the playground with them in the car.

Finally reaching the small diner, Monica and the
two boys went inside to get a table. Sitting by a
window that peered out to the parking lot, Monica
was able to keep a good watch on her vehicle.
Trying to still manage these two boys who have
refused to even settled down still Monica handed
them both a menu to read, which was almost
pointless seeing how Johnnie and George were
very familiar with this place and had already
decided on what they wanted to eat. After ordering,
Monica once again had to remind these two that
they were no longer at the playground. And it is
high time that they settle down now. After the food
arrived, one would think after all the playing that
these two would be half starved. However, these
two barely picked up their food as it seemed way
too inconvenient to stop talking long enough to
take anything else in, other than a few breaths.
Monica began to make it clear that the food they
had ordered better start to disappear. Johnnie began
to eat his fries that he ordered with a cheeseburger.
George, however, began to eat his hot dog first.
Typical meals for two young boys one would
think. Johnnie and George finally settled down and
ate their meals while enjoying a little break herself
while eating her fresh crisp salad that she had
ordered with just about everything in it and French
dressing on the side.

Monica never liked how restaurants always put so much dressing on their salads. She used to often say I can't taste nothing but the dressing. I want to taste the veggies I just paid for. George always tried to sneak a few of Monica's croutons, which Monica didn't mind as long as he left her with more than just a few.

After finally finishing their meal, Monica drove them all back to the house while taking the scenic route that she may enjoy the beauty of the trip at least. Seemed as if after eating the two terrors in the backseat had finally calmed down and were playing with a few toys that they brought along for the trip, to keep them occupied as Monica focused on driving. Or somewhat focused on driving, which is not an easy job with this kind of scenery. Most people seemed to slow down through here, so they get a better chance to enjoy it as they pass through.

After making her way through it, Monica finally pulled in the driveway, and not a moment too soon either. George and Johnnie were beginning to get restless again. As Monica put the car in park, the two young boys jumped out like caged animals. Monica, opening the door and calling for them to come in, went inside and sat in a soft, cushioned chair in the living room. She had turned on the television to watch a few shows and relax while George and Johnnie ran to his room to play a few games on George's game system, and as it seemed that for these two, Soldier Wars would be their reality for the next few hours, which was perfectly fine with Monica, that gave way for her to enjoy some quiet time as well. And maybe even some light cleaning before Tim came home from work. But for now, it was time to just relax in her red velvet chair with the soft cushion.

The house furniture outfit was all red velvet with soft cushions. Having two chairs, a couch and a love seat all of which looked so nice on their cherry hardwood floor. And the white walls gave it just the right touch to still keep it a little bright in the living room.

Tim called home on his lunch break to find out from Monica how Sara was doing. Monica explained to him that Sara and Tammy were getting things in order today and also that she had agreed to take Johnnie for the night, and that the two boys were playing together in George's room. Tim, thinking that was a good idea, told Monica she can spend some money on them if she got bored. Perhaps that's not a bad idea, Monica started to think.

"We could go see a movie or something," Monica said to Tim.

"Sure, honey, whatever you want to do, okay? I need to get back to work. I will see you when I get home. I love you, baby." Tim kissed Monica through the phone.

"I love you too, honey," Monica responded before hanging up.

Sitting back down to think if she really wanted to take the boys back out this afternoon or just let them play here. *Maybe a movie night here would be a good idea.*

Johnnie, pausing the game that he and George

were playing, politely excused himself to use the bathroom. Johnnie had been hiding his struggle all morning, but it had finally caught up with him. Going into the bathroom, Johnnie finally broke down and sobbed for quite some time. After several minutes, he wiped his tears away and splashed some water on his face, then dried his face off on a towel before returning back to Soldier Wars with his best friend George. However, splashing water on his face and drying it off with a towel didn't cover up the fact that Johnnie's eyes were beat red and still watery. Something George noticed right off the bat as soon as Johnnie entered back into the room.

Not really sure on what to say or if he should even say anything, finally mustered up the words. "Are you okay, bro?"

Johnnie, trying to hold it together, whimpered out the words, "I am okay, bro."

Still trying to hold back his tears, Johnnie picked up his controller, so they can return back to their mission. This had not been an easy day at all. However, the distraction of being with George today has helped Johnnie out way more than one could even realize. Perhaps just the companionship of a good friend would have been comforting enough. But being at the park and now doing this mission on Soldier Wars was very effective in keeping his mind from constantly thinking on the death of his father. But Johnnie could never hide his feelings from George. And George could always tell when something was bothering Johnnie, so to try and hide something like this was out of the question. And for George, he honestly was very happy Johnnie was there today with him. He would have been so bored being stuck at home with no one to talk to, for all of their other friends were in school today.

For George, this was the best day off from school he had in a long time; however, he was very sorrowful for his friend Johnnie. Mark had been good to George, and had always welcomed him into their home like he was one of his own sons. As Tim would do the same for Johnnie anytime he would come over to visit his best friend. For these two families had been best friends since before the two boys had even been born. So one could only expect for these two youngsters to be as close as they were. After all, there wasn't a time when these two didn't know each other. Being like brothers from birth, as if they were twins. They were even used to discuss what they wanted to get for Christmas and would often ask for things that would go with what the other one wanted, so they could always match up when playing together.

The other two, Darrell and Randy, they would just get whatever they wanted and didn't put much thought into anything other than what they liked. Darrell was more serious when asking for gifts for Christmas. He would want to even know how much of a budget he had, so he could try to figure out how he could get the most out of what his parents would be spending. Whereas for Randy, he didn't care just as long as he got a lot of gifts.

Johnnie and George, however, always had a game plan on how to build up their toys, so they each had a piece that the other didn't have, making it much easier for when they were together. And when spending the night together, the packing was as if they were moving out. They would try to stuff as much in their bags as they could. And sometimes even leaving toys at each other's houses just so they could finish what they were playing at a later time.

Monica, finishing up some small house chores that needed to be done, decided to call Sara to see how she was doing and made sure everything was okay. Sara, had just woke up and plugged the phone in to answer the call, groggily she picked up the phone, trying to gather herself together.

"Hello." Monica could tell by the way Sara answered that she had been asleep.

"Hey, Sara, did I wake you? You sound like you were sleeping. I am just calling to check up on you."

Sara took a deep breath and tried to focus her eyes. "No, I was laying down for a spell, but I had just got up before you called. Everything is okay here, we have everything done for the most part. I do hope some will volunteer to bring food however. I sure hate to ask for them too, but it will be too much for me to try to take care of. I know Tammy said she will bring some food, and she was going to mention it to some of the family as well, but I suppose I will need much more than that. I will buy something myself to bring as well. But I do expect that there shall be a lot of people that will come. You know Mark had lots of friends and coworkers."

Monica did not hesitate. "I and Tim will pick up something as well to bring. And I can have Tim mention something at work, maybe some of Mark's coworkers can bring some dishes to pass."

Sara, feeling relieved at Monica's support, thought that was a wonderful idea and should be a great help to her. "Thank you, Monica, I am sure some will offer to help out. That really would take a lot of pressure off me and make things a lot easier. How is Johnnie doing? Is he okay? I should really come get him now that I am done for the day."

Monica responded in a comforting voice. "Don't trouble yourself, the boys are doing fine, and Johnnie seems to be taking it well. I think it's a good distraction for him to be able to spend time with George, and anyways, Tim is happy that we are able to help out by doing so, we were planning on keeping him for the night if that is okay with you?"

Sara paused for a minute to think, then responded, "Well, I do feel a bit lonesome without him here and would like to not be alone in this house and having Johnnie home would be a real comfort to me. I can come and pick him up."

"No, that is okay, please don't trouble yourself. I can send him home. Or maybe I can come sit with you for a while. Maybe the boys can play a little longer while we visit?" Monica asked, not wanting her best friend to feel alone.

After all, everything was done around the house, and she would be bored now just sitting around waiting for Tim to get home. "Let me call Tim so he can mention about the food to his coworkers before he leaves to come home."

Sara felt relieved that Monica would be staying for a spell. "That would be great, Monica. Thank you so much. It would be nice to have some company, and thank you for all your help as well. You have no idea how much you have been a blessing to me. I will see you in a little bit, Mon."

"Okay, Sissy, be there in a few, let me just make this phone call to Tim real fast, and then we are on our way." Monica hung up from Sara and gave a call to Tim real fast.

"Hey, honey, I know you're busy, but I need to ask you a question. Can you see if any of the boys there will help out with some of the food? It would sure be a lot of help to Sara if they can?"

Tim reassured Monica that he will just as soon as he gets done with this job. "No problem, honey, I can ask them when we all get back to the shop. I am sure they will be more than happy to pitch in and help out. Mark was very well liked by everyone. It sure doesn't seem right to have him not being here today. Everyone seemed a bit down of sorts. It's not going to be the same without him here. I still can't believe he is gone. I miss him so badly. Mark was like my brother, and now, well, it's hard to believe this is real, you know? We are all a little bit on edge out here today. It just isn't right, it isn't right at all."

Monica almost in tears herself again. "No, it isn't right. And Sara is devastated. I am going over there for a while and going to spend some time with her; she is quite lonely and needs to have some company. Are you okay with picking up something to eat on your way home?"

"Yes, I can do that. How is Johnnie doing? How is he handling all of this?" Tim said, being very concerned.

"Johnnie seems to be okay, but I wonder if it just hasn't sunken in yet. I can tell at times that he struggles a bit, but I really think he is trying to stay strong in front of George. But I do wish he wouldn't hold it all inside, it's not good for him to do so."

"Yes, that is true. Okay, honey, I have to go, be safe and give Sara a hug from me. I love you, honey, I will see you when you get home." Tim kissed Monica through the phone real fast while he was alone for a brief moment, and the guys won't hear it.

Monica responded with a kiss as well. "I love you too, Tim, please be safe, baby."

After hanging up, Monica got the boys together, so they can all go to Sara's house. George and Johnnie raced down the few houses that were in between their homes.

Johnnie reached the door first went right in and made his appearance known with a very loud, "I'm home, Mom."

George, who was right behind him, both dashed up the stairs and headed straight for Johnnie's room to begin a new adventure. Johnnie emptied out his backpack full of toys to see if there was anything he wanted to continue playing with.

Downstairs, Sara and Monica sat in the living room and spent some much needed girl time

73

together. Monica tried to comfort Sara as would be expected. Sara got up from the soft tan couch that almost matched the off-white carpet they had just installed a few years back and offered Monica something to drink.

"I can put on a pot of coffee if you would like some, Monica? Or would you prefer a soda or some tea?"

Monica gave thought for a minute before settling on some tea that Sara had made the other day. After returning with the beverages that Sara had went to get, the two sat for a few hours and talked before being interrupted by the phone as if it was being a rude interruption Sara almost not wanting to respond picked up the receiver.

"Hello?"

The familiar voice on the other end greeted Sara with a softness in his voice, "Hello, Sara, is Monica still there?"

Sara responded before handing the phone over to Monica.

"Hello? Hi, honey, are you on your way home?" Monica asked.

"Yes, I am, but I wanted to know before I grab something if you all have eaten already? If not, I will pick up some pizza on my way, and we can all eat together." "Oh, that sounds great," Monica responded. "I will see you when you get here then."

Monica, hanging up the phone, went back to where she was sitting and let Sara know that Tim was bringing some pizza over for dinner, which was perfectly fine with Sara who hadn't even

74

given thought as to what she and Johnnie would eat for dinner.

After a while, Tim came in with some much needed food, carrying two large pizzas. Sara and Monica grabbed them from Tim and went into the kitchen and prepared the table for their dinner, after which Sara yelled up the stairs for the two boys to come down and eat. Returning back to the kitchen, she sat at the table with Monica and Tim as they patiently wait for the two boys to make their way into the kitchen for dinner. Sara thanked Tim for bringing dinner over.

Johnnie and George both sat down next to each other. Sara had their pizza already on their plates, and they all began to eat. For both homes, dinner was a time for sharing and discussing any and all events of the day, as they would talk over any issues that may have developed over the period of the day.

After dinner, Tim and his family made their way back to their home. Monica had offered to help Sara clean up after dinner, but Sara assured her it was quite okay. Sara never minded doing housework, and it would seem as an escape for a few passing minutes while they got everything back in order before she and Johnnie retired for the night.

CHAPTER 3

The Burial

The next morning, Sara woke up after a good long night's sleep, finally having returned to her own bed, instead of the couch that she had been sleeping on. Feeling a bit refreshed, she went through her normal routine of getting a pot of coffee going. Sara then headed into the bathroom for a nice hot bath before getting Johnnie up. After relaxing for thirty minutes in the steamy hot water, Sara decided it's time to get out and get moving. Stepping out of the bathtub, she grabbed a towel from the shelf and dried off her silky smooth body before wrapping her soft blue robe around her.

Walking into her bedroom, she opened her huge walk-in closet and looked for a nice dress to wear today before settling on some blue jeans and a nice blouse.

It's going to be a long day. "I want to wear something comfortable. Maybe some nice tennis shoes to go with this."

After getting dressed, Sara woke Johnnie up then went to prepare breakfast for the two of them. After having a very quiet and uneventful breakfast, Sara called Monica to ask for another favor.

Monica answered, "Good morning, Sara, how did you sleep?"

"Like a rock," Sara responded. "I was wondering, Mon, if I could trouble you to take Johnnie again today? I will be at the funeral home all day for visitations. And Johnnie would get so bored if he had to stay there with me."

Monica happily responded, "It's no trouble at all, send him down when he is ready. I will bring the boys up when I come later this morning. Oh, and Tim forgot to mention last night that many of his coworkers volunteered to bring some food today. And Tom also said that the company would cater the food for the funeral tomorrow."

Feeling extremely relieved, Sara said, "Thank you so much, Monica. I couldn't get through this without you. You have helped me out so much."

Monica expressed her love and care for Sara and Johnnie before hanging up.

After a short while, Johnnie made his way down to George's house, taking his time as he thought on the day. While Sara finished getting ready to go to the funeral home, so much sadness and loneliness filled her heart. So much depression and stress. How could one even begin to imagine all the feelings that Sara must be experiencing and all the emotions that seemed to be so overwhelming to her?

Johnnie finally made his way up to the door and

knocked on it. George answered the door and welcomed his best friend to come in. No surprise that these two disappeared immediately to George's room, for these two young boys had a serious battle to finish on Soldier Wars. As this battle continued to wage on, the two boys got so caught up in this game that time passed by unnoticed.

Monica was getting some food prepared for the visitation and did some light house cleaning and straightening up while the boys were occupied with the war they were waging in George's room. After a few hours of cooking and cleaning, Monica got dressed in a nice yellow dress with a red flower pattern with some matching yellow high heels and a yellow summer hat with a red flower on the side. Looking very bright and pretty against her smooth tanned skin, the whole outfit flowed well together and was quite elegant. Monica had a sensual walk about her with the kind of hips that would almost make any man break out into a sweat. Finally having everything ready with just a slight touch of makeup. Monica gathered the two boys together and had them carry the food out to the car and place it in the trunk. Monica made a few adjustments before closing the trunk and then got the boys in the car. After making sure everyone was seat belted in, she headed to the funeral home to meet Sara.

At the funeral home, Sara was busy with all the people who had shown up already this morning, somewhat overwhelmed by the number of people who came to see Mark one last time before he was buried tomorrow. Sara, always the worrying sorts, began to wonder if they will have enough food. It was nearly noon now and people would be getting hungry soon. Feeling a bit relieved, however, when she spotted Monica and the boys coming in carrying a few dishes of food, Sara took a few minutes to go and greet Monica. She walked with her to the break area where they were serving fresh hot coffee and a few snacks. Sara and Monica began to get the food set out and some paper plates also with plastic wear.

The boys, of course, sneaked off for some wandering around and perhaps a time of imagination. Always taking every advantage of their surroundings to make a game out of it, they began to imagine themselves as investigators, seeking to find the answers to each mystery. Peeking into several rooms, they acted as if they were looking for clues.

Sara and Monica had everything set out now and ready for the guests as they had returned back to the showing room to greet people and have small talk. Sara was always very popular as was Mark. Sadness had filled the room as people would walk past the dark black casket with the red velvet lining that contained Mark's body. The sadness on people's faces was too much to ignore, making it even harder for Sara who was doing her best to keep it together.

Sara was always known for being a marvelous host. And it was a way for her to use it this time as a sense of strength. Monica stayed by her side and helped out with little things that should arise, even in conversations that she would expect Sara may have struggled with. Being a constant sense of comfort for Sara.

While Johnnie and George continued on their mission to uncover every dark corner of this detective scene, looking for some kind of clues to uncover every kind of mystery that this place should have. Monica had stepped away for a few minutes to go find the two boys who had been gone way too long to not be getting into trouble, finding them wandering all over this place letting their imaginations run wild. Gathering them together, all three returned to Sara, so they can all go sit down and get a bite to eat before Monica took the boys with her for a while.

Sitting and talking for a few after eating, Monica made sure Sara would be okay before leaving her for a while to keep the two boys from getting too bored and finding themselves in some kind of sorts. After Monica and the boys left, Sara found her way back up the stairs and into the visiting room, having taken a seat to try and relax just for a few. Feeling exhausted, Sara would have loved to have sneaked off for a few to lay down for a spell.

While Monica was driving and George was sitting up front next to her, Johnnie let a few tears run down his face before whipping them off. Hoping no one had noticed. George, seeing Johnnie trying to hide it, made no mention of it at all. But rather pretended that it had gone unnoticed.

Later that evening, Sara called Monica to let her know that she was on her way to pick up Johnnie.

After a long day at the funeral home, Sara was ready to get home and relax with a nice hot bath. But first, she must pick up Johnnie and get them both some dinner. After that, it will be time for some much-needed relaxation and then off to sleep. Feeling a bit exhausted from the day, she got to Monica's house, and Monica let Sara know that she already fed Johnnie, and so Sara grabbed something simple to snack on rather than make a small meal for herself.

After getting settled in and some food in her, she went and slid herself into the hot water which had now steamed up the whole bathroom like a sauna and fell into what would have seemed like a deep sleep.

Ahhh, just what I needed. A nice hot quiet bath.

After which Sara made sure Johnnie was ready for bed. "It's going to be an early night tonight, Johnnie, I am exhausted."

"Okay, Mom. I will get myself ready and then play for a while before going to sleep," Johnnie replied.

"Okay, just don't stay up too late, I am going to go lay down." Sara climbed into bed and almost immediately fell to sleep.

Waking up the next morning, Sara went to check on Johnnie, finding him asleep in his bed with his toys scattered all about as if he had forgotten that he even had a toy box. Then hurried down the stairs to get things ready as it was her custom to do every morning. However, today was it. This was the day to truly say goodbye to the man she had loved so deeply. Being a bit anxious today to get it

81

over with, Sara tried to remain calm and focused and everything that was needed to be done before leaving for the funeral home for the last time. After getting herself together, she sat and had a nice hot cup of coffee while relaxing out on the patio.

I never came out here much before in the morning to drink my coffee, it's rather nice out here in the morning time.

Just resting back and drinking her coffee and taking in the wonderful nature scene that was her backyard. The woods and the animals that were scurrying about looking for food, the birds chirping, the squirrels chasing one another in an attempt to steal each other's food of which they have hidden in Sara's backyard. The whole scene was quite enjoyable and refreshing. Sara, so intrigued by the scene, had even forgotten all her worries for a brief few minutes. That was until she heard the sound of Johnnie in the kitchen. Sara got up and went back in to assist Johnnie with breakfast.

Hugging him as she entered back into the house. "Good morning, Johnnie, how did you sleep?"

"I slept okay, Mom, how about you?" Johnnie inquired of his mother.

"Like a rock, I was so exhausted by the time I got home," Sara explained to Johnnie while getting things out for her to cook them both some eggs and toast. After eating, she hurried Johnnie along to get dressed for the funeral. Taking a deep sigh, Sara also finished up getting herself together as well. After an hour, Sara yelled up the stairs for Johnnie to come on. It was time now to leave for the funeral home.

After a short drive that seemed to take a lot longer than usual, however, it really hadn't. Johnnie and Sara held hands as they walked into the funeral home, which seemed to have comforted Sara a bit. Sara wanted to get there early that she may have a few minutes to really say her last goodbye to her loving husband before anyone else showed up. After a few quiet moments and some tears, Sara gathered herself together once again and prepared herself to greet the friends and family who would be arriving soon.

Tim, Monica, and George were the first to show up as Sara had hoped they would of. George and Johnnie went in the back and sat down and played with a few small toys that had brought along. Darryl and Randy also came to the back once they arrived and sat with Johnnie. All four of them began to play until time for the funeral to begin. Monica stayed as close to Sara as she could, as the people began to pour in.

Mark's mother was a mess already. She was crying before she even walked in. Hugging Sara as they held one another as tight as they could and crying as if they had water falling from their eyes. This was it. The funeral was about to start. Sara did her best to not fall apart. She felt a sense of responsibility to remain strong for Johnnie, but how could she? How could one be expected to not fall apart? How could one be expected to keep it together at a time like this? Not being able to hold the tears back, Sara gripped Johnnie's hand tighter, and cried as she mourned this tremendous loss to her wonderful family.

After the funeral had ended, Johnnie just stood there as if now he finally realized what all had really happened. For the first time, Johnnie seemed to appear very aware of the situation. Up until now, Johnnie had been very strong in his emotions, but now, it seemed to be a clear realization what he had known all along. But now, it hit him like a truck. Johnnie for this first time broke down in front of people as he dropped to his knees, he lost all control as he sat there at the grave and sobbed. This was the final goodbye to his hero, the father he had loved so deeply. This was the end.

Now what? What will happen now? A boy needed his father. And for Johnnie, Mark had been the very best father that anyone could have ever had. Sara stood behind Johnnie also crying in anguish before helping him to get back up, so they could go. Not wanting to stay there a minute longer, Sara motioned Johnnie to the car.

After sometime later, they finally returned to their home that had once been so vibrant and now was much colder with a darker feeling.

CHAPTER 4

The Rivalry Begins

After returning back to school, Johnnie
seemed to have a more edgy side to him. This
young boy who was once really funny and
outgoing seemed to be starting to develop a more
serious side to him now. After the death of his
father, Johnnie had begun to change a little in his
attitude. Not so much as being mean to others but
more on the side of getting back in your face real
quick if you had started something with him,
whereas before Johnnie at times was a bit more
passive.

However, being his first day back to school, he
was sure to be tested this afternoon on the
playground during lunch break. Seemed like it had
been running through the school that Wayne was
running his big mouth about Johnnie's father
dying, and that was something that Johnnie was
not about to let slide. Once the boys heard about it,
they began to argue about who was going take out

Wayne until Johnnie got into the group and spoke up immediately saying that Wayne was his come lunchtime, which also didn't take long to get through the school as well. That also had got back to Wayne too who was already looking for a fight anyways.

Wayne wanted to show off for his friend Ricco who was starting his first day at South Bend School. Ricco was part of a group that was over at West Bend Heights. They were some tough kids who liked to bully other kids and made them give them their lunch money or toys. And if you didn't, you were sure to get beaten up by these kids. They thrived off being mean to other kids and making everyone afraid of them.

However, for Johnnie and his band of friends, being pushed around was something that was out of the question. Johnnie fidgeting as the clock slowly ticked by, waiting for lunch break to get here, he was furious at the remarks Wayne had made about his father's passing. Barely being able to even concentrate on his schoolwork for all he could think about was making Wayne pay for what he had been saying. And this time, the fight was his and not someone else. No one was going to step up this time and do it. This fight surely belonged to Johnnie and him alone. He could imagine what he was going to do to Wayne, how he was going to win this fight, and the more he thought about it, the angrier he had become.

If only time would go by faster. He wanted the fight the first time, and now, Wayne was going to get everything that Johnnie wanted to give him the first time plus a whole lot more. George, sitting by Johnnie, noticed very quickly that he was fidgeting quite a bit.

"Hey, bro," George whispered to Johnnie. "Are you okay, man?"

Johnnie whispered back, "Yeah, I am good, bro, just can't wait for lunchtime to get here. I am going to destroy Wayne when we get to the playground."

George smiled. "Heck yeah, bro, take this punk out for sure."

Mrs. Smith noticed the little chit chatter between the two boys and walked over to them. "Is there something you would like to share with the class, boys?" Mrs. Smith asked.

Both boys responded at the same time, "No, Mrs. Smith."

"Then get back to work, and no more talking," Mrs. Smith said as she walked back to her desk and sat back down, keeping a sharp eye on Johnnie and George to make sure they stop talking and got their work done.

Johnnie, still keeping his eye on the clock waiting for it to reach lunchtime, knowing it was almost here. Realized that he hadn't done much work today at all, as he tried to focus for a few minutes to get some work done. Finally, it was lunchtime, the moment he had been waiting for all morning.

George and Johnnie met up with Darrell and Randy as all four had their lunch time together. Darrell being all hyped up about the fight that Johnnie was looking forward to being involved in.

All four sat down together and saw Wayne and his friend Ricco sitting across the lunch room together. Johnnie gave Wayne a cold stare, not taking his eyes off him as he ate his lunch. Johnnie slowly eating his lunch and not saying much as the other three boys made several comments about Wayne meeting his fate. Laughing and joking about what they felt would happen, however, Johnnie not even smiling, just eating his food and occasionally shooting Wayne an angry stare.

After lunch was finished, they began to let the kids go outside. The four boys made their way to the door where Wayne and Ricco had already exited.

This is it. Time for retribution. Walking outside, Johnnie saw Wayne and Ricco over at the slide staring at the door as if waiting for Johnnie to come out. All four boys walked over to Wayne, Johnnie out in the front to lead the way. Wayne stepped forward to meet Johnnie.

"So, sissy boy, you want to get your butt kicked today, huh?" Wayne asked with a smirk on his face. Johnnie, not even responding, just threw a right hook that caught Wayne square across the chin and knocked him to the ground.

"Get up, Wayne!" Johnnie shouted with anger.

Wayne got back up and threw a punch at Johnnie that just missed him. While Johnnie countered with a solid left jab that knocked Wayne back. Regrouping fast, Wayne hit Johnnie as they grabbed each other and began to wrestle. Both finally fell to the ground, and Ricco took a step forward as if to try and jump in before being met head-on by George. Darrell made it known real fast that he wasn't about to let anyone jump in.

"The first person to jump into this fight will have to take me on." Looking around to make sure everyone heard him, Darrell returned his focus back to the fight and began to cheer Johnnie on.

They were rolling on the ground before Johnnie got free and stood back up. Giving Wayne a moment to get on his feet, Johnnie unloaded a tirade of blows and combinations that finally ended this fight. Johnnie being declared the winner breathing heavily looked over at Ricco.

"This is how it is, now you have anything to say?" Ricco with a sly grin didn't say anything, just helped Wayne up.

As they walked away, Wayne stopped and yelled back to Johnnie, "This ain't over with."

Johnnie stared back at Wayne, looking deep into Wayne's eyes with such great anger. "Anytime, Wayne, just bring it."

George was laughing. "You're two for two, Wayne," George said as all of the four boys laughed. "Maybe next time huh, Wayne?"

Darrell, who always loved a good fight, made a remark to Ricco, "Next time, we can have a tag team bout, what you think, Ricco?"

Ricco shot Darrell a glare. "Anytime you feel like you want some, I am always game. You think you're something, next time it will be me and you."

Darrell accepted that challenge. "We can go right now."

Ricco responded to that challenge, "After school,

meet me by the old bell. And we will see who is the man."

"Yes, we will, and I can tell you right now it won't be you," Darrell responded.

"Come on, guys, let's go play," Johnnie said as they all walked away and went off to get some time in on the playground before the lunch bell rang.

After school let out, the four boys who always took the bus home together made their way to the old bell that was out in the yard out front of the school. Ricco and Wayne were already standing there waiting, watching as the four boys made their way over to them. Ricco stood there with a very cocky smile on his face. And Darrell who was never one to turn down a fight let alone a challenge was very confident that Ricco would become another notch in Darrell's victory belt. Wasting no time at which was Darrell's custom, he walked straight up to Ricco and engaged in some conversations of sorts.

"Well, you made it Ricco, that's good. I would have been really disappointed had you actually not shown up. Now it's time to put up or shut up." Darrell got deep in Ricco's face.

"Well, I am sure happy you didn't chicken out, I've been looking forward to this ever since Wayne told me about you guys. Seems he doesn't like you all very much, and I reckon I don't like you all either," was the response Ricco gave Darrell that had made him smile.

Darrell almost laughing pushed Ricco who returned the push with a punch across Darrell's face. Darrell was now riled up for sure after being punched in the face as he went after Ricco like a mad bull. Throwing all kinds of punches and landing most of them. But this fight would not end quickly. One thing for sure about Ricco was he could take some punches. However, Darrell was known for his right hook that was very powerful and would often end a good fight rather quickly.

Wayne cheered Ricco on as Johnnie, George, and Randy cheered on Darrell who was taking some good shot to the face by Ricco. Finally, after a good long few minutes of wrestling each other, Darrell dropped Ricco with a solid punch that rocked him and knocked him to the ground as Darrell stood over Ricco declaring his victory. After a few minutes of celebration, the four boys walked off still hyped up about the win Darrell had received. All four boys had missed to bus and walked home together.

While Ricco got back up, he reaffirmed to Wayne. "This isn't over with yet. I will make sure of that, my friend. This war has just begun."

Wayne helped Ricco gather his stuff together and responded, "They are going down, Ricco. We will have our revenge on them. This is far from over. Just you wait and see."

Both Ricco and Wayne had made it their aim to see these four boys go down. Wayne may have lost both of his fights, and Ricco didn't win for sure either, but in no way were they about to give up and let this go. They were sure of that.

A few days later as they were walking home from the bus stop, Randy mentioned a new family who moved in down the block from them. George hadn't noticed anyone moving in had begun to inquire about it.

"Was there any kids?" George eagerly awaiting his reply.

"Yes, I saw two kids, one was a boy about our age and a girl also," Randy responded in a slightly disgusted way as if hoping they had both been boys.

"Well, maybe we should go over there and meet them later on today. I have to stop at home first and check in, but I am sure we can go right after," George added.

Johnnie, not looking at all excited, remarked, "Yes, I suppose we should at least go down there and meet them. But I also have to check in first."

Darrell began to instruct them as to how they should all meet up. "Okay, we all go check in real fast then we meet back at the camp behind Johnnie's house."

After everyone finally arrived at the camp behind Johnnie's house, they decided to walk down and meet the two new kids who had just moved in down the street.

"I saw them riding their bikes up and down the block, so let's go see what they are like," suggested Darrell.

All four agreed to it and made their way down to meet them. Randy flagged the new boy down as was supposing to ride his bike right past them. "Hey, my name is Randy, and this is my brother Darrell; and these two are Johnnie and George. We saw you just moved in, huh?"

"Yes, just the other day. My name is Steven, and this is my sister Tonya."

Tonya and Johnnie's eyes met, and something sparked within them both, not being able to take their eye off each other. Johnnie, never having felt anything like this before, tried to regain his focus back to the conversation.

"So when will you be joining us at school?" Johnnie asked while still keeping his eye on Tonya.

"Probably next week, I figure, we still have to go and get registered and all," Tonya said while giving Johnnie a slight smile as she brushed her hair back.

"Yes, next week, I am sure of it," added Steven.

"Cool bikes, man," George said as he was checking them out.

"I have a cool bike also," he added.

"Oh, what kind do you have?" asked Steve.

"Well, it's a freestyle bike, I can do tricks and stuff," George responded, feeling good about himself that he was able to share that with the new kid as he was trying to impress him.

"And what about you, Johnnie?" asked Tonya. "What kind of bike do you have?"

"I have a freestyle bike also, but mine is black and white, where George, well, his bike is red and black, but I don't normally do tricks on mine, I just like to ride it," explained Johnnie.

"Well, maybe we can go riding together sometime," said Tonya with a flirty smile.

Johnnie also smiled a little too much for George's liking, and the other boys had begun to notice the liking that these two had taken to each other also.

"That would be great," Johnnie answered, trying very hard to keep his composure, but failing miserably.

Darrell piped up with a loud voice, "Hey, we have a camp, if you want to join, Steve."

"Yeah, you both can join," Johnnie added, making sure that Tonya wasn't left out. For it was Darrell's intentions to exclude her mainly because she was a girl. And they have never had a girl in their club ever. And it was Darrell's aim to keep it that way. However, after Johnnie had included her, there wasn't much Darrell could do now. And she was sure to join.

"Yeah, that sounds cool, I would love to join your club. What's the name of it?" asked Steve. "I would love to join also," Tonya added while staring at Johnnie.

"Um, well, we actually never gave our club a name," Darrell said with some embarrassment.

"Yeah, we just always hangout, and I have this place back in the woods behind my house," Johnnie added.

Tonya, brushing her hair back and smiling, asked, "So it's your club, Johnnie?"

"Well, yes, it is. I started it. But George helped me build it and so did Darrell and Randy," Johnnie responded, trying to include everyone as to not make himself above the rest.

However, this was Johnnie's club, and they all knew it. But Johnnie could see the disapproval on Darrell's face about Tonya being with them altogether. But it was too late, for Johnnie knew he had got what he wanted as soon as he invited her in. George also was not so happy, but not wanting to make an issue out of it acted as if he had not even noticed what was going on with Johnnie and Tonya.

"Well, we will have to put all our heads together and come up a name, I guess, I mean we can't exactly be in a club with no name, right?" Tonya said with quite a flamboyancy, not realizing her words were like a dagger into the heart of Darrell who was not about to let some girl come in and name their club.

Being very irritated, Darrell looking over at Johnnie added, "Well, I am sure we will come up with something that fits us perfectly."

"Well, let's go check it out then. I am eager to see this club you all have built." Steve not wanting to wait, for this was the first club he had ever been asked to join before.

"Sure, follow me, guys," Johnnie said with great confidence as he was trying to impress Tonya to assure her that this was in fact his club, and he was the leader. Taking them back into the woods where the camp was.

Tonya began to immediately get excited about the way it was designed. Looking around and smiling ever so big.

"Oh, what a wonderful club this is, Johnnie. I love it. This is so cozy I could make this into a really comfortable camp with a few added touches."

Darrell, having had enough of this girl club, spoke up, "It's perfectly fine the way it is, and it sure don't need a girl's touch."

Johnnie shot Darrell a look of disgust while he was talking.

And Tonya looked crossed at him as well responded, "Well, everyone knows a girl's touch makes everything better." Johnnie laughed until seeing that Darrell was not amused.

"Anyways, this is it," added George. "So I guess the next order of business is to come up with a good name for it."

All six members sat down and began to think about what they shall call this club of theirs. Johnnie, completely satisfied with not having a name, wondered what they will come up with, but as for him, he added very little input. Other than the fact that he didn't want a name for the club of course. Tonya obviously wanted it to have some reference to Johnnie's name such as "Johnnie's Crew or Johnnie's Rebels," which was quickly dismissed by Darrell and Johnnie.

"Well, I don't think we really need a name, do we? I mean it's just for us to hang out is all. And we don't do anything really but talk and play games." Johnnie added in hopes to be able to keep them all from really going any further with this idea that he was obviously was against. George also agreed with Johnnie.

"Yeah, I think Johnnie is right, why do we need a name for? It's just a place for us to meet together and have fun. Anyways, I vote for no name."

Johnnie also spoke up, "I agree with George, let's not waste our time with trying to name this club."

Tonya did not like the idea but agreed with it for Johnnie's sake as she relaxed back on a long log that they used for sitting. "Do you guys ever sleep out here?" Tonya inquired with such great curiosity.

"Yes, we do sometimes," Johnnie responded in hope that Steve and Tonya would be able to sleep out here with them.

Johnnie found it very hard to conceal his liking toward Tonya, for she was extremely beautiful. With long blonde hair that seemed to glow against her silky soft tanned skin. Johnnie had thought she was the most beautiful girl he had ever seen and was mesmerized by every word she had uttered. Never had anyone caught his attention so quickly. And for Tonya, well, she had no trouble at all making advancements toward Johnnie, for she also took quite a liking to Johnnie. She had thought he was the most handsome young boy she had ever met in her entire life. And was more than eager to get to know him. As for the rest, they all took a liking to Steve right from the beginning. He just seemed to fit right in with the group and was more than happy to be a part of something so quickly after moving in. Johnnie walked over and sat on the same log that Tonya was laying on.

Asking her and Steve, "Do you think you both will be able to stay out here sometimes with us?"

"Oh, I am hoping so," Tonya responded with desperation in her voice.

"Yes, I do think so, Johnnie," added Steve who was very excited about the idea himself.

"Perhaps this Friday, we can get together and

sleep out here," he added.

"Oh, wouldn't that be just so great, Johnnie?" Tonya said in hopes that he would invite them to come stay out there with him.

"Yeah, sure it would. I will ask my mom about it tonight and see if I can't get her to let us do it," Johnnie responded. "I am sure she will."

George and the rest of the gang also wanted to do it. Randy hadn't said much concerning Tonya, but he was paying close attention to the interaction that had been going on between her and Johnnie. For Randy didn't care much whether a girl joined the club or not and had felt his brother's attitude of the whole idea was very silly indeed. Randy rather liked the idea of having new members in the club and wasn't too concerned about what their gender was just so long as everyone got along.

The next day at school, everyone was talking about the two fights that had taken place the day before. And Darrell was very proud of the fact that he was the winner in the stories being told around the school yard. Darrell loved any attention he could get. And reveled in this opportunity to be the tough guy who won the school yard fight. For Darrell, it pleased him to be able to brag about it and have others talking about him also. And it was very noticeable to the others. Johnnie made a statement about it that didn't seem to make matters any better.

It actually only fueled Darrell's ego when Johnnie said, "So you're the new big shot around here, huh?"

Darrell smiled as big as his cheeks would let

98

him. "I sure am, Johnnie boy, I am the man now. And no one is ever going to beat me." Laughing out loud as he began to flex his muscles in front of all those who was looking in his direction.

Ricco was also being aware of the things that were being said around the playground. As him and Wayne began to think on how to get even with Darrell and Johnnie, and Wayne also not forgetting about George either, for he wanted revenge on the whole group. But Johnnie was his main focus. And he was for sure going to find a way to make Johnnie pay for his embarrassment. As the boys laughed and had a good time with their victories, they had no idea that there was a rivalry that was taking place, and that it was far from over with. Ricco was not the kind to let this go, and Wayne wasn't either. It would only be a matter of time before they would come up with some kind of plan to get even. And that was exactly what they were spending their time on. Talking over many ideas, but the only problem was that they were outnumbered and needed to figure out a way to even up the odds. But what they didn't know was come Monday, the odds was gonna get even worse. For that is when Steven would be joining the group at school along with Tonya. And making it worse was the unknown fact that Steve was taking karate classes three times a week, while Tonya was also taking karate as well as gymnastics.

As the school week had drawn to a close, Johnnie was excited about having Tonya and Steve join them back at the camp for an all-nighter. Everyone met up at Johnnie's after dinner back at the camp area. It was the first for Steve and Tonya. They had both brought their pillows and blankets with them as the others did as they always had. Johnnie and Tonya sat next to each other all night as they all shared stories about each other and Steve and Tonya shared about themselves as well. It was a good time that they all was having together while getting to know their new friends. Everyone was sharing and talking all night and the more they shared the closer they all felt to each other.

Darryl had talked about his fight with Ricco as well as the fight Johnnie and George had both had with Wayne. Tonya was impressed that Johnnie had not only been in a fight, but had won it as well. Johnnie felt good that Tonya had heard that story he was proud to be able to have her know that he had won. It was a good night of stories and laughs as the night had ended with some jokes and laughing.

On Monday, as they all went back to school, Johnnie was happy to find that Tonya was in his class, and Steven was in the same class as Randy and Darrell. Darryl was a year older then randy but had been held back a year. Having all being in the same grade, they all were able to be together during the lunch recess. Of course, Ricco and Wayne were there also. Wayne took notice of Tonya right away and wasn't afraid to let her know it. Seeing her out in the playground with Johnnie and his friends didn't make Wayne very happy at all.

It didn't take long for Wayne and Ricco to try to

make trouble because of it. Wayne was more than happy to try to get Tonya's attention in front of Johnnie. And decided that was exactly what he was going to do. As Wayne had walked over to where Tonya was, he immediately tried to strike up a conversation with her when he had saw that Johnnie had walked over to talk to George.

"Hey there, my name is Wayne, what's your name?"

Tonya, unaware of the situation between Wayne and Johnnie, responded in her normal, soft pleasant voice, "My name is Tonya, it's very nice to meet you."

"My pleasure," responded Wayne with a smile.

George had taken notice of it and made Johnnie also aware of it. "Hey, Johnnie, look over there, bro." Johnnie turned his head to see what George was pointing at.

"Oh, well, let me go see what this is about," Johnnie said as he walked toward Tonya and Wayne.

"Hey, Tonya, what are you up to?" Johnnie asked.

"Just meeting Wayne, he seems to be nice, don't you think, Johnnie?"

Wayne interrupted, "Yeah, Johnnie, don't you think I'm nice?"

Johnnie gave Wayne a look that could have killed him, while Wayne stood there with a big grin on his face knowing that he was getting Johnnie riled up.

"Ain't nothing nice about Wayne," Johnnie responded.

"Oh, um, what's wrong, Johnnie?" Tonya asked with astonishment.

"Yeah, Johnnie boy, what's wrong?" Wayne added as if he didn't know already.

Johnnie had enough of Wayne's game. "Okay, Wayne, that's enough. Tonya is with us, so why don't you beat it."

Wayne was still grinning. "Why don't we let Tonya decide that?"

By this time, Steve and George, as well as the two brothers, had joined Johnnie and Tonya.

"I got a better idea, Wayne, how about we meet after school and settle it?" Johnnie said with great anger.

Tonya being surprised by the whole thing wasn't sure what to say. Steve spoke up, "Is there a problem here with my sister?"

Wayne being the usual smart mouth as he responded, "No, the problem is with me and Johnnie boy. But that will be settled after school."

Johnnie agreed, "Yes, it will, Wayne, and I will give you another beating since you didn't learn the first time."

Steve was not happy that his sister was brought into the situation. "Well, whatever your problem is, leave my sister out of it."

Wayne never liked being told what to do and was way too cocky to let anyone tell him either responded, "I will talk to whoever I want. Ain't that right, baby?" Wayne said as he had looked at Tonya.

"I am not your baby," responded Tonya with disgust.

"That's enough, Wayne. I will see you after school at the old bell." Johnnie ever so angry now that he could almost hit Wayne right here.

About that time Ricco walked up. "Come on, Wayne, we will handle this after school."

Darrell looked intensely at Ricco. "Be careful how you say we."

Ricco turned his attention to Darrell. "Oh, you got a problem with what I said, Darrell?"

Darrell had enough of this foolishness from these two, "Yeah, and now, you have a problem too, Ricco."

"Well, I will be at the bell also, if you think you want to settle it?" Ricco said as he and Wayne were backing up to walk away.

Darrell made one last comment, "I will be there too, Ricco.

As they all walk away, Darrell said out loud. "I hate that freaking jerk."

Johnnie tried to calm Darrell down a bit. "Let it ride for now, Darrell. We will see them after school."

After school, Johnnie and Darrell met up and walked together with the rest of the crew to meet Wayne and Ricco at the old bell who was, of course, standing there waiting for them already. Johnnie dropping his stuff went right after Wayne, and Darrell had grabbed Ricco as the four boys began to fight. Everyone was cheering it on for everything had always gone through the school fast when there was going to be a fight.

Johnnie and Wayne both threw punches at each other, while Ricco and Darrell were wrestling on the ground. All four boys were fighting as hard as they could until they all four began to become exhausted. Johnnie and Wayne fought to what would become a draw between the two. While Darrell had gotten the upper hand on Ricco and clearly won his fight. Johnnie and Wayne separated from pure exhaustion.

Johnnie made it clear to Wayne that he was tired of this. "This ends here, Wayne, I am sick of this crap from you." Wayne just smiled as if it's a joke to him.

Ricco chirped in, "This will never be over with, Johnnie."

Johnnie, tired from the fight, looked at Ricco with a fire in his eyes. "I will end this, Ricco."

Ricco laughed. "We will see, Johnnie."

As they all went their separate ways, Tonya apologized for this whole mess, thinking it was her fault, not knowing that this feud had been going on for a while now.

Even after a few years went by, the feud never settled, while Johnnie and Tonya became even closer together. All six of them became inseparable. And one of Tonya's friends even joined the group, who had taking a huge liking to George.

Sara who had been alone for the past few years after the death of Mark had finally decided to meet someone. After having a few dates with Mike, Sara began to start having some feelings again for the first time since the passing of Mark.

Mike seemed like a wonderful man. Full of passion and desire. A real sweet talker for sure.

And Sara had begun to take a real liking to him. Sara hadn't felt these feelings for a very long time. Mike knew how to make her feel like a woman again. Always telling her how pretty she was and making mention of how nice her outfits looked on her. It was something that Sara had missed so very much and needed so badly.

Sara was trying desperately to slow things down, for they had really just met, and she didn't want to rush into it. But Mike had a passion about him that was irresistible to Sara. She needed to feel it and craved it so badly. Her thoughts were on Mike ever since they first met. It had been way too long since anyone had complimented her the way Mike had been doing.

Sara wasn't really sure, however, how Johnnie was going to react to this new situation. Ever since Mark had passed, it had only been the two of them. But Johnnie was always very understanding, and Sara was hoping he would understand this as well. She needed him too.

She couldn't stop what she was feeling for Mike, nor did she want too. It was time for her to start dating again. She was tired of feeling lonely and needed to feel that love again that she had missed with Mark.

CHAPTER 5

Another New Beginning

I t was late afternoon, and Johnnie would be home soon from school. Sara was anxious and nervous as she waited for him to get home. Today, she was going to take Johnnie to the park and talk to him about Mike. They had been dating now for two weeks, and it was time that she told Johnnie. Not quite sure how he was going to handle the news though made Sara nervous, but she was excited to finally be able to have Johnnie involved in the relationship now. Sara was hoping that Johnnie would be excited as well. He had been busy with his friends and with his club that for him, the passing wasn't as difficult, but for Sara, it was almost as if her life had partially ended. But now, Mike had made her feel alive again, and it was time to let Johnnie know all about it.

Johnnie, finally coming home from school, came in and began to tell Sara about his day. After which Sara told Johnnie that they were going to the park.

"Mom, is it okay if George comes with us?" Johnnie asked with excitement.

"Not this time, Johnnie, I want to spend some time with you." Sara had hoped he wouldn't ask any questions.

"Okay, Mom, when are we going?"

Sara grabbed her purse. "Right now, if you're ready."

Johnnie was ready to go. "Yes, Mom, I am ready to go now."

Sara and Johnnie hadn't been to the park in a long time, and it's a nice ride there. The two of them enjoyed the drive as they listened to the radio together, singing and laughing like they used to do before Mark had died. Johnnie had forgotten what it was like to feel like a family. Things had been rough for Sara and Johnnie since Mark's passing. Finally as they had pulled into the park, Sara told Johnnie to come and sit on the bench with her, so they could talk for a minute before he got distracted with all the toys that was there for him to play on.

"Johnnie, I wanted to bring you here, so I could tell you something. I met someone a few weeks ago. His name is Mike, and he is a wonderful man. I have been dating him now for two weeks, and I want to invite him over for dinner, so you can meet him."

"Okay, Mom, as long as he is good to you. But he better not hurt you." Johnnie felt a little uneasy about the situation, but seeing how excited his mom was about him, Johnnie tried to be good with it. He did not want his Mom to be lonely anymore.

"He is good to me, Johnnie, and I think it might work out." Sara said as she had hoped to have gained Johnnie's approval. Johnnie and Sara held hands as they sat on the bench together and talked.

"As long as you're happy, Mom. That is all that matters." Sara had hugged Johnnie.

"I love you, Johnnie."

"I love you too, Mom."

"Okay, go play, Johnnie. I know you've been waiting to get on those toys."

Johnnie took off to go play, seeing only one other kid on the playground. Johnnie ran over to him.

"Hi, my name is Johnnie," extending his hand out to shake this stranger's hand.

"Hi, my name is Jason." Reaching back to meet Johnnie's hand and shaking it.

"Do you want to play with me?" Johnnie asked Jason.

"Sure, what do you want do to?" Jason responded.

"How about the monkey bars?" Johnnie asked, as he was hoping Jason would say yes. The monkey bars was his absolute favorite.

Jason never really played on the monkey bars with anyone before, and now, he was very excited to finally have someone to play with. Shortly after they started playing together on the monkey bars, Sara saw an ice cream machine.

"Hey, boys, do you want some ice cream?" Sara yelled over to the two boys.

"Yes," Johnnie and Jason responded at the same time. Sara yelled back very loudly,

"Okay, I am going to go get you both an ice cream and use the bathroom. You both be careful and don't run off, Johnnie." Sara walked into the public bathrooms while the boys still played on the monkey bars.

As Johnnie and Jason were playing, some kids walked out of the woods. Jason recognized the boys who used to pick on him. Jason, not sure if they would start a fight or not. He decided he should let Johnnie know that there might be trouble.

"Hey, Johnnie, there might be some trouble, and I don't want to get you involved in it. I have had some issues in the past with these kids, and I don't know if they will start anything or not, but this isn't your fight, so if they start something with us, just take off, okay?"

Johnnie looked at the boys as they walked toward them. "I don't think so, Jason, I don't run from fights, and certainly not when one of my friends needs me. If they want a fight, then they will get it from both of us."

Jason smiled. "I like that. I have never had a friend before."

Both boys dropped from the monkey bars as the, five boys who stepped out of the woods, began to get real close.

"Well, you have a friend now, Jason, and I'm not letting you take them on alone. Johnnie said very seriously.

"So look who we have here if it isn't our old

friend from the street," one of the kids said.

Another one of them asked, "What are you doing in our park?"

Jason with a loud laugh responded. "Your park, huh? I didn't know you owned it."

Johnnie looked intensely at the five kids waiting to see which one was going to make the first move.

"Yeah, this is our park, and you're not welcome here," said another one of the bullies.

Jason responded with a cocky laugh. "Well, you're welcome to try to make me leave if that's what you want to do."

As the five boys made their move, Johnnie caught one with a straight punch to his face and then found himself in a battle with two of them at the same time, while Jason tangled with the other three. This was Jason's first time actually being able to use all he had been learning while training with Chao Ling.

Johnnie was having a hard time with taking on two at one time, this was a first for him. But he was giving it all he had and was throwing hard punches that landed. Jason was handling the other three by himself and was really enjoying being able to use the martial arts that he had learned. Jason was throwing them around while kicking and punching them like he had never done before and was giving these three boys one heck of a fight. Johnnie took a little more of a beating but came out on top nonetheless as the five boys decided they had enough. Johnnie and Jason stood together as the five boys took off back into the woods. Sara returned with ice cream and saw the five boys running off and began to ask Johnnie what had happened. So Johnnie explained as Sara got mad at him for being in another fight.

"Johnnie, I am getting tired of all this fighting!" Sara yelled with great anger. "I don't know what has gotten into you.

Jason spoke up immediately, "It wasn't his fault. Those boys were after me, and Johnnie helped me out like a true friend would have. Really it was all my fault."

"Why are they after you?" Sara asked Jason.

"Because they like to bully other kids, and I had problems with them before. And they don't like me."

Johnnie also added to the conversation, "Yeah, Mom, we weren't doing nothing wrong, just playing on the monkey bars when they walked over to us and started running their mouths to Jason."

Sara sat down on the bench and looked at Johnnie. "I just don't like you fighting, and I am sure you didn't start it, but you can't keep fighting all the time."

"I know, Mom, honestly, I know. And if they hadn't walked over, I wouldn't of today either. But you know I am not going to run and leave someone on their own," Johnnie responded in a very sensitive voice that made Sara excuse this situation altogether.

"You both eat your ice cream, and then we need to go, Johnnie."

"Okay, Mom," Johnnie responded as he and Jason sat on another bench as they talked while eating their ice cream.

"Hey, Johnnie, I am very sorry I got you in trouble," Jason said, feeling real bad about the situation. He had never had a friend before and sure didn't want to get Johnnie in any trouble.

"No worries, my friend, I am not in any real trouble. My mom just doesn't like me fighting," Johnnie responded. "I have been in a few before already. And it bothers her every time."

"Yeah, well, it was a good fight though, and you handled yourself pretty good," Jason said with a smile that obviously meant he was very impressed with how good Johnnie could fight.

"Thanks, you did really good also. Where did you learn to fight like that?" Johnnie being curious as to how he had learned martial arts.

Jason began to tell Johnnie all about Mr. Ling. And how it was these bullies that had beaten him up before in front of Mr. Ling's place. And how he had taken him in and begin to train him and teach him how to defend himself. After finishing their ice cream, Johnnie talked Sara into letting him and Jason play for a few more minutes before having to finally go.

Sara still had a few things to do yet today and needed to get back to the house. For she wanted to go ahead and invite Mike over for dinner tonight and needed to get back and make preparations. For she had no idea as to what she was even going to cook.

After a few minutes, Sara yelled to Johnnie, "It's time to go, Johnnie, say goodbye to your friend and let's go."

Johnnie reached out his hand to shake Jason's hand again. "It was nice meeting you, Jason, I hope to see you again."

"Yes, me too, my friend. I will never forget you, Johnnie. We will forever be friends," Jason said, feeling very sorrowful. He had no idea if he would ever see his only friend again.

"Thank you for the ice cream," Jason said as he walked off and headed back to the orphanage.

Johnnie and Sara got into the car to head back home. Johnnie watched Jason as he walked away wondering the same thing as Jason. Perhaps one day they would meet again. Johnnie felt very sorrowful as well as he pondered this thought. For whatever reason, there was a strong connection between these two. Sara had been thinking all the way home as to what she could make tonight for Mike. For Johnnie, the thought of meeting Mike had begun to become stressful. Johnnie hadn't had another male in his life since the passing of his dad, and this would definitely be something that he would have to adjust to.

The relationship between Mark and Johnnie was something that could not be replaced. And Johnnie had the kind of personality that if he didn't like someone, they would know by the way he would act around them. Johnnie was never good at faking anything, either he liked you or he didn't. But you always knew where you stood with him.

After arriving back home, Sara went to work on getting things ready for the dinner tonight that she was going to invite Mike over for. After seeing what all she had, she began to get things together.

After which Sara decided, she had better call Mike and invite him.

"Hello," Mike said as he answered his phone.

"Hello, Mike, I was wondering if you wanted to come over tonight and have dinner with me and Johnnie." Sara asked, hoping he would be able to.

"Yes, that would be great, honey, what time shall I come?" Mike responded.

"Well, how about six o'clock? Would that be a good time for you?" Sara said with great anticipation.

Mike responded with excitement in his voice as well. "Yes, that would be great.

"So I will see you this evening at six then."

"Perfect, dear, see you at six." Sara smiled as she hung up the phone.

Sara began to scramble around to make sure the house was in order and very clean. Being so very nervous and wanted everything to be perfect. Sara couldn't help but to keep thinking how much she was hoping that Johnnie would like Mike. It had been a few years since there had been a man here for dinner with it just being her and Johnnie all the time. And this was a big step she was taking. When Mark died, Sara had felt that she could never love again, but Mike had deeply affected her. And it was time to see how Johnnie would respond to it. Sara had been so lonely since the passing of Mark and was ready to try to love again. The closer it got to six o'clock, the more nervous Sara had become. Sara was always good under pressure, but this had really got her in some kind of sorts. Sara called Johnnie down from upstairs so that they could sit and talk for a few minutes before Mike arrived.

"Johnnie, come over here and sit. I want to talk to you for a second," Sara said, still being very nervous. Johnnie had sat next to Sara feeling her nervousness. That was something Johnnie was good at, always being able to read people's feelings.

"Yes, Mom, is everything okay?" Sara smiled to try to hide her nervousness.

"Yes, Johnnie, everything is fine. I just wanted to tell you that Mike will be here soon, and I wanted to ask you to please be on your best behavior. And if you don't like him, please don't make any fuss, we will discuss it after he leaves."

Johnnie sensed how important this was to Sara. "Yes, Mom, I will be very good tonight, and afterward, I will tell you what I think of him."

"Fair enough, Johnnie." Sara agreed. "I will call you down when he gets here."

"Okay, Mom." Johnnie went back up to his room to continue his video game until time for dinner with Sara and Mike.

As Sara began to finish preparing the food for the oven, she slid the chicken into the oven, began to fry some potatoes and got the green beans ready. *Hmm, perhaps I will make some muffins.* While making the batter for the muffins, Sara thought about the situation at the park. *Can't help but wonder why Johnnie always finds himself in a fight, I mean I know he doesn't start these fights, but why is it him who always has to get caught up in them?* She put the muffins in the oven with the chicken. *It's almost six o'clock, and Mike should be here any minute. Everything is just about done and should be ready by the time he arrives.*

Shortly after Sara got the table set and food all set out, Mike knocked on the door. Sara hurried herself to answer the door.

"Hi, Mike, come in and make yourself comfortable. The food will be ready in just one second. Sara had called Johnnie, to come down for dinner."

Mike had a seat in the living room as Johnnie came down the stairs and went straight into the kitchen to make sure his mom didn't need any help.

"Johnnie, go ahead and have a seat. I will go get Mike. Mike, the food is ready Honey, come into the kitchen."

Mike got up and followed Sara into the kitchen as they all sat down to eat together. "Mmmm, everything looked so very good Sara, and it smells so wonderful. I can't wait to dig my teeth into this wonderful meal you have created for us," Mike said with a huge smile on his face as he looked into Sara's eyes.

Johnnie watched every move and gesture that Mike had made, as he watched on with careful eyes to make sure that Mike was being absolutely sincere in all that he was saying and doing. Sara smiled and brushed her hair back as she began to dish out the food. Johnnie thanked his mother as she put the chicken on his plate.

"Well, Sara, what a nice young man you are raising," Mike said as he looked at Johnnie.

"Awe, well thank you, Mike," Sara said with a

smile as she looked at Johnnie and gave him a fast wink as to say thank you for being so polite in front of Mike.

Johnnie said nothing as he just continued to look on and watch every move his mother and Mike made, following each conversation ever so carefully.

"So, Johnnie, do you like to play any sports?" Mike asked as he took a bite of his chicken.

"I don't play sports, but I do enjoy to watch baseball," Johnnie responded and then glanced over at his mother.

"Oh, well, baseball is a good sport, but I do prefer football," Mike responded.

"This food is very delicious, Sara, you are a wonderful cook," Mike said as he took another bite.

"Well, thank you, Mike," Sara said while blushing just a bit, for it had been a long time since a man had complimented her cooking, other than Johnnie of course, but the compliment of a seven year old isn't quite the same as a compliment from a handsome man who you are developing feelings for.

After finishing up the meal, Sara moved everyone into the living room for some social time where they all could talk and get more acquainted. Johnnie, not wanting to go, went along not wanting to upset Sara, but he rather of went back to his room. However, Johnnie did recognize this as another opportunity to gauge the seriousness of this relationship that was still developing. Mike and Sara sat on the couch together as Johnnie sat on the chair adjacent to them, so he would be able to watch everything with a clear view. Still not sure about how he really felt about this whole situation, but not wanting to make it all too obvious. Johnnie continued to be more involved than he had wanted to be. However, Mike was the perfect gentlemen, and Johnnie could find no fault with him as of yet.

After some small talk, Sara decided to put in a movie for them to watch. After a while, Mike decided he better get going.

"Well, it's getting late, so I guess I should probably get going," Mike said as he stood up and started to walk toward the door. Sara got up with him and walked to the door with him.

"Thank you for coming over and having dinner with us and spending time watching a movie as well," Sara said as she kissed Mike on the cheek.

"It was my pleasure, dear, and the food was really delicious," Mike responded as he opened the door and waved to Johnnie.

"Take care, young man, it was very nice meeting you," Mike said to Johnnie before heading out the door to leave.

Johnnie responded quickly before heading up the stairs to go to bed. "It was nice meeting you as well."

Sara stopped Johnnie before he was able to get up the stairs. "Hold on a minute, young man, come give me a hug before you run off."

Johnnie ran over and hugged Sara. "Good night, Mom, I love you."

Sara hugged Johnnie back. "I love you too, son.

Tell me what you thought of Mike," Sara said before letting him go up to his bedroom.

"He was okay Mom. He seemed nice enough."

"Brush your teeth before you go to bed." Sara said as she let Johnnie go upstairs for the night.

CHAPTER 6

Growing Together

Early the next morning, Johnnie was up early and took a quick shower and was eager to get out and hang with George. As Johnnie was showering, he began to think about his new friend Jason and how he was doing. Still thinking on the strange connection that had been between the two, Johnnie wondered if there had been a reason that those two had met. Anyways, it was Saturday, and that meant one thing. It was time to get the group rounded up and have some fun. Johnnie was especially excited to see Tonya today. He hadn't been with the group since school yesterday and was eager to see what's going on.

Johnnie, being full of energy, ran down the stairs and into the kitchen where Sara was preparing breakfast.

"Well, young man, what's got you in sorts this morning?" Sara asked Johnnie as she handed him some eggs and bacon.

"The toast is on the cupboard, Johnnie."

"Okay. Thank you, Mom," Johnnie responded as he grabbed some toast and buttered it for him and Sara.

"I am hoping the gang can all get together today. Do you mind if we stay in the camp tonight, Mom?" Johnnie asked with great expectations.

"No, I don't mind, just make sure everyone's parents are okay with it first. And remember the rules, no one goes home by themselves after dark, if they come and don't want to stay the night, their parents have to be notified that they are coming home, and I will also need to know, so I can walk them home." Sara reminded Johnnie so as to keep from having any unwanted issues.

"Yes, I know, Mom, everything will be okay. No one will want to go home anyways," Johnnie said as he finished his breakfast and went to call Tonya and the rest of the group.

Johnnie got his shoes on and headed out the door to meet with Tonya down the street. For whatever reason, he could not wait to see her, and she also was excited that he was coming to see her. Johnnie felt that maybe he should tell Tonya how he felt. *But does she feel the same way? I have never felt this way before about anyone.* Johnnie walked down to meet Tonya. George and the two brothers Darrell and Randy all would be on their way soon. Steve was just getting up as Johnnie arrived. And Tonya was already sitting on the porch awaiting Johnnie's arrival.

"Good morning, Johnnie." Tonya greeted him with a big warm smile that glowed as if the sun

121

was shining on her face.

"Good morning, Tonya, how are you this morning?" Johnnie asked returning the biggest smile he could while starring into her lovely blue eyes. Johnnie was feeling something in the pit of his stomach that made him quite uncomfortable.

Still smiling, Tonya motioned for Johnnie to come sit by her on the porch. "I am good, Johnnie, and how are you today?"

"I am good also, sorry I did not see you yesterday after school. I had to go with my mom, and then her new boyfriend came over for dinner."

"Oh, how did that go? Do you like him?" Tonya questioned.

"He seems okay, but I am seriously going to keep an eye on him," Johnnie said with a scowl on his face, which made Tonya chuckle.

"Oh, Johnnie. I am sure everything will be fine." Tonya still laughed at Johnnie as he seemed to be slightly embarrassed that he had let his emotions show, which was common for Johnnie who was not very good at hiding his emotions. Johnnie looked up and saw

George as he was coming down the street, and Steve poked his head out the door to let Johnnie know he will be out soon after he took a bath.

"Hey, George," Johnnie and Tonya both said at the same time as if they knew what the other was going to say beforehand.

"Hey, you two, where is Steve?" George asked.

"He is taking a bath, but will be out in just a few minutes. He doesn't take long," responded Tonya.

Right about that time, the two brothers began to

walk down the street to meet the rest of the gang.

"Here comes trouble," George said jokingly while laughing.

"Yeah," responded Johnnie. "Trouble for sure." Johnnie made a funny face as he agreed with George. Tonya laughed out loud at the silly face that Johnnie had made.

"Hey, you two," George said as he greeted the two brothers.

"Hey, Darrell and Randy," Johnnie said as he also greeted them.

"Hey, guys," said Tonya as she scooted closer to Johnnie as to make more room for everyone to sit on the porch if they wanted to.

"Hey, everyone," Darrell responded.

"Hey, peeps," said Randy, as he took a seat on the other side of Johnnie.

"So where is Mr. Steveola?" jokingly asked Randy.

George answered real fast, "Oh, he is taking a bath, something you two needed to do this morning also." George laughed.

"Oh, Georgie boy has jokes this morning," Darrell said while throwing George a quick look and then picking him up as to try to show his strength.

"Get him, Darrell," Johnnie piped in as they all laugh.

Tonya watched Darrell and George play wrestle as she said," "This is gonna be one of those days, isn't it, boys?"

Randy slightly pushed Johnnie toward Tonya. "It's always one of those days with these two."

"Yeah, it is Randy," Johnnie responded as he pushed Randy back as they all laugh and made jokes.

Steve finally made his way outside to meet up with the others. "Hey, guys, what's the plan for today?" asked Steve.

Johnnie spoke up. "Well, I was wondering if you all wanted to stay at the club place tonight. We can make a small bonfire and tell stories or something."

"I'm down with that brother," George responded immediately.

"Yeah, me too, bro, that sounds like fun," Darrell said as Randy also agreed. "Yeah, okay, let me make sure it's okay for me to come as well," Steve said as he went to walk in the house before Johnnie stopped him.

"Steve, hold on. I was wondering, Tonya, if you would also be able to join us?" Steve looked back at Tonya.

"You want me to ask for you as well, Tonya?" Steve asked before going into the house.

"Yes, Steve, see if it's okay if I can go, too." Tonya responded as she stared into Johnnie's eyes very lovingly.

After a few minutes, Steve returned to find George and Darrell wrestling in the front yard again.

"Everything is set for tonight, so we all are going to stay the night at the camp," Steve announced as he watched Darrell and George continued to wrestle until they both were exhausted.

"Do these two ever stop?" questioned Steve.

124

Laughing out loud, Johnnie responded, "Nope, they never stop. And it's always a close battle between these two." He looked over at George who seemed to be almost ready for another round, but this time, he was motioning to Randy.

"That's right, we never stop, but I am the champ, ain't that right, Randy? George shouted as he smiled at Randy.

"Is that a challenge, George?" Randy said as he was getting up off the ground from where he had been sitting.

"Just thought you might want a shot at the title that your brother never wins," George said laughingly while glancing over at Darrell who was rolling his eyes.

"Never?"

I do believe I have had your number on numerous occasions there George" Darrell said as he responded to George's comment as he took another deep breath.

"It was just too early for this this morning, and I would have won had you not got me from behind."

"Yes, I am sure, but seeing that you're still breathing hard, I will go ahead and declare myself the winner as usual."

While George and Darrell was focusing on each other, Randy tackled George down to the ground.

"Oh, here we go!" Johnnie yelled. "It's on now."

Tonya sat and watched as these boys continued to wrestle each other as they bragged about who was better. Johnnie of course was focusing more on his conversation with Tonya, which hadn't gone unnoticed by Steve and the other three boys.

It was all too obvious that these two had taken a liking to each other, and for the group, that was fine for they had started to like Tonya being around also. And Tonya also had met a young girl named Ann who was very pretty. And she was wanting Ann to come and spend the night as well. And this would also give Tonya more of a say about things if another girl was to be injected into the group. And Ann was eager to come and hang out since she knew the boys from school and had liked George for a while. However, this was a little fact that as of yet no one even knew about, not even George.

"Johnnie, do you think it would be okay if my friend Ann joined us tonight? I have been wanting her to stay over for a while, and this would be a great opportunity for you all to really get to know her," Tonya asked.

"Yeah, sure, Tonya. I don't see why not. I mean it's just us hanging out anyways, right?" Johnnie replied.

"Great, I will give her a call later on," Tonya said eagerly while hoping that Ann would be able to come over and stay.

After George and Randy was done wrestling around the six of them went to the park to hang out and play until it was lunchtime. But while they were there, Tonya and Johnnie went off on their own for a little while and sat on a big rock and talked for a bit. Meanwhile, the other four boys where playing on the playground and pretending to be superheroes.

After a while, Johnnie and Tonya emerged to join

the others. Getting right involved in what was going on, and until finally, it was time to head out and get back home for lunch. After which Tonya called her friend Anne and invited her to come stay the night. It was a very nice day out and looked as if it would be a very nice night of which to stay out at the camp all night. It was late spring now, and summer was coming quickly, which meant soon school would be out, and they could hang out much more often and later too. Later on that evening after Ann Stone had met up with the group, they all decided to head over to the camp in the woods behind Johnnie's house.

It wasn't long before George and Ann began to show their feelings for each other, which made Tonya and Johnnie happy because now they wouldn't be the focus all the time when they were all together. As they all had arrived and began to sit around the camp, it didn't take long for the boys to begin to let their imaginations run wild as they started telling ghost stories as they was trying to make the girls scared. However, for Tonya and Ann, this was not something that was going to happen, these two were not afraid of ghost stories but rather could tell a few good ones themselves.

As the evening went on, Sara came out and invited them all to come in for some dinner with which she also invited Mike. After she had cooked up some hamburgers for the whole group and Mike as well, they all laughed and joked as they ate. It was for sure a good evening for them all, but Johnnie couldn't help but think that there was something about Mike that he just didn't like.

George who had known Johnnie forever picked up on it after watching him very carefully as he didn't respond much to Mike as he tried to interact with the group.

Later that night after everyone had settled down back at the camp, George pulled Johnnie aside and asked him if they could talk. Johnnie of course assumed it was about Ann and was ready to try to help make these two into a couple. But as they walked away from the group, Johnnie was taken by surprise when George had asked him if he was okay. Johnnie of course responded that he was, but George knew different, but by now, Johnnie wasn't focused on Mike and Sara anymore and had returned his attention back to Tonya.

"Johnnie, I noticed tonight that while Mike was talking, you seemed to not pay much attention nor laughed like the rest of us did," asked George.

"Oh, well, I just didn't think he was that funny is all," Johnnie responded.

"Hmm, talk to me, Johnnie, we have been friends since we were born, what bothers you about Mike?" George asked hoping that Johnnie would open up to him.

"Is it because you miss your dad?"

"No, George. That isn't it at all. Actually, I don't know what it is exactly, but there is something about Mike that I just don't like, and I am not sure what it is at this point. But something about him just doesn't sit well with me," Johnnie said with a serious concerned look on his face.

"Well, I have never been through what you have been through, bro, but I can tell when something is bothering you. And maybe it's just that this is all very sudden for you?" George said while trying to help Johnnie figure this out.

"No. It's something else, George, I don't know what it is, but there is something about him that just isn't right. I mean he does seem nice and all, but I feel like it's not at all who he really is. I don't know, George, if I am even making sense at all to you, but I can feel it."

"Well, my friend, I for one have a good idea what you mean, and you and your mom are very close, so I am sure it could be some kind of way to be trying to protect your mom or something."

"Yes, we are, George; and yes, I am very protective of her, maybe too much I don't know, but I am going to keep a good eye on this guy for sure."

"Okay, Johnnie, and if you need me to help or just to talk to, I am here for you, my brother. You know I love you and will do anything I can to help you out," George said as he was trying to comfort Johnnie.

"I love you too, my brother, and I know you would, I really appreciate you so very much for that. Come on, we better get back before they come looking for us."

After returning to the group, Johnnie went over and sat next to Tonya and grabbed her hand and held it, while George returned back to Ann and very nervously put his arm around her. Ann smiling scooted closer to George as she brushed her hair back.

As the rest of the group looked on, Tonya asked,

"What is this? Are you two now a couple?"

"George, not knowing how to respond, said, "Well, if she wants to be, we can."

Ann, being a little embarrassed, responded, "Well, that is up to you, George."

"I think you two would make a cute couple," Tonya said while nudging Johnnie to also comment.

"Yes, indeed. I also think you two would make a cute couple," Johnnie added. "Well, then, if he wants to be with me, he needs to ask me then," Ann said while looking directly into George's eyes.

"I am asking, Ann, would you be my girlfriend?" George said while his face turned red.

"Why sure, George, I would be honored."

"Well, there you go. Now you two are official," said Tonya while holding Johnnie's hand a little tighter.

"Well, what about you two?" asked George who was looking at Johnnie and Tonya.

"Yeah. What about you two?" Darrell chirped in. "I mean you two have been wanting to be together since day one.

"Yeah, Johnnie. Why don't you ask Tonya as well," added Randy who had been watching these two for some time as they had tried to act like they had not liked each other as much as they did, but they were not doing a very good job at hiding it at all. In fact Tonya had been swept off of her feet by Johnnie.

"Yeah, come on, Johnnie. Ask Tonya already," Steve said while laughing.

130

"Yeah, okay. Tonya, will you be my girlfriend?" Johnnie asked.

"Why, yes, I will, Johnnie," Tonya said with the biggest smile she had ever had on her face.

"Finally," said Randy. "You two should have already been together."

"Yeah, no kidding," added George.

"Well, we are now," Johnnie said as he tried to put up a macho front to try to mask his embarrassment.

As the night drew to a close and it began to get dark out, Johnnie lit up some lamps that he had brought out with him, so they all could see if for some reason someone may have to walk away from where the bonfire was. It got very dark at the camp site at night. And they needed light to see where they were going if anyone had to go use the bathroom, as well as to make sure nothing was getting too close to them. There was a lot of animals and small critters in these backwoods.

As the night drew upon them, Johnnie had pulled out some snacks that he had packed in his bag and handed them out to the group. Tonya also helped him. It was a nice night out, and it was already starting to feel like summer. And they all began to talk about what they wanted to do this summer. George and Johnnie had once taken a camping trip together back when Johnnie's father Mark was still alive.

Mark and Tim were very close friends and had planned a family vacation together one year. Of course, Randy and Darrell being real brothers took all their vacations together. So as they all sat around the camp that night, they all talked about past vacations and experiences. Tonya and Steve also talked about the many camping trips that they had taken where they did a lot of boating and swimming and fishing. Johnnie and George used to go fishing a lot back when Mark was still alive, but since then, they had only been once. That was when George's dad Tim had a weekend off and took them up to the lake. As for the brothers, they usually went to amusement parks every year which was their favorite thing to do, and they always looked forward to it.

*****

As the night went on, Sara and Mike enjoyed a quiet evening alone inside watching movies and cuddling on the couch, which was something Sara had not done since Mark had passed away. Not realizing how much she missed it and needed it, this was for sure working on Mike's behalf. Sara had missed being held and touched. And one thing Mike knew was how to make a woman feel needed. It was something he had honed his skills too. And Sara was eating it up. As the night went on, Sara began to really fall for Mike, and he could feel that he had her right where he wanted her. It was so hard for Sara to be alone for this long when she had felt so much love from Mark, and this was something she more than craved. And tonight, Mike pulled out all the stop and made sure he was saying and doing all the right things.

Sara would have gave anything for this night to last forever, but unfortunately, it was getting late, and it was time for Mike to go home. Although he would have stayed the night, but he knew what kind of woman Sara was and didn't want to push his luck too early until he was for sure that he had her on the hook for long term. As the last movie finished, Mike gave Sara a good night's kiss and got up to get ready to leave.

"I hate for this night to end Mike, it's been so wonderful," Sara said almost hoping Mike would stay.

"Yes, it has been the most amazing night of my life, Sara. Being with you makes me feel so good," Mike responded, as he looked deep into Sara's eyes as he continued to slowly work on seducing her. Knowing exactly what to say.

"It feels good being with you also, Mike. I have really enjoyed this night with you. Thank you so much for coming over and having dinner with us and spending time with me."

"No need to thank me, honey, I really enjoyed it also, and I look forward to our next time together. I am sure I will sleep good tonight as I dream about you," Mike said with a smile that stretched across his face.

Sara also smiled, as she leaned in and gave Mike a kiss, as Mike also leaned in and kissed Sara as he put his arms around her and held her for a few minutes.

"Well, honey, I guess I will see you later. I will call you tomorrow if you're not busy."

"No, I won't be busy, and you can call me

anytime, Mike." "Okay then, I will, Sara, you have a good night, and we will talk tomorrow."
"Okay, Mike. Good night, hun."

As Mike walked out the door, Sara sat back on the couch and began to replay the night over in her head and was surprised that she couldn't stop thinking about Mike and had already began to miss him. It had been a long time since Sara felt this way. Mike really had made her feel needed again and loved, and this was something she could not resist. But it was late, and Sara was tired, so it was time to end this night and get some rest; she knew the group would be up in the morning, and she wanted to be up to cook them all breakfast.

As Sara went to sleep, the group was out back still wide awake and taking their heads off about everything and anything that came to mind. Mostly stories about things they have done or wanted to do. And then back to scary stories which was what Darrell and Randy loved to do. And they were quite good at it. Whereas for Johnnie, he was more of a listener than a talker, which served him well for this was one way that Johnnie had learned to read people, which would serve him even more later on in the years to come. Something George needed to learn but could never quite get the hang of was keeping his mouth shut long enough to pay attention to important details of conversations. Johnnie was getting real good at reading between the lines. Where George would have to be explained certain thing by Johnnie when there was an issue that he didn't pick up on. However, very little got past Johnnie.

Finally after a long night, they all fell asleep until later that morning when Sara came out and woke them all up for a nice breakfast, which consisted of eggs, toast, and bacon. After which, they all split up and went to their own homes for a while.

During this time, Johnnie took some alone time to think upon the things that were bothering him, mainly Mike. As Johnnie continued to try to figure out what it was about Mike that he just didn't trust. He couldn't help but wonder if it was just him or if there really was something about Mike that he just couldn't get a grip on. But either way, he was troubled and wasn't really sure why at this point. However, one thing was for sure that until he figured it out, he was going to watch Mike very closely with his mother.

As Sara got ready for her day which was filled with laundry and cleaning, she thought much about Mike and was going to make some time to call him a little later on that afternoon. Sara had felt so good about Mike and couldn't keep her mind off him at all. She wasn't quite sure why, but Mike had affected her way more then she had realized until she found herself steadily keeping her mind on him all the time. Feeling slightly uneasy about the whole thing actually, even though he made her feel so good, and she had missed being held and romanced, which was something that Mark was very good at. As Sara pondered this, she began to wonder if it was more of missing Mark than anything else, but one thing was for sure, she really enjoyed being with Mike and the way he

135

treated her, and she had missed being with a man so much, and Mike was doing a great job in making Sara feel like a woman again. As for Mike, he really liked being with Sara and couldn't wait to be with her again.

As Sara was cleaning, Johnnie came down and began to help her out some, which was something he had never done before, but Johnnie was growing up some and realized he needed to help out more around the house and take the pressure off of Sara, which showed the maturity of this young man seeing how Sara had never asked him for help. However, Johnnie always was more mature than others his own age anyways. He had a real gift for seeing things in a different light than others did, and he was always able to feel things and recognized a need that was there. Johnnie helping out was something that was never hard for him to do, for he had always like pitching in to get things done. Sara was appreciative toward all that Johnnie was doing to help her out, especially the way he hardly ever complained and always seemed to be strong when things would happen that was out of their control. One thing for sure was that Johnnie was always a thinker and very positive in his attitude. That was something that was handed down to him from his father. Mark was always good at seeing the good in everything and being positive when things were not going so good. And Johnnie was for sure a lot like his father even right down to being very dependable. Johnnie was always there for all of those he was close to and even some that he wasn't close too. For this reason alone gave many people much respect for Johnnie. And when he needed something he very seldom had to ask, which was good seeing as that he never liked to bother anyone unless he absolutely had to.

George was at his house trying to think of a way to be with Ann again today. And he knew Johnnie at some point was going to be with Tonya, so for George, it was just a matter of getting Tonya to want to invite Ann over again, which shouldn't be hard seeing that Ann was one of Tonya's best friends. Of course, George would call Johnnie later and try to make it happen.

Sara let Johnnie take over the rest of the cleaning when she had decided it was time to go get lunch ready for the two of them when the phone rang.

"Hello," answered Sara.

"Hey, Sara, it's Mike. I was wondering what you and Johnnie were doing for lunch?"

"Oh, well, um, I was just about to start making something for the two of us."

"Well, I was hoping to take you two out for lunch this afternoon if it would be alright with you?"

"Sure, Mike, that would be great. What time did you want us to meet?"

"Well, I could come get you both now if you would like?"

"Yes, that would be great, Mike, me and Johnnie will be ready when you get here."

"Perfect. I will be there in about thirty minutes or so."

"Sounds great, Mike. I will see you when you get here then."

"Great, Sara. Be there soon then, hun."

"I will be waiting," Sara responded before hanging up.

After Sara had hung up, Sara told Johnnie to get ready for they were going out to lunch with Mike, and he was on his way to come pick them up. Johnnie noticeably not liking this idea didn't say anything, just went and did as Sara had told him, but she knew he wasn't happy about it by the expression on his face, which troubled Sara and made her start to think if maybe she was moving too fast with Mike. She hadn't considered if it was too early for Johnnie for her to start dating again, and maybe, she needed to slow things down. But for Sara, she did not want to slow down. She had missed all the things that Mark used to do, and this was refreshing to say the least. But either way, she knew she was going to have to sit down and talk to Johnnie about this and find out exactly how he was feeling about this whole matter. Anyways for now, it would have to wait. There was no time for it now as Mike was already on his way. This conversation would have to take place another time.

Mike took Sara and Johnnie to a little fish and chips diner that ran along the expressway. Not too far from where Sara and Johnnie lived. But yet it was a place that they had never been to. This was not the kind of place that they usually would have gone too, but the food was okay. Not the high-end kind of food that they we're accustomed to. But Johnnie didn't mind because they had great hamburgers and fries.

After eating, Mike wanted to go for a walk at the

park that was only a few miles away, but Johnnie was wanting to get back home, so he could spend some time with Tonya. But Sara, not wanting to disappoint Mike, said yes, and so they went and Johnnie, of course who wasn't happy about it, at least tried to act appropriately.

Finally after an hour or so at the park, Mike was ready to go and took them back home and once they had gone in, Johnnie hurried to the phone and called Tonya and began to make plans to come down and see her. Right after Johnnie had hung up, Sara checked her messages and told Johnnie that George had called. Johnnie stopped and turned around and decided to make a fast phone call before going down to see Tonya.

"Hey, George, my mom said you had called, what's your plans?"

"Well you know I was wondering if you were going to see Tonya today?"

"Yes, I am George, I was just about to go down there now."

"Do you think Ann will come over?"

"Well, I can ask Tonya when I get down there and then call you and let you know."

"Yeah, that sounds good, bro, call me as soon as you find out."

"Okay, George, I will talk to you in a few minutes or so."

After hanging up, Johnnie ran down to meet Tonya at her house and found her already outside waiting for him so they both sat on the porch together. Johnnie told Tonya that George wanted to see Ann.

"Oh, I guess I could call Ann and see if she wants to come over."

"Yes, that would be great," Johnnie responded as Tonya went inside to call Ann.

After several minutes, Tonya returned and told Johnnie that Ann would be here in a little while.

"That's great, do you think I can use your phone and call George?" Johnnie asked.

"Sure you can, come on in, I will show you where it is." Tonya and Johnnie both went inside as Johnnie followed Tonya.

"Here it is, Johnnie."

"Thank you, Tonya, I will make this fast."

"Hello," George said as he answered the phone.

"George, Ann will be here in a little while. Do you want to come on down?" Johnnie asked.

"Yeah, give me a few, Johnnie, and I will make my way down there."

"Okay, George, that sounds great, see you when you get here." Johnnie walked back outside and sat back on the porch next to Tonya.

"That was fast, is he coming down?" Tonya asked Johnnie.

"Yes, he will be here in a few minutes," Johnnie responded as he reached over and grabbed Tonya's hand.

After a few minutes, Steve came out and was talking to Johnnie as George was coming down the street.

"Hey, Johnnie, how are you, bro?" Johnnie shook Steve's hand.

"I am good, Steve, how are you doing?" Steve saw George coming.

"I am good also, here comes George."

George took his time as he walked up. "What's going on, my brothers and sis," George said while finding a spot on the porch to sit down. "It's nice out today, so what do you all want to get into?" George asked.

"I don't know, George, I just feel like relaxing today. Maybe just hang out and chill for a while," Johnnie responded.

"What do you think, Steve?"

"Well, Johnnie, we could go to the camp and hang out."

"Yeah, we could do that, what do you think, George? Once Ann gets here, we could shoot down to the camp and hang out for a while."

"Yeah, Johnnie, I'm good with that."

After a little while, Ann finally showed up and was happy to see George standing there with the group. Trying not to seem excited to see him, she tried her best not to smile, but she could not keep from it as she was too overwhelmed by her feelings for George.

"Hey, Ann, we are going to go down to Johnnie's camp," Tonya said as she was getting up from the porch.

"Okay, that sounds like fun to me," Ann replied.

"Well, let's go then," Johnnie said as he was getting up from the porch as well.

As they were walking back to Johnnie's, Mike's car was coming up the street and pulled into Sara's driveway. George had looked over at Johnnie and was going to say something until he saw the expression on Johnnie's face that showed his

141

disgust. George knew this was not the time to get into this conversation and decided it was best to not say anything at all.

Sara came out to meet Mike when she saw Johnnie and the group coming down the street. Smiling at them as she waved to them, she was walking to greet Mike.

"Hey, honey, how are you doing?"

"Hey, babe, I'm doing good. I thought I would come by and see if you and Johnnie wanted to go to the park or something today."

Sara motioned for Johnnie to come over to them. "Johnnie, come here for a minute," Sara said as she was standing next to Mike.

"Hey, guys, I will meet you in the back at the camp, let me see what my mom wants real fast."

As the group split off to go back to the camp, Johnnie walked over to where Sara and Mike were standing. "What's up, Mom?"

"Mike asked us to go to the park with him for a while."

Johnnie wanted to stay with his friends so he blew it off real fast. "Actually, Mom, I was going to hang out with the group at the camp, but its okay if you want to go, we will be okay back there."

Sara was not happy about Johnnie's response. "Are you sure you will be okay?" Sara asked while giving Johnnie a look that let him know she was upset at his response.

"Yeah, Mom, we will be good, go have fun with Mike."

Sara looked back at Mike then back to Johnnie.

"Well, okay then, I will grab you all some lunch on the way home."

Johnnie turned to walk off. "Okay, Mom, that sounds great, see you when you get back."

Sara tried to stay calm at Johnnie's decision. "I love you, Johnnie, and you guys be safe back there."

"No problem, Mom, I love you too," Johnnie replied as he hurried to catch up with the rest of the group.

Sara and Mike pulled off and decided to just go for a nice drive and maybe a walk through the park trail. Things between Sara and Mike continued to move fast, and soon, they became a serious couple. Mike began to start making plans for him and Sara to spend much more time together. And it wasn't long before they were together almost all the time.

As for Johnnie, his focus was on Tonya; and as time went on, these two also fell in love together. Johnnie was so in love with Tonya that she was all he thought about. And Tonya just adored Johnnie to death and was always looking forward to their time together. As fall came to a close and summer was finally now here, school was about to be over with, which was great. That meant more time together for Johnnie and Tonya as well as the whole group in general.

Ann and George had gotten a bit more serious also, but there had been a few issues along the way. Of course, Wayne helped that out by purposely flirting with Ann to get George angry. By which it worked and resulted in a fight between Ann and George before George and Wayne had another fight. This time, Ricco had jumped in, and the two were beating George up before Randy had walked out of the school and saw it. He ran over and grabbed Wayne off George and threw him to the ground then grabbed Ricco and punched him as George was getting back up to his feet. By that time, Wayne was back up and coming at George as the four boys fought until finally, Ricco and Wayne had enough and took off. Shortly after George and Ann had worked things out and now was working on being a couple once again.

After many altercations with Wayne and Ricco, summer break was upon them, and this meant a nice long break from fighting this war that never seemed to end. Now it was time for peace and time to enjoy the summer with no problems from Ricco and Wayne. It also meant more of Mike being around, which didn't make Johnnie happy one bit. But nonetheless, it was something he could do nothing about. Sara seemed so happy with Mike that Johnnie didn't want to say anything at all.

CHAPTER 7

A Long Hot Summer

I t was a hot summer morning, and school was finally out for the summer. Vacation time had finally arrived. Early mornings and long nights. This was what we lived for. More time for hanging out and having fun with no homework and a much needed break from Wayne and Ricco. This was our time to do what we wanted to do and just enjoy our time together as best friends and lovers and whatever we did was going to be according to our own imaginations. This was our summer. And it was going to be the best one yet. For love was fresh and new and the group had grown stronger together over the past year especially with the addition of three new members. For us, we had a long year behind us that taught us a lot. Even more about ourselves than anything else really. We we're stronger than we thought and better than we imagined. We were fighters and protectors. We learned that standing up for ourselves and for others was the right thing to do regardless of whether or not we got into trouble for it. We learned that we would stick together no matter how hard the trial was or difficult the situation was. We were brothers for sure. A real family and now we had sisters also. Girlfriends who would be there for us. We had stood tall in the face of fear and triumphed victoriously. For we truly was our brother's keeper. Unified together in love and strength, there was no doubt we had each other's back no matter what was to come our way. This was our pack, our group, even our own brotherhood. One that would not exclude females or lower them as a lesser vessel, but our mates, our equals. We were one, and this was how it was supposed to be. Real friends sticking together through thick and thin. Never turning our back on one another. No matter what. This would be the beginning of our legacy. And that which is within us is far greater than anything we had faced or will face. We are courageous and we define our own moments.

This was Johnnie's revelation. It had been a tough year for him, but he had survived it and was ready for the time that was ahead of him. Everything to Johnnie was a lesson. He knew there was always something to gain from everything he had encountered. This was something Mark had taught him and Johnnie embraced it. This was something that he would never forget. Even though

Mark passed away so early in Johnnie's life, the things he had taught him would forever remain.

Mark was a wise man, and Johnnie had inherited much of the same trait. Johnnie loved being a student of life, and this was something he would find later as a common bond between him and Jason. Johnnie often wondered what happened to his friend Jason who he had met that day on the playground at the park. He often wondered why he had such a strong connection to someone that he would probably never see again. Or perhaps maybe one day, they would run into each other again. And what would become of that day? Would they recognize each other? Or would they just pass each other by on the street as if they had never even known each other? Who was to know the future? One thing was for sure, and that was Johnnie had never forgotten his friend that he had only saw that one time.

It was an exciting time. The fun they had shared and the fight they had. Johnnie now was getting used to fighting and was starting to actually enjoy it a bit. Thanks to his rivals, he had gained more experience than he had expected in the past year. And now, his reputation had begun to grow as a leader and someone that you didn't want to mess with. And not only him but the whole group for that matter had now became somewhat of a notable group that could handle themselves very good.

Darrell was always known for his fighting, but now, the rest was also gaining a tough reputation that made them very well respected in the neighborhood and around the school yard. For

Johnnie, it was important though that they did not come off as bullies or a group that would push people around. For they had made sure to protect others so that people would understand that they were not troublemakers but rather problem solvers. With the exception of Darrell, of course, who would always find himself in a dispute over meaningless things, but then again, that was just his nature.

Darrell loved to argue and debate no matter what the topic was. He had an opinion for everything. Everyone knew he was always ready to back up his mouth any time it came down to it. Maybe a little too ready at times. Johnnie had to step in many times and bring peace to a situation before it got way out of hand. But nonetheless, Darrell was a brother, and he was a loyal friend right down to the end.

Randy was more of a jokester himself unlike his brother. However, one thing they did share in was the fact that neither one would take crap from anyone. Randy was just more reserved in the fact that he would rather make light of a situation than argue about it, which at times did cause a few problems, but that's just how it was when not everyone could take a joke or when the joke was ill timed or of poor taste. Either way, for Randy, a joke was a joke and nothing more. And George was of course one who always jumped into things without thinking about it first. Many times, Johnnie had to cover his butt.

George, on most days, thinking seemed to be a last resort, and usually by the time he did think about it, it was already too late, and Johnnie had to come and help clean up the mess. One thing about George though, no matter what, he was always very entertaining.

As for the other three new members, Steve was a great addition to the group mainly because of two reasons. One, he had much of the same ideas that flowed with the way this group was. And two, he was very good at martial arts and wasn't afraid to fight. As for Tonya, she was a very sweet girl but took no crap from anyone and was always ready to mix it up if that's how it was going to be. For being as sweet as she was, her attitude was equal to it, and one thing was for sure, she could back it all up. Ann was mild tempered and didn't like fighting at all and would rather avoid it if at all possible. Ann was more of a peacemaker than anything else and was always trying to find a good way to solve problems before things got out of control.

All in all, this was the group, but there were also other friends who came by from time to time and hung out. Johnnie had a lot of friends, and at times, the group could be as big as ten to fifteen kids. But that wasn't very often, and it was usually limited to a Saturday, but now that summer was here, it could be any size at any giving time. But the inner circle or core group was almost always together. They had all became like a very close family that was there for each other.

Johnnie, needed this after the death of his father, and Tonya was a big help as well also; she would listen to Johnnie as he talked about his father and

149

how he missed him when he would open up about it. Had it not been for Tonya coming into his life, it would have been much harder than what it was. Johnnie's love for Tonya ran deep and so did her love for Johnnie. It was rare that the two would meet at such an early age and fall this deeply in love with one another, but the connection that they had was stronger than normal, and it was unique to say the least. It was genuine unadulterated true love. The kind of love that could not wait. And this summer would be a summer that brought many things to Johnnie, but one thing that was going to remain for sure was the love between him and Tonya.

The first day of summer vacation and Johnnie was up early and already thinking about Tonya. But first things first, before he could go running off with her for the day, a shower and some breakfast was in order.

The two brothers were already up and outside sitting on their porch waiting for the rest of the group to finally awaken out of their sleep. Darrell was going to invite them all to come over today and hang out at their place. Randy and Darrell had lots of stuff to do in their backyard, such things as a nice pool and a trampoline. Darrell was already trying to figure out how he could talk his parents into letting him have a pool party today to celebrate the first day of summer vacation. Of course, Randy was more than willing to help out with that plan. One thing these two boys loved to do was have parties and would use almost any excuse to throw one. Their parents didn't mind because they always felt that the stuff they had bought needed to be used.

Pool parties were fun for Randy and Darrell's mother Christina, she loved to make up a bunch of sandwiches and cookies for all the guest. And she was good at it. Making sure she always had lots of punch and soda pop on hand as well as chips and dip. Of course, her cookies weren't made from scratch, but you couldn't tell that she bought them pre made, and all she had to do was bake them. So in essence, they were still fresh and hot from the oven. Thomas and Christina were known for their parties, so it was no big surprise that the two boys also like to have parties as well.

George was usually one of the first to show up for these parties, of course, he loved to just be anywhere where he could jump in a pool or eat food. Johnnie, on the other hand, was more for the fellowship with the group and everyone being together.

After a quick shower and some breakfast, Johnnie was just getting up to go call Tonya when the phone rang. Johnnie answered the phone.

"Hello." It was Darrell.

"Hey, Johnnie boy, you got any plans today?" Johnnie paused for a moment.

"Just was going to call Tonya and see what she was going to do."

"That's perfect because you both have plans now, so when you call her, ask her if she can come over for a pool party, and hurry, bro, we are starting just as soon as you all get here."

Johnnie sounding excited at the idea of having

151

the whole group together for a pool party, "Heck, yeah, bro, a pool party, that's what I'm talking about. Let me make this call then we will be on our way, I hope."

Darrell did not waste any time working out his plan. "Hurry, bro, and I will call George."

"Okay, Darrell, see you as soon as we can."

After hanging up, Johnnie hurried and called Tonya. "Hello, is Tonya there?"

"Yes, she is. Hold on one minute, Johnnie, and I will get her for you." Mrs. Flowers said as she went to get Tonya.

"Hey, Johnnie, good morning," Tonya said with a nice cheerful sound in her voice that always made Johnnie smile.

"Good morning, honey, hey, listen, Darrell and Randy are throwing a pool party and want us all to come."

Tonya got excited. "Oh, great, what time does it start?"

"Well, it's an all-day pool party that start as soon as we get there this morning and will run until this evening. They will have lunch there for us and everything."

Tonya hurried to get Steve's attention waving for him to come to where she was at. "Steve, Darrell and Randy are having an all-day pool party that is starting as soon as we get there this morning and will run all day into the evening. Lunch will be provided, now go ask Mom if we can go." Steve ran off to find his mom before returning after a few minutes and told Tonya they could go.

"Okay, Johnnie, we can go. We will be there just

as soon as we can get ourselves together."

Johnnie with excitement in his voice said, "Perfect, I will see you there in a little bit. I love you, Tonya."

"I love you too, Johnnie, see you soon."

After hanging up, Johnnie went to talk to Sara about the whole ordeal. "Hey, Mom, you know how you've been so busy lately? Well, how about you take this day to yourself and just relax?"

Sara looked strangely at Johnnie. "Son, what on earth are you talking about?"

Johnnie responded, "Well, Darrell and Randy are having an all-day pool party starting now and running till this evening. Mr. and Mrs. Hilton will be providing lunch and everything."

Sara nodded. "Christina loves to make food for parties. Okay, well, be safe and have some fun I guess. And tell Christina to call me."

Johnnie responded as he was turning to run up the stairs. "Yes, of course, Mom." He was hurrying to grab his stuff and get out the door, but Sara had to stop him just to get a kiss and a hug before he hurried off.

As Johnnie was walking down to Darrell and Randy's house, he met George on the way.

"Hey, George, how are you, bro?"

George stopped to meet Johnnie in the middle of the street. "Hey, Johnnie, bro, listen. I got a favor to ask you, as soon as Tonya gets there, can you ask her if she can call and invite Ann?"

Johnnie of course had no problem with that request. "Yes, I sure can, bro. Actually, let's go back to my house real fast, and I will call Tonya, and then we can go to Darrell's."

George liked that idea even better. "Yeah, that will work, Johnnie, let's do that."

Johnnie and George walked into the house as Sara was just sitting down to watch some television.

"Back already, and hello, George." George always smiled as Sara when she talked to him.

"Hi, Mrs. Steele."

"Yeah, Mom, I need to make a quick phone call first, and then George and I are going down there."

Johnnie called Tonya once again, but this time, Steve answered. "Hey, Johnnie, did things change?"

"No, Steve, but can you have Tonya call and invite Ann for George?"

Steve paused as he yelled for Tonya. "Yeah, bro, I will have her do it now then we will come down."

"That's perfect, Steve, thank you."

"You're welcome, Johnnie."

After hanging up, Johnnie and George were back on track and heading to the pool party. Shortly after they had arrived, Tonya and Steve came down. Tonya began to let George know that Ann would be there shortly, and she was able to stay the night. That meant for George that he got to spend the entire morning, day and evening with Ann, which made him very happy.

Timothy, who was also a friend of the group, had also shown up already and was eager to get in the pool as he ran and jumped right in. Not waiting for the rest to get in for he was a bit high strung, but in general, he was a good kid. Timothy's cousin Nate who also went to school with the group had just shown up about fifteen minutes after Steve and Tonya did. Nate was a tall kid who was at times a bit clumsy. Nate could eat a lot but never put on any weight. He was as skinny as the smaller kids.

As the party went on, more kids came, but some didn't stay but a few hours, and then they had to go. Thomas Hilton decided instead of Christina making sandwiches that this time, he would fire up the grill and cook hamburgers and hot dogs. Since after all, they were celebrating the first day of summer vacation. And Thomas decided to stay home today from the office. As he was cooking, he waved Johnnie over to see how he was doing.

"Hey, Johnnie, how are you doing, young man? I have been wondering about you ever since your dad passed away. He was a good man, Johnnie, and a very good friend."

Johnnie not wanting to allow himself to feel the emotions since this wasn't a private setting and didn't want the others to see him crying held back his emotions with great restraint.

"I miss him terribly," is all Johnnie said.

"Well, yes, I can imagine you would. If you ever need to talk to someone, I am here for you Johnnie, you can come talk to me anytime you need to."

Johnnie, with a half-smile, responded, "Thank you, Tom, I really appreciate that."

Thomas did not want to keep Johnnie from all the fun, but just wanted to let him know that he was there for him and to make sure that Johnnie was okay. "Okay, Johnnie, run along and have some fun. These burgers will be done in about a half an hour."

While playing in the pool, George and Johnnie decided to come up with a game that they all could play, which really meant that everyone was going to get hit in the face with a ball. George named it pool dodge ball. And the only way to keep from getting hit was to go underwater or catch the ball. If you got hit, you had to get out of the pool. Or if you threw the ball and someone caught it, you also had to get out of the pool. As they all were having fun playing, Christina was inside making up some potato and macaroni salads to go with the hamburgers and hot dogs.

Since Johnnie was going to be gone all day, Sara decided this was a good opportunity to invite Mike over for a nice romantic lunch and some private time out back on the swing, which was something she had been wanting to do for a while; but with the group always back there at the camp, it seemed like too much of a distraction to really be able to enjoy a nice swing and some fresh lemon tea with Mike. After calling Mike and getting everything arranged, Sara began to get everything together that she would cook for their lunch. Perhaps a nice meatloaf with fried potatoes and some green beans. That was Mark's favorite. As she had thought about that, she sat down for a minute. *Oh, how I do miss Mark so much.* Putting her head down on the table for a few minutes, Sara began to cry. *Am I doing the right thing by dating Mike? Is it good for Johnnie? Or is it too early for the both of us? I really do like Mike, and he is very sweet to me. But*

Mark was my everything. And I still love him so much. Oh, how my heart still aches every time I think of him. Mike is coming, and I need to get things ready.

Sara decided that cooking Mark's favorite meal just seemed inappropriate at this time. Perhaps some fried chicken with mashed potatoes and gravy with some fresh homemade biscuits was a much better idea. And maybe some string beans to go along with it all. After making sure she had everything she needed, Sara began to make some fresh tea with lemons and set it outside in the hot sun. After which she made some ice for the tea that they would be having later on while out back on the swing together. While Sara was doing some light cleaning and a load of laundry, she decided to turn the romantic lunch with Mike into a nice picnic out back as well.

*****

After a few long game of pool dodge ball, the hamburgers and hot dogs were finally done, and it was time to eat lunch. Christina had baked a bunch of chocolate chip cookies for desert, and everything was now ready. As they all sat down to eat, Thomas who was a regular churchgoer had prayed over the meal before they ate. For some reason, this simple prayer over the food had somewhat inspired Johnnie. Not really sure why, but now wasn't the time to ponder on this thought.

*****

Mike was just pulling up at Sara's house and was walking up to the door. Sara had been trying to watch for him, but she had to go out back and set the picnic area up with a nice blanket and some pillows. Not hearing Mike at the door as he stood there knocking for a few minutes who had now begun to get aggravated. When Sara came back in and was walking back to the kitchen, she heard the knock on the door and went to let Mike in.

"Hey, Mike, come on in, sorry I was out back preparing our place to eat."

Mike answered Sara back with a bit of a rough sound in his voice as he was very unhappy for having to wait outside for this long. "Well, I have been standing out here for over five minutes knocking on your door."

Sara, feeling a bit embarrassed, once again apologized. "Oh, Mike, I am very sorry, I was trying to look out for you to see when you arrived, but I had to run out back real fast just to get this all set up for us."

Mike tried to keep his cool for the moment. "Where is Johnnie?"

Sara smiled a bit. "Johnnie is gone for the day, so I thought we could have a nice picnic out back seeing how no one is back there today at the camp."

Mike, seeing all the trouble that Sara has gone through, decided to let his anger subside. "Yes, well, I guess I understand that." Sara gave Mike a hug and then led him out back and took him to the picnic area and then went back in to bring out the food that she had just finished cooking a few minutes ago.

"Wow, Sara, look at all this wonderful food, it looks great and smells even better. You really went all out for our lunch," Mike said as he began to help himself to the food.

"Yes, I wanted to have a nice quiet afternoon with you since Johnnie was going to be gone until sometime this evening."

Mike liked the sound of that. "So I have you all to myself for the whole entire day with no kids around at all?"

Sara finished the food that she had taken a bite of before responding. "Well, yes, that was the plan."

Mike responded with a nice smile. "That sounds just wonderful, dear."

*****

As Johnnie and the group were eating lunch, they were still finding it hard to really settle down still hyped up from the games and swimming in the pool. Thomas and Christina had set up some games for after lunch to give them all something fun to do while they waited to get back in the pool. Thomas had set up some lawn darts and a beanbag toss game while Christina had set up a badminton net. The food was so good, and the group ate a lot. But now it was time to get back to having some fun, as they all finished up eating, they headed over to where the games was set up at and began to pick teams for the games.

Johnnie and George decided to challenge Tonya and Ann to a game of lawn darts. Johnnie let the girls' team go first as they would alternate each turn with Tonya and Johnnie both keeping score. A few other kids went for the beanbag game while the two brothers went for badminton with Timothy and Nate for a friendly two against two game of family versus family. Everyone was having such a great time with the games that it was almost two hours before they all decided to get back into the pool again.

After which they decided to have a cannon ball contest to see who could make the biggest splash while jumping into the pool. By which it was roughly decided that Darrell had won that contest. Followed up by a relay swim race using floating batons.

*****

As Sara and Mike were finishing up their picnic lunch, Sara took all the stuff back in the house while Mike waited for her on the swing. After returning, Sara poured them both a nice glass of tea and added some ice to it that she brought back from the house. As they swung together and was holding hands, Mike began to express his love for Sara and his plans to one day marry her. Being slightly overwhelmed, Sara didn't know exactly what to say. She was taken back to earlier this morning when she had sat at the table and was thinking of Mark. Sara knew now that things were moving way too fast, but she also felt a deep sense of love for Mike that she couldn't deny. However, at this point, Sara had more questions in her heart than she had answers. Not knowing how to respond, she decided it was best to just smile. At least until she had gathered her thoughts.

"Mike, I really do love you, and I want us to be together and I hope we work out and see where all of this takes us. But I am concerned that maybe this is moving a little too fast for me and Johnnie. I mean we both still miss Mark, and Johnnie still struggles at times, just as I do as well."

Mike did not seem to look very happy at how Sara had responded. "Well, I am very sorry that you feel this way. I had supposed that we were moving in the right direction, and everything seemed to be going so well. I know I haven't been able to spend as much time with Johnnie as I had hoped, but I am truly in love with you, Sara. And I would like to spend the rest of my life with you."

As Sara tried to reassure Mike that she also loved him and was wanting the same thing, that perhaps they just needed to slow it down just a little and let things fall into place. "We have so much time ahead of us, Mike, and there is no real need to rush anything at the present moment. And besides with Johnnie out of school for the summer, we have plenty of time to be together all summer and see where we are at this fall."

Mike tried to be reasonable. "Yes, I agree, let's see how this summer goes and then this fall, we can see how we feel and where we are at with each other. I think that is a great idea, honey, we can enjoy our summer together and get a better feel for how we do together as a couple. Plus, I do want to take you and Johnnie to a few places this summer, and I am sure Johnnie and I will get along great. He seems like such a smart young man."

Sara agreed with all that Mike said. "Yes, Johnnie is very smart, and he will come around in time, but right now, he is very distracted with his friends and his new girlfriend. So I don't want to push him too much. He has had a rough year, and I would like for him to just be able to enjoy his summer, and then maybe this fall, we can shift and start trying to do things more as a family." Sara held Mike's hand as they continued to swing together.

"Yes, that sounds like a good plan to me as well, honey." As they continued to talk, Sara tried to shift the conversation into another direction and tried to discuss their families and things such as that.

It was mid-afternoon now, and Timothy and Nate had to both go as they had made plans to go to the movies together that evening, and Nate had brought extra clothes for him to stay a few days at Timothy's. As they headed out, it was back to the main group once again. They were all starting to get bored with the pool, so they all sat around on the deck chairs that were around about in a circle on the deck as they all just sat and talked. Laughing and joking and trying to make up stories just for fun.

Johnnie was in one of his quiet moods though.

He often would get like that at times. For the most part, he was very talkative and quite funny. However, he did have times when he was more reserved and didn't say much at all as he would just sit and listen.

George, on the other hand, was never short on words and barely at time stopped talking. He loved the attention and would often poke fun at the others just for laughs. Johnnie was also good in making jokes on others, but at times, he just didn't seem to want to be bothered with it.

Darrell, on the other hand, was not good at being poked fun of; however, when it came to running his mouth, he was exceptionally well at it. Tonya also being able to hold her own when it came to arguments and joking with others wasted no time to give it back to George. Tonya was very clever and witty. Johnnie never spoke much about his thoughts and would often just keep them to himself. But one thing was for sure, Johnnie was a thinker and always had something on his mind. This was a trait he inherited from Mark who was always thinking on many different subject concerning life issues.

As the evening came to a close, the group had begun to decide what was going to be the plan for the night. Johnnie hated leaving Tonya at night when it was time to go home. Tonya became everything to Johnnie, and she was always on his mind. However, they couldn't stay at the camp every night either. George had finally gotten up the nerve to get Ann's phone number. Now these two could spend more time talking even when they were not together in person.

As for Sara and Mike, their night was also beginning to wind down. But not before Mike had leaned in and gave Sara a very long kiss while they were swinging together out back by the garden. The whole scene was very romantic, just as Sara had hoped it would. Mike was ready to take this relationship to the next level and was trying to test the boundaries to see how far Sara was willing to go. But tonight was not the night, even though Sara created a very romantic time for the two. It was starting to get late in the evening, and she needed to find out when Johnnie was coming home.

"Well, Mike, this has been a wonderful day, and I have tremendously enjoyed our time together, but I should probably find out when Johnnie is coming home and see if he is staying in tonight or somewhere else. Do you want to do something together tomorrow?"

Mike looked at his watch. "Yes, of course I do, honey. And I have also enjoyed our time together. Thank you so much for inviting me over for this wonderful time. The food was terrific, and the whole scenery was amazing. I love spending time with you, and I look forward to seeing you tomorrow as well. Do you want to walk me out?"

"Yes, of course. I am happy you enjoyed our time together, and I am so very happy that you came over to be with me. Soon, I will get Johnnie to spend a day with us, but right now, he needs his friends, and I know he is head over heels about Tonya."

Sara and Mike slowly walked to his car as Mike gave Sara another nice long kiss before getting in his car to leave. "Well, my love, I guess this is good night."

Sara gave Mike a hug that lasted for several minutes. "Yes, I guess it is, honey, be safe on your way home and call me when you get there so that I know that you got home safely."

Mike got into his car. "Yes, of course, baby. I love you and good night."

"Awe, Mike, I love you too and good night, babe."

After Mike pulled out and headed down the street, Sara went into the house to call down to Mrs. Hiltons to see when Johnnie was coming home and if he was going to want any dinner. After which, it was time for some relaxation on the couch with some television shows.

Johnnie wasn't hungry for any dinner and wanted to go to Tonya's for a few hours before coming home. Sara was fine with that. She rather began to enjoy her alone time. It was the only time she could just relax and breathe for a while and try to not think upon the things that were heavily on her mind. But no matter how hard she tried, her mind always drifted to Mark and Mike. Still being torn between this decision of whether the timing was right or not and still not quite sure if Johnnie was ready for all of this. Soon, she would have to sit and talk with Johnnie concerning all of this, but it wasn't a conversation that she was looking forward to at all. However, it was a conversation nonetheless that was going to have to happen regardless.

Sara needed to know Johnnie's real feelings about the whole matter concerning Mike. She knew Johnnie was avoiding spending any real time with Mike. One thing Sara knew was her son and when something wasn't right with him. And it was time to find out.

Johnnie knew that Sara was happy with Mike. But he still felt that there was something not right about him. And wasn't sure if he should say anything or not. Whether Johnnie liked Mike or not, he could tell that his mom was very happy, and that was something that Johnnie was also happy about. Maybe he didn't like Mike, but he did like seeing his mom happy again and smiling a whole lot more often, which was something that she had lost for a long time after Mark had passed away. *How could I ruin that for her?* Johnnie had thought to himself many times. For a young boy, this was a very difficult thing indeed to wrestle with. Johnnie was good at hiding his thoughts, but his feelings was a different matter entirely. One could always tell when Johnnie was troubled or concerned with something. And if he was angry or upset, you for sure knew that. But in this case, he was just worried that maybe Mike wasn't the right one for his mother. Still not sure why, but Johnnie didn't want Mike and Sara to be together.

As the night began to come to a close, Johnnie and Tonya found it hard to say good night. But Johnnie knew it was about time for him to get home. Tonya was holding Johnnie's hand when he leaned over and whispered in her ear.

"Tonya. I love you." Tonya was feeling overwhelmed by the words that meant so much to her.

"I love you too, Johnnie."

After a kiss on each other's cheeks, Johnnie made that short walk home and was ready for bed as soon as he came into the house. It had been a long day, and he was exhausted. All the playing and swimming had done him in and he was heading to bed for some much needed sleep.

As for the rest of the group, they were all exhausted as well. The party once again at the Hilton home was a success. The brothers always knew how to kick off the summer vacation. After a few weeks had went bye, vacations began to take place, and the group was somewhat separated until they all had taken their vacations.

Tonya and Steve went camping for a week and then to an amusement park for which they stayed a few days. George went out of state to visit his family and had visited some out of state family while sightseeing as well. The two brothers also went camping, but they stayed for two weeks and did a lot of fishing and swimming. Randy did a lot of boating, which was his favorite. Darrell, however, wasn't that fond of boats and preferred to just fish off of the shore. There was also a nice game room that was filled with pool tables and video games, which no doubt got the boys in trouble a few times during their stay. Mainly over billiard games with other kids that ended in arguments and an occasional fight. No matter where these two boys went, they always made a reputation for themselves.

Johnnie, on the other hand, didn't do much as for a vacation. Sara and Mike took him to the zoo and to some art museums, which Johnnie loved to do anyways. But he remembered the times when Mark would take them to great places, and now, they just did things around the city. Mike didn't make the kind of money that Mark made. However, he did alright to get by.

When Tonya finally had returned home from her vacation, Her and Johnnie was happy to be reunited. They had missed each other terribly and was eager to spend some much needed time together. Steve wasn't ready to come home though. He loved the amusement park and never wanted to leave. It was routine to have to listen to him complain when it was time to go. But for Tonya, she was missing Johnnie and was eager to get back home to him. Tonya was the highlight to Johnnie's summer as well as his year. Her love for him made all the difference with everything he had to go through. She often encouraged him, and that was something he had lacked since the passing of his father. Johnnie needed it so much. He had struggled with having to fight at school with Wayne and Ricco, and he missed his father all the time, and now with having to deal with Mike, which was not easy for him. Tonya was exactly what Johnnie needed. She knew how to handle him and keep him focused on getting his schoolwork done and trying to be a good leader for the group. It was strange in a sense that with how tight this group had been before Tonya and Steve arrived, that it would be Tonya and not George who became the biggest support to Johnnie, and most of the time, it was her who always had his back.

Tonya learned fast how to read Johnnie and knew his temperament and his attitudes. It had become very easy for her to know when Johnnie was troubled. Even when he's hiding it, which he was very good at doing, unless Tonya was with him. She could pick up on everything with Johnnie and always seemed to know how to handle it. For Johnnie, she was his godsend, his angel that came to him when he needed it the most. And he truly loved her with all of his heart.

As Sara and Mike got to the middle of summer, Mike really began to push for Sara to give him a deeper commitment. He knew that Johnnie wasn't a big fan of his and began to try to win Johnnie over in hopes that it would improve his chances to get Sara to marry him. The truth is, Mike could care less about Johnnie, but he knew if he was going to get what he wanted from Sara, he was going to at least have to act like he really liked Johnnie. Johnnie, on the other hand, wasn't interested in spending time with Mike at all, but Mike was trying to get Sara to make Johnnie come with them, so she would think that he really wanted Johnnie around. One thing Johnnie was good at was picking up on people who was trying to play games, and he knew Mike wasn't being sincere. Sara felt that it was important for Johnnie to be more involved as well and began to make more plans including him, which of course wasn't at all what Johnnie wanted to do. But for Sara,

Johnnie would do anything to please her and make her happy. Even if it meant spending time with Mike who was always trying to act like Johnnie's friend when he knew he wasn't. But for now, Johnnie would play the game and wait for his time to expose Mike. Sara might have been fooled, but Johnnie sure wasn't. The more he was around Mike, the more he felt uneasy about him. Sara, on the other hand, only saw Mike as making efforts to be like a family, and for her, that was important. Tonya naturally didn't like Mike either, if for no other reason, then the fact that she knew Johnnie didn't like him. And that was a good enough reason for her.

George and Ann began to grow together finally, for they had their struggles early on, but now, things were smoothing out rather nicely for the couple. George really began to fall in love with Ann who was deeply into George, and the two became very passionate about each other. Still though, they would have the occasional fight that would usually result in a few days on not talking to each other. Rarely did the group do anything without them all being together, but as the summer went on, Johnnie and Tonya began to do more things on their own and also had double dates with George and Ann, while the two brothers and Steve drew closer together and did more things together as well. Timothy began to hang around a lot more often also and was now officially part of the group as well.

Timothy and Steve became very good friends and Steve would often stay over at Timothy's. As the weeks went on through the summer, the group found themselves at the beach swimming and playing games and often went fishing at the old pond way back behind the camp. It was a long walk though, but it was well worth it. For it was rarely fished, and you could easily catch some big fish out of there. No one even really knew it was there except for the group. It was so far back and kind of hidden, even for its size. And it was a nice place to relax and just fish and have some fun. Mark used to take Johnnie back there, and they would fish alone and just spend time together. Just the two of them. Sara would make them some sandwiches and pack a small picnic box with water and chips to go with it. It was great memories for Johnnie, and now, he was making new memories out there with the group. Johnnie had asked Sara to not mention it to Mike. This was a special place for Johnnie, and he didn't want Mike to be a part of it. Sara was not pleased with Johnnie's request, but she did understand what that place meant to Mark and Johnnie, so she honored his request and never told Mike about it.

However, the group was different, now that Mark was gone, Johnnie felt that there was no reason for the pond to be abandoned. But if he was going to share it with anyone, it was going to be with his group. They were his family, and Johnnie loved them like his real brothers, and Ann had become like his real sister. And Tonya was his world.

Sometimes, Johnnie and Tonya would go to the pond alone and just hold hands walk along the bank of the pond while they talked as they took in the whole scenery of wilderness, and they would just sit and listen to the water run. The pond, for the most part, was clear and still; but in this one area, it did branch off into a little stream where there was a small bridge that you could walk across or sit on. It was mesmerizing and a very romantic setting for Tonya and Johnnie. With the birds chirping in the background, and sometimes, you could hear the sound of frogs. Every now and then, a fish would jump out of the water and make a splash as it got some bug or some other kind of food from the surface. It was a lovely place for sure, and being in the middle of the woods made it even better, for it was completely surrounded by trees. And there were many different kinds of flowers all over the place, and the fragrance would often fill the air with a sweet aroma. It was common to see squirrels and chipmunks running around out there as well as an occasional raccoon. And sometimes, even a few snakes, which Johnnie hated, but it was no bother to Tonya for some reason she happened to like them. There was only a few paths that were there, but the trails went on forever. One could explore for days out there and never find the end to it. The woods was massive, and the pond was huge.

For this group, it was like having their own little private lake. Sometimes, the group would get a good game of hide and seek going on out there or a friendly war game of paintball, which was usually a team sport for the group, where Johnnie and Randy would both be the leaders, and one by one, they would pick their teams.

George was usually Johnnie's first pick until Tonya came along. Then Johnnie always made sure that Tonya was with him, which was fine with George because he wanted to have Ann with him so that meant he was going to have to go with Randy so that each side would have a girl on their team. For Johnnie and George, it made it even more fun because up until now, they had always been together, and now, they get to hunt each other and shoot at each other. Of course, that made the competition more fun and competitive. The trash talking between the two in itself was fun to just listen to.

As the summer went on, they spent as much time together as they could at the camp and out at the pond. They had as much fun as they could, and each pitched in to bring snacks and drinks. Always an adventure in the back woods. For Johnnie, he specially loved it when they could just go off and explore. This was his favorite thing to do back there as a group. Johnnie always loved to look for new things and experience new things. And so they did it as often as they could throughout the entire summer.

CHAPTER 8

Standing our Ground

As summer came to a close, fall began to come in. The weather at South Bend Heights rarely changed as in other places. It was a little cooler and not as hot, but the weather never really got cold there. All year round, the group was able to be at the camp with no worries of it being too cold, and snow was a rarity.

School time was once again approaching, and the group was not ready to go back yet. They all had enjoyed their summer so much that the end of it brought a sense of sadness, knowing that their time would now be limited because of early nights and early mornings once again. No more staying up late at the camp telling stories or just hanging out there and talking all night. It was back to the grind.

The group had enjoyed their break away from

Wayne and Ricco. But this season would bring even more challenges for the group. Ricco was able to get a friend named Paco to transfer schools and come over to where they were as well as his girlfriend Sammy. Sammy and Ricco made a good couple together. They both liked to cause trouble and fight. Sammy had always thought she was better than everyone else and liked to shoot her mouth off all the time. For Sammy, being a bully was a way for her to gain popularity. She loved to push people around. Ricco being much of the same, was never a loss for words when it came to making someone feel small. Ricco and Sammy relished in making people afraid of them. That is why they hated the group so much because they would not back down to anyone. Rather allow the bullying, the group would intervene and stick up for others. Sammy was accustomed to being the top girl everywhere she went. But here it would be different. Tonya had established herself as a dominant and very popular girl at this school and had gained much respect as well as popularity. Sammy, however, was going to test that and see just how tough Tonya really was. Sammy felt by knocking Tonya down a bit would put her on top, and she could run this school with Ricco. That was the plan. It was an all-out war between the two groups.

This couldn't have come at a worse time for Johnnie. He had other things to deal with, so his patience with Wayne and Ricco was wearing very thin. For this fall brought on new challenges for Johnnie. Now that Summer had ended and the last bit of it had slipped away rather quickly, it was now fall. Mike had proposed to Sara as he had been waiting to do. Sara had finally said yes to Mike, and for Johnnie, this meant another new beginning, one that he was not looking forward to. He had hoped his mother would have continued to put it off and was very surprised when she had accepted Mike's proposal. This was for sure something that Johnnie wasn't ready for. Now he had wondered if he did the right thing by not really speaking his mind about the situation. *But was it too late? Was there still something he could do to try to get his mom to rethink this? And if so, what could he do?* She had already accepted, and now, plans were being made.

Back to the grind, a new school year has begun. The group was together for the most part, but Darrell and Steve had separate classes from the rest of the group. As they all met up in the playground before school started, it was apparent that this year would be much of the same with Ricco and Wayne. Johnnie had noticed how they kept staring over at them with some new kid and some new girl with them as well.

George came up behind Johnnie and grabbed him from behind to get his attention. "Hey, bro, forget them fools we are going to have a good year. Just ignore them unless they start something."

It didn't take Darrell long to see them looking over at them and talking among themselves as they stared at the group. "Yeah, Johnnie, no worries this year. If they want some, then we will give them some more of what we gave them last year. No one is going to run this school but us, bro," Darrell said while starring back at Wayne and his friends.

Tonya also noticed how the girl was looking straight at her. "I wish they would start something," Tonya said. "I hope that girl can back up her ugly looks. If not, she is going to get hurt. Especially if she keeps looking at me like that." Ann chuckled as she watched Tonya stare back.

"We better get to class, Darrell," Steve said as he grabbed Darrell to pull him away. "We will see you guys at lunchtime."

"Okay, Steve, see you at lunchtime, bro," Johnnie responded as the group all headed to class leaving the scene to Wayne and his group who was still standing there looking at the group before finally going to class themselves. Johnnie was in no mood for this crap this year, and if they wanted another year of fighting, Johnnie was going to make real sure that they paid a great price for it.

George was getting very tired of Wayne and was ready to go ahead and get the fighting started, so he could get at Wayne for all the trouble he had caused the previous year, and since they were already eying up the group, George figured it was going to come down anyways, so he was ready for it. Tonya and George both sat on each side of Johnnie in class with Randy on the other side of George. Unfortunately, they found Ricco in their class as well who being alone seemed to keep his mouth shut for the time being.

However, Darrell and Steve had the pleasure of Wayne and Paco in their class for the year, which was not something they looked forward to. And

Wayne and Paco made sure that they let Darrell and Steve know that they were going to be the top dogs this year. Wayne walked in running his big mouth to Darrell which of course was a huge mistake.

"Well, well, well, look what we have here, Paco. Two of the loser group members," Wayne said with a smirk on his face.

"So I see, Wayne, how interesting will this be?" Paco commented.

Darrell and Steve were known for not taking any crap whatsoever, responded quickly, "Look at this, Steve, we got a few from the Special ED class visiting us today, are you two idiots lost?"

Laughing as he responded to Darrell, Steve added his comments in as well. "I hope you fight better than Wayne and Ricco does if you're going to run your mouth to me, kid."

Paco made sure that Steve understood why he was here. "I came to this school to fight you, guys, so don't think for one minute you are going to make me scared."

Steve laughed once again. "I never saw someone transfer schools before just to get beat up. Looks like you came to the right place though because if you're looking for a fight, then we can do it right now."

Paco not being one to back down from a fight either stood his ground with Steve until Steve got in his face. "Let's do it now, punk."

Paco had pushed Steve back and that was all it took, and it was on. It took all of three minutes for the school year to officially begin before the first fight between these two groups was underway. Steve hit Paco with a round house kick that knocked him down, and as soon as Paco was back on his feet, Steve hit him with a series of punches. Finally, Paco was able to grab Steve and get in a few punches himself while Darrell and Wayne made sure that each other stayed out of the fight.

The whole scene was a mess as the desk and chairs had been knocked over and pushed all over making the room look like a disaster area. Finally, Steve got Paco in a choke hold that allowed their teacher to grab him and pull him off, as she took the two boys down to the office. As the two boys sat in Principal Hardwell's office, he was shocked that there was a fight going on.

"Wow, what do we have here? So you two want to start the school year off like this, huh? So who wants to go first and tell me what happened?"

Steve spoke up, "It's real simple, this jerk started talking crap and pushed me, so I kicked his butt."

Paco responded, "You didn't kick nothing, and this is far from being over with." As Principal Hardwell listened to the two boys, he realized that this was a more serious issue than he had thought as first.

"You two are not going to keep on with this nonsense. I am giving you both a three day suspension, and when you come back, I don't want any more trouble out of you two, do you both understand me?"

Steve nodded and then responded, "As long as this kid leaves us alone, we don't have any problems, but I am not taking no crap from

179

anyone."

Paco added, "I don't care what happens, you can suspend all me year long. It doesn't matter to me, but I do know that this isn't over with by a long shot."

Principal Hardwell was being disgusted with Paco's attitude. "Then you're going to find yourself in a lot of trouble this year, young man, now go sit out in the lobby and wait for your parents."

While she was gone, Darrell made it clear that if Wayne wanted some, then they could also do the same. However, for Wayne, he wanted to wait till lunchtime. By which time the news of Steve and Paco had already spread throughout the school.

As they went outside for lunch, to Darrell's surprise, Wayne never even approached him. But some looks were giving their way nonetheless. Ignoring it though, the group went about their business and did the usual and found a spot on the steps that would fit them all as they sat and talked until lunch break was over. The whole school was filled with a buzz from the fight though, and everyone knew the history between these two groups, and it was only a matter of time before another fight was for sure to come. You could feel the tension between both groups already and now with a fight on the first day, it was promising to be an interesting school year. Most of the kids didn't like Wayne and Ricco anyways. But most of the school had lots of respect for Johnnie and his group. Mainly because they always helped out other kids and never bullied anyone. Even though

180

they were established as the more dominant group in school, they always used it to help protect the other kids from bullying. Whereas Wayne was known for pushing kids around and running his mouth to everyone, and Ricco was no different. He loved to push kids around and intimidate them. Even at times, taking lunches from other kids who could not defend themselves. Even though they were feared, but it was Johnnie's group who got all the respect. And everyone knew that the group was not something you wanted to mess with as well, even though they never started fights; their reputation for ending fights was becoming legendary.

Even Tonya at time had been in a few scrapes with snobby girls who thought they were better than everyone else. That was one thing that Tonya could not stand, was for someone to act better than everyone else. And Tonya was quick to say something that usually ended up in a fight. Because Tonya would take time to help people, it was easy to forget that she had a bad temper and an attitude to go with it. And if one thing was for sure, she could back it up and did so when needed. She was taught to not back down, the same with Steve. Their parents never got mad if they got into fights just as long as they weren't the ones who started the fight. This is why they were put in to martial Arts classes. Steve and Tonya's dad wanted to make sure his kids could defend themselves and wanted them to always stand their ground and not back down to anyone who started a fight. Which suited these too just fine. They never wanted to back down anyways. And if you wanted a fight they were going to give it to you. But for now all was quiet.

Lunch passed without incident and the day was about over now. Wasn't much longer when the kids all got home from school. Johnnie had set up a meeting at the camp when they were at school, so everyone knew to just come over once they got done with their after school chores and homework. Johnnie ran through everything as fast as he could to make sure that no one was back there waiting for him. He had felt that he should always be the first one there since it was his camp. Johnnie was funny like that, certain things bothered him. For his age, Johnnie took being a leader very seriously, this was one thing he had learned from Mark and had held true to it as to honor his father. After the rest of the group had finally arrived, it was time to talk about the situation at hand.

Johnnie, being the first to speak, put his cards on the table. "Here is why I wanted to talk to you all. You all know last year, we had a huge problem with Wayne and Ricco. Well, it appears that now they have a new friend, and he seems to want to get right in and make himself known. I am not going to tolerate any more crap from them at all. I don't care if I get kicked out for the whole school year. If they want a war, I will give it to them. I am sick and tired of Wayne and his crap."

After Johnnie had finished talking, George stood up next to him. "I'm with you, Johnnie, I am sick of it also, and if this is what they want, I am ready to go all the way with it."

As Darrell and Randy also stood up, Darrell added, "You know I'm down, bro, I have already had my first fight, and I'm sure there will be more to come. But whatever they want is fine with me."

Randy also added, "I have been sick of it from day one, I never liked Wayne. Not even since kindergarten. If this kid wants a war, I'm down to ride also.

Steve finally stood up. "I don't know these kids, but I do know that if they come at us, I'm not backing down, especially after the way Wayne disrespected my sister last year. And as far as Wayne running his mouth with his little friends, well, I got something for that."

Tonya grabbed Johnnie's hand. "And if that girl keeps looking at me like she has a problem, then I will for sure give her a problem, you can bet that." Johnnie nodded in agreement.

"Okay then, we all stand together, and we take each other's back, and we make sure we win this war."

This meeting was a huge turning point on how things were going to be handled from now on. There was not going to be anything let go or ignored any more. In the past, a lot had been said by Wayne and Ricco that was not acted upon by the group, but the day of letting them run their mouths was over with. There had already been a lot of fights, but there could have been a lot more had the group not let some things slide. But this was a new day, and nothing was going to be overlooked anymore. As for Wayne and Ricco and Paco, they thought it was fun to provoke this

183

group, but they had no idea how far they had pushed them, and now, the fight was about to escalate to new heights. And Sammy thought she was being cute giving Tonya some dirty looks, but she had no idea what she was in for either.

As the week went by, Steve was finally back in school as well as Paco. Things seemed to have simmered down for the time being. But you could sense that there was tension between the two groups. And Paco was way too eager to make a name for himself. Seeing Johnnie walking down the hall, Paco started off toward him and made sure he bumped right into Johnnie. This was his way of trying to make a statement.

"You got a problem, Paco?" Johnnie said as he got in Paco's face.

"Yeah, I got a problem, and it's with you and your little friends."

As the anger began to rise up in Johnnie, he pushed Paco. "Then do something about it, punk."

Paco, with a cocky smile, hit Johnnie in the face as the two boys started fighting in the hallway. Both boys threw some good punches, but Johnnie threw Paco to the ground, and about that time, one of the teachers had grabbed Johnnie and another grabbed Paco when he got up from where he slid after Johnnie threw him down. The fight for the most part was pretty even, but being as that, Johnnie was the one standing by the time the teachers broke it up signified that he was the winner by the rest of the kids.

As both boys entered Principal Hardwell's office, he was shocked to see Paco already back in his office for fighting. "Are you serious? Didn't you just come back from fighting? I see I'm going to have some problems with you this year. And, Johnnie, I have seen you in my office a few times last year for the same thing as well."

Johnnie did not say a word, but Paco had a smart mouth on him and made a comment that pissed Johnnie off. "Yeah, well, it's hard not to want to punch these kids when they look like this."

Principal Hardwell, however, was not in the mood for his attitude nor his smart mouth. "Well, Paco, let's see how a week's suspension suits you then. As for you, Johnnie, you get three days suspension. And I don't want to see either of you back in my office for the rest of the year, do you understand?"

Paco once again being smart. "I can't make any promises."

Johnnie was shaking his head. "As long as they keep starting fights with me, I will keep fighting with them."

Principal Hardwell had heard enough. "Then you both will have a lot of time off this year. Now get out of my office. I am calling both of your parents to come pick you both up."

Sara was irritated that she had to go pick Johnnie up from school because he had been fighting again. As Sara and Johnnie was riding home, Sara began to question him. "Johnnie, why are you always fighting with these kids?"

Johnnie explained the situation. "They keep starting fights with us. And we aren't going to take their crap."

Sara was not real pleased with Johnnie's answer. "This has to stop, Johnnie. You can't just keep fighting all the time."

"Mom, listen. I don't want to keep fighting, but they won't let up, and I refuse to back down to these punks."

Sara being extremely frustrated with the situation. "I don't know what to do, Johnnie."

Johnnie always had a way of talking to his mom that could bring a sense of calmness to her. "Mom, it's okay. I and the group will handle this, everything will be fine. I promise."

Sara had reached over and grabbed Johnnie's hand as she drove. "I just don't want to see you or anyone else get hurt."

"Don't worry, Mom, we can handle this. But we all have agreed that we will not back down to anyone. That is what my dad would have wanted me to do. He taught me to stand my ground and stick up for those who couldn't stick up for themselves."

Sara was almost in tears as soon as Mark was brought up. And it had been a long time since Johnnie had mentioned him. "Your father was a good man, Johnnie. And he lived what he taught you. I miss him so much."

Johnnie saw the pain in Sara's eyes. "I miss him too, Mom. So why are you with Mike then if you still love Dad so much?"

Sara tried to respond, "It's hard to explain, Johnnie, but Mike makes me feel things that I haven't felt since your father's passing. Your father made me feel like a real woman, and he loved me so much. Mike isn't quite the same, but he does make me feel alive again, Johnnie."

After Sara had said these things to Johnnie, there was no way he could try to stop it from happening now. He loved his mom more than anything, and if this is what she needed, then he couldn't interfere. After he got home, Johnnie spent the rest of the school day in his room playing video games while waiting for Tonya to get home.

It was the next week before Johnnie was able to return back to school. But while he was off, it was apparent to him that this wedding was going to happen sooner than he had anticipated. All while he was off, he had to endure spending time with his mom and Mike and all he wanted to talk about was getting married. Sara wasn't a hundred percent on board, but for Mike this seemed like it was all he wanted to do.

Sara stilled missed Mark and wasn't sure if she would ever get over it. And that scared her especially since she had already accepted Mike's marriage proposal. Still not having a date set yet though, she was hoping to push it back a while, but she could tell that Mike wanted it to be as soon as possible.

At this time, Johnnie had more pressing matters concerning their rivals and how he was going to put an end to it. If he could. It seemed to be getting worse with more people Wayne was able to get on his side. Johnnie was beyond frustrated with the situation and would often wonder just how far this was going to go. The only thing that Johnnie knew for sure was that he wasn't going to back down.

Before Johnnie could get back, George and Wayne had another fight that got them both three days out of school. George had a black eye from it, but Wayne took some hard punches to his ribs that had bruised them which was making it difficult for him to move around. The very next day, Johnnie had returned to school, and for now, everything had seemed quiet. Over the next few weeks, there was no real action. Only a few brief comments from both groups, but nothing major had come from it.

In the meantime, Mike had finally gotten Sara to commit to a wedding date which was not easy. Sara had felt that she would never get over Mark, so she was trying to just move on the best she could and thought maybe this would help. This of course only added to Johnnie's frustrations. Had Tonya not been there for him to help him work through this, he may have lost it at some point. He never could feel comfortable with Mike, and now, he was going to be family. Reluctantly, he agreed to be in the wedding, but it was only to please his mother. He was trying his best to be there and support Sara the best he could.

During the course of the next few weeks, Christina Hilton and Monica Reid helped Sara with all the wedding plans, including the invitations and the food menu. They all three looked at dresses and came up with a beautiful blue and white color theme. To make things easier because the wedding was going to come quickly, Sara decided on having the wedding catered. And Christina Hilton had secured her Pastor for the wedding along with their church, which had a huge hall for the reception.

Everything was going smoothly, and it looked as if this wedding was going to be wonderful. Johnnie had agreed to be the ring bearer but not by choice. During this time together, the three ladies talked often about the situation that the group had been having with these other boys.

"Let me ask you both a question while we are all together," Monica asked.

"Sure thing," responded Sara.

"What do you think about all of this trouble that the boys have been getting into? I mean I have never seen them in so many fights, and me and Tim just don't know what to do with George and all of these suspensions," Monica said with great frustration.

"Well, Monica, I have had a lot of talks with Johnnie, and I agree with him. What are they supposed to do, just take it from these other kids?" Sara said as she looked at Christina who hadn't responded as of yet to the question.

"Well, Darrell has always been a handful for us, but Randy was never really in any trouble until now, and to be honest, we are at our wit's end with it also. We don't know what else to do. We have tried everything from spankings to grounding. But it just seems to never stop," Christina said to Sara hoping that she could give more of an insight since she and Johnnie always talked over things that was going on.

Sara tried to be confident in her decisions with Johnnie. After all, she was on her own now with Mark being gone. "Well, I don't discipline Johnnie for it because they have been bullying him since last year. I don't like it either, but to be honest, Mark taught Johnnie to stick up for himself and for others. And I don't feel right about trying to make him take crap from these other kids."

Monica was so tired of George fighting. "But isn't there anything we can do to stop this? I mean I don't want to take George out of that school. It's a good school, and all of his friends are there."

Sara tried to calm them both down. "I feel the boys need each other and need to stay together. Let them work through it. So far, they have all stuck together, and I think it has drawn them all closer together as well. And I know Johnnie needs them all right now."

"Yeah, I agree," added Christina. "After all, it really isn't their fault, is it? These boys just keep starting fights with them all the time," Sara said to Christina and Monica.

The weeks went on, and the wedding came, and now, it was official, Sara and Mike was married. Sara had decided with all that Johnnie was going through that moving into Mike's house was not the right answer, so Mike had now moved in with them and was in the process of selling his house. Johnnie had made it clear that he wasn't about to move away from Tonya or his friends, and Sara knew how much he needed them right now. So she gave into this one for Johnnie, but it wasn't what she had wanted. She didn't want Mike living in the house that Mark had made for them, and Johnnie didn't either, but what was he to do? He wasn't about to leave his group or Tonya. This was the only option. This is where the group was and the camp was. He couldn't just up and leave. Sara felt that she owed Johnnie to give in and stay here for him. But this would never be a home like the way it was when Mark was here. And as for Johnnie, he wasn't home much anyways. All his spare time was with group unless he had something planned for just him and Tonya. Mike didn't care anyways if Johnnie was gone all the time, he rather preferred it. Johnnie could have disappeared, and it wouldn't have affected Mike at all.

Through the next several weeks, the tension between the two groups would grow again. Sammy had tried to spread some rumors about Tonya until someone went back to Tonya and told her about it. And it was time for Tonya to confront Sammy. This was a fight that had been building up for a while, and Tonya had been waiting for just the right moment to bring it all to a head.

At lunchtime, Tonya waited until everyone was outside and then confronted Sammy in front of everyone. This was a moment that everyone knew was coming. Finally, Tonya was going to show Sammy just who was in control here. As Tonya walked over to the group with the whole gang in tow, she pushed Ricco out of the way who was about to grab her until Johnnie made an advancement toward him. That's when Ricco backed off. Johnnie had a look in his eyes that set Ricco back a little. Wasting no time, Tonya grabbed Sammy and started punching her. While she was hitting Sammy, she was repeating everything that Sammy had said about her just so everyone knew that Sammy was a liar. When Ricco went to grab Tonya off Sammy, Johnnie grabbed him and threw him to the ground. Once Ricco got up, he and Johnnie started fighting hard. Both threw punches at each other and some at the same time.

This had turned out to be quite a show for the rest of the students. Tonya no doubt won that fight, and finally, Darrell and Steve broke up the fight between Johnnie and Ricco when they saw a teacher running over to stop the fight. Once again, Principal Hardwell had another fight on the playground between these two groups. This was something that he was beyond tired of. And now, he had two girls added into the mix. Not wasting time, he called them all into his office and immediately handed out suspensions. Tonya and Sammy only got three days a piece, but Johnnie and Ricco both got five days each. And another warning that he didn't want to see either one of them in his office again for the rest of the school year.

During Johnnie's time off from school, Sara and Mike both agreed that Johnnie should do some chores while he was off from school. This way, he was still being productive and not just playing video games. Tonya also was not allowed to just hang around and do nothing. She was giving a list of things to do as well, which mainly consisted of laundry and dishes. However, once they got their list of chores done for the day, they were able to spend time with one another. George was also with them until his suspension had ended, and he was back to school.

After the ladies had talked about the situation during the wedding preparations, the parents were a little more insightful into the situation. Tony and Tammy Flowers, who were the parents of Steve and Tonya, also got with the other parents and had discussed this as well. And their input into the situation was much needed. For Tony's background was one of a militant background, and he wasn't about to tell his kids not to fight back. Tony was in the Special Forces and had no plans on making his children take any crap from some punks.

Sara and Tammy became pretty good friends after Johnnie and Tonya started dating. Sara just loved Tonya, and Tammy thought the world of Johnnie as well. Tony was impressed with Johnnie and how he carried himself, which said a lot about Johnnie for Tony to feel this way about him. But he was quite fond of Johnnie and liked having him around. Ann had missed George and Tonya not being at school. She had been so used to being with them all the time that she felt herself getting a bit lonely in their absence. But with Steve and the two brothers around to make sure Ann was taken care of there was no real concern. But Tonya was her best friend, and it just wasn't the same with her not being there.

After everyone's suspension had been fulfilled, there were very little incidents for a while. For it had seemed as if things had calmed down for a bit. The group had settled into the school year and was focusing on their own things with little involvement from Wayne or Ricco. Tonya had established herself as someone that was not to be messed with and had very little problems throughout the rest of the fall. Sammy had not been talking as much either after her fight with Tonya only produced some humiliation.

Paco was in and out of school as much as he was in and out of trouble. While Paco was out of school on a suspension, he was picked up for murdering a few gang rivals and was sentenced to a juvenile facility. Shortly after the school year started, Ricco and Wayne were both arrested for stealing several cars together. Ricco was currently on probation for stealing already and was supposed to be tending school regularly which he was not doing as he was told by the court, which brought on more trouble for him.

As for Johnnie, his home life had been a struggle. There had become a friction of sorts between him and Mike. It wasn't long after the wedding that Mike began to drink a lot more and was starting to be a bit abusive toward Johnnie and Sara. At first, it was just drunken name calling until one night, he hit Sara and knocked her down. Johnnie was in his room and only heard the yelling which was starting to happen more and more often.

Every year, Mike took a layoff for the winter months when things began to slow down a bit. And this year, he took it early in the fall which he normally would work through. So he had been home much more often and had begun to drink all the time. This was a situation that Sara had no idea was going to happen. She thought Mike worked year round and only had an occasional beer every so often. Sara was also unaware of how much Mike drank during this time and how violent he would get. Sara wasn't used to be being around a bunch of drinking and didn't feel comfortable around it at all, and really didn't want it around Johnnie. But every time she would bring it up and try to talk to Mike about it, he would get mad and start yelling at her.

As the fall went on, the problem became much worse for Sara as well as Johnnie. After about a month and a half into the layoff, Mike got really drunk and started fighting with Sara and slapped her. When Johnnie saw that, he was filled with anger and pushed Mike away from Sara only to find himself now being hit and knocked down as well. Sara, had gotten up to grab Mike to stop him from hitting Johnnie, was slapped again; and then Mike grabbed her by her hair and dragged her into the bedroom and slammed the door behind them. Johnnie could hear Sara crying as Mike began to do things to her. Not being able to get the door opened, Johnnie didn't know what to do. Mike would get off on hurting Sara and would make her get naked and forced her to have sex with him after he would beat her.

This was the first time in Johnnie's life that he felt as if he was helpless and could do nothing to help his mother or himself. Johnnie had become afraid of Mike and Sara was also. She was more afraid of what Mike would do to Johnnie. Mike never really tried to get to know Johnnie as he pretended to in the beginning. And now, he acted

195

like he hated Johnnie and didn't want him around. Sara and
Johnnie were both afraid as much as they were ashamed to even tell anyone. So they both began to make excuses for things like bruises, and Sara started making excuses as to why she couldn't have company over or meet up for lunch with any of her friends. She would always make up something about being busy doing housework or having to go out and wouldn't be able to meet up.

Johnnie began to hate Mike with a passion. And would often think about killing him. This of course bothered Johnnie because this wasn't like him. But with all the problems he had been through at school with Wayne and Ricco, the last thing he needed now was to come home to the same thing. This of course became a major problem for Johnnie. He was always taught to stand his ground and protect those who couldn't protect themselves. So how could he let someone beat his mother and not do anything about it? There had to be something he could do to stop his mother from getting hurt.

Johnnie began to think of ways he could put an end to his mom being abused and decided to start saving up to buy a gun. Every week, Johnnie would put part of his allowance up in a safe place, and all the change he would find he would put in a jar also. Even finding bottles and taking them back to the store to get the deposit from them. Johnnie wasn't a murderer, but enough was enough. It was too much to deal with and something needed to change. He couldn't cope anymore having to deal with it at school and also at home.

Everyone began to see Johnnie's attitude begin to change, and his tolerance for Wayne and Ricco was gone, who was temporarily back in school while awaiting their trial. If they even looked his way, he was ready to rip into them. The anger in Johnnie was at a boiling point, and you could tell he was about to explode. Tonya was one of only a few who actually knew what all was going on. She was the one person who could make Johnnie calm and be at ease. And when he was with her, it was the only time he felt any real happiness. Tonya was always with Johnnie making sure he was okay and comforting him the best that she could. For Johnnie, Tonya had become his whole world. The one person he knew he could always count on to be there for him no matter what.

Johnnie's love for Tonya continued to grow even while the worse things became. Had it not been for Tonya, Johnnie would have lost his mind. But she was the one person in his life at this time that understood what was going on and would take time to listen to him, which always made him feel better. There were things that he told Tonya that no one else knew. Not even George.

However, he did talk to George quite often about what was going on but it was limited, and George was in the process of trying to find someone who could get them a gun. But this was not an easy task as it was hard to get anything in their area. So they would have to find someone outside of their community to help them get what they needed. In the meantime, Johnnie was saving what he could to hopefully be able to afford it.

As the fall season went on, things got real bad at home for Johnnie. Mike began to hit him quite often. Sara was so scared all the time that she was living in constant fear and would try every day to be as perfect for Mike as she could just so she and Johnnie wouldn't get hit any more. She began to get on Johnnie to not say anything to Mike at all to make him upset. This of course didn't work for either of them because they weren't the problem. The problem was Mike, and no matter what they did, it was never going to be good enough. Mike was violent and abusive no matter how good they were. And the things he would say to Sara and the names he would call her was beyond degrading. It was hateful. Sara didn't know what to do or how to get any help. And she was afraid to tell anyone in fear of what Mike would do to her and Johnnie.

Sara's dream home had now become her prison. A place of daily torment. The love that used to fill this home had turned into fear, hatred, and anger. This once bright, joyful filled house became a dark place of torment and abuse. Mike began to make Sara do things that she was ashamed of. Things that she hated, but if she didn't do them, then he would get mad and beat her some more. Sara who once felt like a real woman was now feeling as if she was nothing. Mike had broken her down and destroyed all self confidence that Sara had once had. The hope of a new life and a chance to love again had been destroyed.

CHAPTER 9

No Other Way

The winter season was upon South Bend Heights. The weather rarely changed there, so it wasn't much different than the fall season. Only a small fluctuation in the weather from summer to spring and then from fall to winter. But it very seldom changed dramatically, and snow was very rare for the people of this city. A good sweatshirt or jacket was usually all you needed to stay sufficiently warm.

As the new season began, it was not without its share of difficulties. The one good thing for Johnnie and the group was Thanksgiving, and Christmas break were in this season which meant a nice break from school and more time for hanging out at the camp or other places. For most of the group, it was a time to relax and enjoy family time and extended friend time, except for Johnnie, it just meant more time to try to not be home with Mike, which wasn't a problem since he would rather spend his time with Tonya and the group anyways. Johnnie's school grades this year had suffered from all the drama he had to endure this year. It had become very hard to focus on his studies with so much going on and the constant worrying about his mother.

Johnnie faced so many challenges in his young life, but this was proving to be the most difficult. Not since the death of his father had he so much to endure. How much more did this make him miss his father? Johnnie never forgot the things that his father had taught him and that was the one thing he held on to the most. So much had happened in the past few years, and often, Johnnie would sit and wonder why things had turned out the way they did. Why did everything have to change when it all started out so good? Every year seemed to bring new problems and new challenges to face.

For the rest of the group, winter was an exciting time. George had always looked forward to the winter month. It was the season that he and Johnnie would get together and work out their Christmas list, and the Thanksgiving Parade in town was always something they looked forward to. This year, Tonya and Steve would be a part of their winter traditions. The two brothers always loved the parade and the snack food that they sold there. It was always such a wonderful family time, and everyone went into the town for it. It was common for the group to do most things together. Johnnie looked forward to the winter break, just so he could be with Tonya all the time as well as the group. And he was for sure planning on not being home as much as possible, so that way, he wouldn't have to deal with Mike.

Sara wanted this winter to be a time for the family to get closer together in hopes that Mike would get to know Johnnie better, and then maybe, things would get better for everyone. Sara always kept thinking that there was something that she could do to improve the situation so that Mike wouldn't be so angry all the time. Her hopes was to find a way to get him to stop drinking all the time, and maybe some family time would be the answer. If only she could get Johnnie to cooperate and stay home for a bit instead of running off all the time. She remembered how the group used to come and stay all the time, and now, they only would go back to the camp area. She rarely saw them anymore, and it was the same with Johnnie now also. She knew it was because they all hated Mike. He was rude to everyone, and even Sara's friends had begun to stray from the house. But they obviously had begun to get tired of the many excuses Sara had as to why she couldn't do things now, since she had to hide the bruises that she got from the beatings that Mike gave her on a regular basis.

Johnnie never wanted any of his friends to come into the house because of the way Mike would act and say in front and to them. Johnnie was ashamed of how things had become at his home, and he was too embarrassed to talk about it most of the time. However, when he did talk about it, it was usually only to Tonya and George.

George had been trying everything he could to

establish a connection to get Johnnie a gun, so he could protect himself and Sara from Mike. Finally, after some time, a friend from school got a hold of a handgun and told George that he would sell it to him. George called Johnnie right after they had talked.

"Johnnie, I was able to finally get what you had been asking for. He wants fifty dollars for it, and it's loaded already."

Johnnie knowing he had to make this deal couldn't wait any longer, he needed this gun. "Set it up, George, I will have the money ready."

Johnnie was still short, but he knew he could get it if he had too. But he hated to have to lie to his mom to get money. Lying wasn't something that Johnnie ever liked to do; he was always taught to be honest no matter what, but he had to get this money, and Sara would never give it to him for this reason. He was still twenty dollars short. So he told Sara that he was going to go out with the group to roller skate and needed some money. This was one of only a few times Johnnie ever lied to Sara. He hated it, but he felt it was something that he had to do to protect his mother as well as himself.

George met up with Johnnie back at the camp before anyone else came. Johnnie had set it up that way, so no one would know about the money he was giving George so that he could purchase the handgun for him. This was something that they hid from the rest of the group. George didn't want anyone to know that he was involved in this, and neither did Johnnie. After giving George the money, they sat and talked about the situation with Mike until the others began to show up. George wasn't sure about doing this, but Johnnie was persistent on getting this handgun. George was afraid that if he didn't and something really bad did happen, he would feel guilty for not doing it. It was a hard place to be, but Johnnie was his brother, and he loved him and was willing to do whatever he could to help him out.

Once the rest of the group finally all got there, it was time to have some much needed fun. Johnnie had suggested that they go back to the pond, which was the group's favorite place to hang out. So after a short while, they all walked back to their secret pond and played. Johnnie wasn't into it as much as he used to be. He would stare off into the distance or stand at the edge of the pond and skip rocks. It wasn't hard to tell what he was doing. He had a lot on his mind, and everyone knew it. And they would try their best to distract him and try to keep him involved.

The next day, George made contact with his friend and set up a meeting place for the two of them to meet up and make the deal. He had the money that Johnnie had given him and just needed to find a place that they could both be at, which wasn't hard to do, but they didn't live close, so it would take some work to get the time set to where they could be together. And it needed to be somewhere with a bathroom, so they could meet in private. George was very nervous about this. Sam, his friend, had suggested a park, but George didn't want to do it out in the open, and he was afraid their parents would see the transaction. George had suggested the mall, but how to get them both there at the same time was going to be tricky, and they would both need a good reason to go to the mall; but neither was going to buy anything so how would they work that out?

Finally, George agreed to the park because it was just easier to meet up at a set time. Once they got that set, then it was a matter of getting their parents to take them their right at the exact time together. To make it easier, George suggested Saturday morning, which Sam agreed too. Later on that day when the group was together, George had pulled Johnnie aside to go over what had transpired earlier that day with Sam. Johnnie knew that George was taking a huge risk for him and surely didn't take it lightly. This was something that they had never done before, and they were both nervous about it. Johnnie didn't want George to get caught doing this for him.

"Be very careful, George. If you get caught, we are both in trouble."

"No, just me. I will never tell anyone who I was getting it for."

"I would never let you go down alone for something you are doing for me. You're my brother."

"I know, Johnnie, don't worry, everything will go smooth."

"Yeah, well, just be careful, and thank you for doing this for me. It means a lot to me that you would do this," Johnnie said as he almost started to tear up.

"I love you, Johnnie. You're like my real brother. I would do anything to help you." George said as he had hugged Johnnie.

"I love you too, George."

After returning to the group, Johnnie sat down next to Tonya. She could tell he wasn't okay. As she grabbed his hand to hold on to it, as she whispered into his ear, "Is everything okay, babe?"

"Yes. Everything will be okay, honey."

"Okay, good, then I don't need to worry, right?" Tonya gently whispered trying to keep things very low, so no one would hear them.

"No need to worry, Tonya, everything is going to be alright," Johnnie said to try to ease Tonya, so she wasn't so worried about him.

The next day, George and Sam both worked out the time frame for Saturday with their parents. George had worked it out for a picnic, which he knew would get his mom to do it. That is something she loved to do with the family. And of course, Tim would do it just to make Monica happy. The only real concern that George had now was getting the package and bringing it back home without anyone noticing it. This was a major concern for George. He knew if he was caught, he would be in very serious trouble. So what George planned was to pack a book bag with toys and put the gun in there once he got the opportunity when no one was looking. All he had to do was take a few other toy guns, and hopefully that would work.

As Johnnie was sitting in the living room watching television, he heard an argument started between Mike and Sara. Johnnie could almost cringe. No argument with Mike ever ended well. Once he started, there was no end until he hurt someone. Johnnie almost knew what was coming. He could hear his mom pleading for Mike to stop. He knew she was afraid, and Sara knew she was going to get hit if she couldn't calm Mike down. But Mike had been drinking all morning and was in a bad mood since the time he woke up. When Johnnie heard things getting knocked around, he jumped up and ran in to help his mother. Mike had her on the ground and was choking her. When Johnnie saw this, he ran to try to push Mike off her and was met with a backhand that knocked Johnnie to the ground. While he was getting up, Mike was looking at him intensely.

"Oh, you want some more, you little punk kid? I will give you some more."

As Mike got off Sara, he began to head toward Johnnie as Sara tried to grab for him to try to stop him, but he was already out of her reach. Johnnie clinched his fist.

"I'm tired of you hitting us, you piece of garbage," Johnnie said as he swung at Mike. This only made Mike angrier.

"I will show you who is a piece of garbage, you little punk. You want to try and hit me, I will teach you a lesson that you won't never forget." Mike picked up Johnnie and threw him across the kitchen, then proceeded to kick Johnnie in the ribs.

"Who's the tough guy now, you little punk?"

Sara got back on her feet, grabbed Mike and tried to get him to stop.

"Mike stop, please stop, Mike. I will do anything

you want, just don't hurt him anymore."

As Mike turned to Sara, he smacked her one more time and knocked her down to the ground. As her head hit the floor, she laid there crying.

"Get up, Sara," Mike said with such anger in his voice. "I said get up!"

After Sara got up, Mike took her into the bedroom and locked the door. He made Sara get undressed for him and lay down on the bed. This was all Mike had wanted, but Sara hated to have sex with him when he was drunk and was trying to avoid having to do this.

After a few minutes, Johnnie got up and went and took a shower then got dressed and left to go to Tonya's. He couldn't stay there one minute longer. He knew this had to end and was hoping George could pull this off for him so that he could protect him and his mother. If he had the gun today, surely Mike would have been dead already.

When Tonya came out and saw that Johnnie was upset and had been hit, she immediately took him back to the camp, so they could be alone and talk. She knew Johnnie didn't want anyone else to know. As they got to the camp, she held Johnnie as he cried in her arms. He was so tired of all the crap he had been going through and knew that Mike had to go one way or another. He knew that Sara was too afraid to leave him now because he had often threaten to kill her and Johnnie if she did. She was terrified. Mike's temper which was out of control. He was so violent. Sara was sure he meant it. Johnnie and Tonya stayed together all day into the late evening. Just the two of them. As they sat and talked, it became clear to Johnnie that he needed alone time with Tonya. They very rarely was ever alone because they were usually all together. But Johnnie was enjoying his alone time with Tonya, and she was also. There wasn't much that they didn't talk about, and it gave Johnnie a sense of peace just being with her. Something that he had rarely felt these days.

Saturday morning had come, and George was at the park playing on the swings when his friend Sam had finally showed up. As they met up, they went off away from everyone else and made the transaction.

"Hey, Sam, did you bring the gun?" Sam looked around. "Yeah, I brought it, you got the fifty bucks?"

George looked to make sure no one was looking. "Yeah, I brought it."

After making the transaction, George went back to the spot where his parents where and slipped the gun in his bag while he was pretending to look for a toy. After a few minutes, he returned to Sam, and they went off and played on the swings together.

Later on that day as they all met up over at the two brothers' house, Darrell was talking to Steve about a situation where Paco had made some comments about him to some other kids. Steve had been talking to this girl on the playground, and Paco had also shown interest in the same girl and wasn't real happy to see her talking to Steve.

Before George and Johnnie met everyone at Darrell's and Randy's, George had called Johnnie to meet with him first. When George stopped over to Johnnie, they headed up to his room where George pulled out the gun and gave it to Johnnie. "Here you go, bro, please never tell anyone that I got this for you."

Johnnie was very thankful that George had done this for him. "Don't worry, George, I will never tell anyone where I got it from. I promise you that."

George took a deep breath. "Thank you, Johnnie, and please be careful."

As Johnnie was putting the gun in a safe place, he responded back to George. "Don't worry, George, this is only for if I have to do it."

George did not understand why they just didn't kick him out. "Johnnie, why does your mom let him stay here with everything that he is doing to you both?"

As a very serious look came over Johnnie's face, he responded, "She is really scared, bro, he threatens to kill her if she does. And he always tells her that if she tells anyone that he will hurt us both really bad, so she is too scared to go to the police or anyone else. This is why I needed your help getting this gun, George. I have to protect my mom. I love her so much, and I can't let him do this to her anymore."

"Yes, I understand, Johnnie, I just wish there was another way. I don't want to see you get into any kind of trouble like this. I am scared for you, Johnnie, you are like blood to me."

Johnnie hugged George. "You will always be my brother. No matter what. I have no choice, George, I have to do this. She is my mother. And I can't let this keep going on. I have to do something, even if

209

killing him is the only way to end this, then that is what I will do."

After talking for a few, Johnnie and George headed out to meet up with the others over at Darrell's and Randy's place. When Tonya and Ann saw the two coming down the street, they both got up and went to meet them. Johnnie met Tonya with a hug as George grabbed Ann's hand, and then they all walked back together. Talking along the way, Ann had missed George, and Tonya always missed Johnnie when they weren't together. Likewise, George had been waiting to see Ann as well, and of course, Johnnie always hated being away from Tonya.

As they were altogether at Darrell and Randy's playing, Johnnie couldn't help but think about what if he had to actually use the gun. He was scared, but more scared about what was going to happen to his mother if he didn't do something. He knew he wasn't a killer, but one thing was for sure, and that's he was a protector and would do it if he had to. Tonya could sense that Johnny was troubled. Every so often, she reached over and held his hand to comfort him. Both would smile as she did that. It did comfort Johnnie. He knew that Tonya loved him and she meant everything to him.

It was late in the evening when Johnnie came home and found the living was all tore up, and there was a vase smashed on the floor. Everything was quiet as Johnnie walked through the house looking for his mother. After searching the whole house, he looked out the back window and saw Sara sitting on one of the swing benches. She was just sitting there, so Johnnie went out to meet her and see if she was okay.

"Mom, are you okay?" Johnnie asked her as he sat down next to her on the swing.

"Yes, I am fine, Johnnie. I guess you saw the living room," Sara responded as she put her arm around Johnnie.

"Yes, I did. What happened?" Johnnie asked.

"You know, Johnnie. Just another fight between me and Mike. I fear it's getting worse, son, and I don't know what to do about it."

Johnnie could tell Sara was becoming even more afraid. "Everything will be okay, Mom. Things will get better soon," Johnnie said as he laid his head on her shoulder.

"I don't know, son. I just wish I knew what to do."

Johnnie didn't dare tell Sara about the gun or his plan to kill Mike. For now, he was just trying to comfort her.

"Where is he now?" Johnnie asked.

"He went out to the bar. That's what we got into a fight about. I didn't want him to go out drinking, and he got mad about it and started tearing up the living room before I finally gave in and told him to just go," Sara explained.

"Things are going to change soon, Mom. Things will be good again. I promise," Johnnie said, knowing what he was going to do.

"I hope so, son, I don't know how much more I can take of this."

Johnnie went back into the house and cleaned up the broken vase and fixed all the furniture that had been thrown about, putting everything back in its place. As he was doing so, he was thinking to himself that this was the last straw and now he had the means to end it. Sara came in and locked up the house and headed to bed after checking in on Johnnie who had retired to his bedroom after cleaning everything up in the living room.

"Thank you, Johnnie, for cleaning everything up," Sara said as she hugged Johnnie.

"You're welcome, Mom," Johnnie said as he sat back down on his bed.

"I am going to bed, Johnnie. I will see you in the morning."

As Sara was walking out of the bedroom, Johnnie said to her, "I love you, Mom." Sara smiled for the first time all day.

"I love you too, Johnnie."

Going into her room, Sara got undressed and climbed into bed and fell asleep, after being exhausted from the fight with Mike earlier that day. Johnnie stayed up for a few hours and played some video games while he tried to relax. This whole ordeal with Mike had him on the edge to where he could not rest.

Just as Johnnie was about to turn in for the night and try to get some sleep, he heard Mike come home. After a few minutes, Mike had come upstairs and went into the bedroom. It wasn't long when Johnnie heard his mom telling Mike to stop.

"Mike, you're drunk, I don't want to do this when you're drunk you know this. I'm very tired, Mike, please stop," Sara said, trying to almost plead with Mike to just let her sleep.

"You can't give me any love? What kind of a wife are you when you can't take care of your husband?" Mike said as he got more aggressive with Sara.

"Mike, I said stop, I don't want to do anything tonight. Please stop you're hurting me," Sara said as she began to try to fight Mike off.

Finally, Mike, being frustrated and drunk, slapped Sara and began to try to force her to do what he wanted before he heard to door open violently.

"Get off of her, Mike!" He heard Johnnie say from behind him.

"Well, you little punk, who do you think you are coming into my room like this?" Mike said as he got up and headed toward Johnnie.

Before he could hit him, Johnnie pulled out the gun he had bought earlier that day and fired three shots that hit Mike and sent him fast to the floor. As Mike laid there bleeding, Sara sprung out of bed and ran to Johnnie.

Still trying to process what had just happened, Sara grabbed him. "Johnnie, what did you do?" Sara frantically asked as she was shaking.

"I ended it. He won't hit you anymore, Mom," Johnnie said as he dropped the gun on the ground, slumped down the wall and sat on the floor.

Sara stood there not knowing what she should do. After gathering herself, Sara went and called for an ambulance. However, it was too late as Mike laid there on the floor, he was already gone. Johnnie had killed him with the three shots that he put into him. When the police arrived, they took both statements from Sara and Johnnie. But because Johnnie had cleaned everything up and put all the furniture back in its place and Sara didn't at this time have any visible marks, they had to arrest Johnnie for murder.

As they took the body out of the house, Sara was pleading with the officers to not take Johnnie to jail. But at this time, they had no choice and until they could further investigate the situation they had to take Johnnie into custody. As they took Johnnie out, Sara followed still trying to plead with the officers as they put Johnnie in the back of the police car.

One of the officers finally grabbed Sara and explained the situation to her. "Look, we are just doing our job. We have to take him in, pending an investigation. You can come down to the station once we get him processed."

As they finally drove off, Sara just stood there watching them when Monica and Tim came over. Everyone had heard the shots and the sirens. Most of the neighbors where outside at this point. Monica took Sara into the house, so she wouldn't have to deal with the neighbors who began to ask questions. Thomas and Christina had also heard the sirens and saw the flashing lights. Once everything had settled down, they also came down to make sure that Sara and Johnnie were okay.

As they all sat in the living room, Monica went into the kitchen and made some hot tea for everyone as they all sat and listened to Sara explain what happened. She told them about all of the abuse and how Mike had been beating her and

Johnnie. Then she explained that Johnnie had shot Mike while trying to protect her. Everyone was in shock and no one knew how Johnnie was able to even acquire a gun at his age. No one could believe what had transpired tonight. It was so hard to imagine Johnnie killing anyone. They had known for a long time something was going on and knew Mike had a drinking problem. No one liked him because of the way he would talk to everyone and they all knew he treated Sara very poorly. Everyone's heart sunk at the thought of Johnnie being arrested for killing him.

CHAPTER 10

Going Away

Once they got down to the station and got Johnnie processed, they had to put him in a separate holding cell because of his age. They could not talk with him as of yet because he had no lawyer present, and Sara had made it clear before the police had pulled away that no one was to talk to him until she could get a hold of her lawyer. It wouldn't be until sometime tomorrow morning before Sara could do so. In the meantime, Johnnie had to sit in a cell alone and just wait.

Early the next morning, Sara was awake and had barely slept all night. As soon as her lawyer's office opened, she began to call and set up an appointment to come in and talk with him making it very clear that it was an extreme emergency. As soon as they got an appointment set up for as early as they could, Sara started getting herself together.

After putting on some coffee, she took a quick

shower and got herself dressed before returning to fetch the coffee that was ready by the time she had returned. After pouring a cup of coffee, Sara sat down on the couch and tried to get her thoughts together. She was tired from the long sleepless night and was trying hard to keep her mind focused on what all she was going to have to do today. She was scared. Sara had no idea what was going to happen to Johnnie. Her mind was going in so many different directions and thoughts all at the same time.

After finishing her coffee, Sara headed out to meet with her lawyer. As Sara went into Mr. Powers' office to meet with him, she was very nervous. As she went in, Mr. Powers greeted her and offered her a seat. Sara sat down and began to explain the situation and all that happened. She went into great detail of everything that she and Johnnie had been through and what had transpired the previous night.

Mr. Powers made her explain everything, starting at the beginning of how it all got started. Sara was in tears as she explained the beatings and how Mike had been abusing her and Johnnie. After taking the time to hear her story and ask several question, Mr. Powers agreed to take on the case and then began to make preparations to go down and meet with Johnnie and talk with him. After which, he was going to talk with the arresting officers. As Johnnie's lawyer, he was going to have to interview everyone.

Johnnie was happy to see his lawyer come in. He knew Sara would get him a good lawyer, and they knew Mr. Powers already, and Johnnie was quite comfortable with him, which made him feel more at ease. Mr. Powers had been a friend of Marks from childhood. As they sat and talked for some time, Mr. Powers realized how his story and Sara's story had perfectly matched in all details, with the exception of the things that Sara had said that Johnnie had no idea had happened. It was so very difficult for Sara to talk about everything, but she knew it was important if she was going to help Johnnie. She was embarrassed and ashamed, but more than that, she was afraid of what was going to happen to Johnnie if she didn't tell him about what all happened.

After Mr. Powers interviewed Johnnie, he met with the arresting officers and got their statements and also was able to look at the report they had. It became clear to Jeff the officers didn't even want to arrest Johnnie, but there wasn't enough evidence to support their story. Johnnie explained to Jeff Powers that he had cleaned up the mess, and by doing so, he had erased all traces of what had happened prior to the shooting. The laws did not favor Johnnie since there was not a law against raping your wife. Sara did not show any signs of physical abuse, so they had no choice but to arrest him for the murder of Mike Johnson.

The officers wanted to make a deal with Johnnie, to try to get a lesser sentence for him. They did not want this to go to court in fear that he would spend the rest of his child years locked up. As Jeff Powers talked to the arresting officers, he was able to make a deal that would have Johnnie out after three years. It was the best they could do.

Johnnie's lawyer explained to him that with there being no real evidence and with his history of violence in school with suspension for fighting, he felt their best bet was to take the deal and not risk going to court. As Sara heard the deal, her first reaction was to not take it. She didn't want Johnnie doing any time at all, but Mr. Powers had finally convinced the two that this was the best way to go. To Johnnie, it did make sense, he knew he had been in a lot of trouble at school for fighting, and this wasn't going to look good at all for him if it went to court.

After signing the deal that they had gave to Johnnie, they let him see Sara for ten minutes before taking him to processing. Being that Johnnie was the only transfer for juvenile, they decided to transfer him first thing in the morning. It was a long night for Johnnie. He had barely slept a wink all night. As he was laying on his cot thinking of how it was going to be there. All he knew of juvenile facilities is what he had seen on television or movies. He was scared to say the least, not knowing what was going to happen. As he laid there, he couldn't help but wonder if he was going to the same place where Ricco, Wayne, and Paco was. This troubled Johnnie greatly knowing he was going in alone and did not know anyone else that was there. He had never been in this kind of trouble before, but one thing he did know was that he was going in alone, and that wasn't going to be good for him if they were all there together.

In between his thoughts on this situation, he

would think of Tonya and how she must be so
worried about him as well. He felt so bad for
having to do what he did. But he couldn't see any
other way and felt it had to be done. He was
already missing Tonya and couldn't help but
wonder if this was going to affect his relationship
with her. And if so, how would it be when he got
out. Would she even visit or write him knowing
that he had killed someone? He wondered about
George and if he was okay. Time seemed to pass
by slowly as Johnnie laid there all night thinking
upon all these things. Not knowing the answer to
any of them. It was the longest night of his life.
Full of worries thinking on the many things that
had entered his mind that night.

Three years was a long time to be away from
Tonya. And what about Sara? After all of this, now
she was all alone. Johnnie had felt so sick to his
stomach as he thought about his mom and all she
had lost already, how would she be able to handle
losing Johnnie for three years or if forever if he
didn't make it back out. Who would take care of
her? And as for Tonya, would she wait for him?
Would she still be there when he got out? Would
she even be able to still see him after all of this?
What did her parents think of him now?

Shortly after the sun was up, one of the guards
came for Johnnie. "Get up, Johnnie," the guard
said as he stood just outside of the cell looking in
at him.

As Johnnie got up off the cot that he had laid on
all night, the guard raised up a pair of handcuffs
from his side. "I need to put these on you. Come to

the door and turn around and put your hands through the hole," the guard said as he instructed Johnnie.

Johnnie did as he was told and then stepped forward away from the door as the guard had gave him further instructions to do once he had placed the handcuffs on him. After opening the cell door, the guard had instructed Johnnie to step out and then he had grabbed his arm and walked him to where a car was waiting for him, to transfer him to the juvenile facility.

After Johnnie was placed in the backseat of the police car, he was taken several miles away to where he would be reprocessed again, and where he would live for the next three years. The ride took a few hours and very little was said along the way. Johnnie just sat in the back looking out the window as they drove him to the facility, sitting and thinking as he continued to wonder what would happen to him there.

Once they arrived, they took Johnnie out of the backseat of the car and walked him inside where he would be reprocessed once again. He was more than nervous. Being so scared not knowing how this was going to be for him. Johnnie was trying not to show any emotion at all, as he was trying to fight back his tears, refusing to cry at all or show any kind of weakness. Once released into their custody, the transporting officer turned and walked out as he left Johnnie in their custody.

CHAPTER 11

The House

After being taken back into an area for processing, Johnnie was given a new set of clothes to wear and his bedding as well as basic necessities. He was made to change before they would take him into population. Once Johnnie was processed and ready, he was escorted to what would be his new home for the next three years. They stepped through the gate, as they called it, which was a cage with a door on it. Everyone was standing there waiting for the new arrival to enter in.

Once Johnnie walked through some of the inmates especially those whom he knew began to say things to him and cuss at him. Some even telling him what they were going to do to him. He saw Wayne and Ricco and knew this wasn't going to be good for him. This was exactly what he had feared. The guard got Johnnie to his cell, he left him there to get settled in. Johnnie had never felt so alone in his entire life. He had no friends here, and those who did know him hated him.

Johnnie had trouble fighting back the overwhelming fear that was gripping him now. He was in a foreign place with nothing but enemies and strangers. As Johnnie put his stuff on the top bunk that was the empty bunk of the two, he heard a voice come from behind him.

"So I get the new guy," Vincent said, who was now Johnnie's new roommate.

"Yeah, I guess so," Johnnie responded as he was putting his stuff away.

"You respect my space, and I will respect yours. You get into my stuff or cause me any problems, and I will be your biggest problem," Vincent said as he began to make it clear that he had seniority.

"I'm just here to do my time, nothing more, nothing less," Johnnie said as he paused to address Vincent.

"Good, then we shouldn't have any problems. My name is Vincent, any beef you have here with other people, keep it out of our cell. Your problems are not my problems. Understand?" Vincent said as he was laying on his bed.

"I always deal with my own problems," Johnnie replied as he was making his bed.

It wasn't long before Wayne and Ricco had purposely walked past Johnnie's cell door real slow, taking time to look in. You could hear them both laugh as they continued to walk on.

"Friends of yours?" Vincent asked.

"No, no, they are not friends at all," Johnnie

answered as he took a deep breath.

"What's your name?" Vincent had asked Johnnie.

"Oh yeah, my name is Johnnie."

Vincent looked out the cell door turned back and looked at him. "Well, Johnnie, whatever problem they have with you, it's your problem alone. Don't try to get me involved in it," Vincent said as if Johnnie didn't hear what he had said just prior to them walking past their cell door.

"Yeah, I heard you the first time that you said you won't get involved in any of my problems," Johnnie responded.

"Do they know you?" Vincent asked.

"Yeah, they know who I am. And no, we are not on good terms, and yes, there will be a problem. Anything else you want to know?" Johnnie said with great irritation in his voice.

This was what he had feared would happen. He felt trapped with nowhere to go and no help in sight. Johnnie had always had the group with him in all the fights that he had with Wayne and Ricco, but now he was going to have to stand on his own against them

"No, that about sums it up. They won't come in the cell. So as long as you're in here, you're safe. They won't disrespect me. But once you're outside, anything goes. So just watch your back. You don't have any friends in here?"

As Johnnie climbed up on his bunk to lay down, he responded, "No, I don't know anyone in here accept the few who don't like me," Johnnie said as he laid down.

"It's going to be hard to make friends with them against you. They are already making it clear that you're on their hit list," Vincent explained to Johnnie as he was watching them make their rounds and pointing to the cell where Johnnie was, before he had also laid down on his bunk.

Vincent was somewhat feeling sorry for Johnnie and not expecting him to last long in here. Later on that day as they all went to the cafeteria to eat lunch,
Johnnie could not find a place to eat by himself, so he took a spot at a table that had less people. Not knowing anyone, he just sat down and started eating. The few that was at that table just looked at him, but no one said a word. They were curious about him, but he never even looked up at them as he sat there eating and not paying them any attention. Johnnie wasn't really interested in any small talk. He really just wanted to gather his thoughts as he was still trying to take everything in and process the whole situation that he was now in. It wasn't long before Ricco and Wayne happened to walk past Johnnie as he was eating.

"Look what we have here, Wayne, looks like someone got lost? Where are your friends at Johnnie? Or don't you have any?" Ricco said with a laugh in his tone.
"You're sitting here with these dorks, kind of fit right in, don't you, Johnnie?"
Wayne added as he leaned down to mock Johnnie.

"You make the first move, Wayne, and I will make the last move. That goes for you too, Ricco." Johnnie said as he was using his anger to mask his fear.

"Patience, Johnnie, patience. There's no hurry. We got all the time in the world. You're not going anywhere for a while, so we can take our time," Ricco said as he motioned for Wayne to walk away with him.

Trying to keep it silent, Johnnie took a deep breath and released it as they walked off. Johnnie knew from now on he would have to watch his back every moment of every day. The rest of the cafeteria period, Johnnie never said a word. It wasn't long after that that everyone had to go back to the main population area. For Johnnie, it meant going back to his cell and try to relax a bit and do some thinking.

As he laid on his bunk, his cell mate Vincent came in. "So I see your friends stopped to chat with you in the cafeteria. Hope everything is okay?" Vincent said as he sat on his bunk for a few minutes.

"They're not my friends and no everything isn't okay. But that isn't your concern, is it, Vincent?" Johnnie responded in a serious tone as he was very irritated about the whole matter. Sitting there thinking about the whole situation and what if it had been him in this situation.

"Well, if they come in here for you, they will have to fight me also. No one comes in my room to fight," Vincent said to Johnnie in hopes that he would find some kind of comfort in his words as he spoke them.

But for Johnnie, there was no comfort. Everything seemed to have brought him to this point. And what would be the end of it was what he was fearing the most. There seemed to be no way out of this, and he was greatly outnumbered. But one thing was for sure. He wasn't going down without giving them all he had. And if he was going down, he was planning on taking as many with him as he could.

Later on the next day as Johnnie was walking to the steps to go down to the main area, Wayne just happened to be walking his way. As they went to walk past each other, Wayne purposely leaned into Johnnie, bumping into him as he spoke, "Your days are numbered, Johnnie boy."

Looking into Wayne's eyes as he responded, "So are yours, Wayne. I don't care what happens. How many there are. I simply don't care. When the time comes, you die first."

Wayne knew by the seriousness of the look in Johnnie's eyes that he was more than serious and meant every word he had uttered to him. As he walked off, there was a fear in Wayne's heart. For the first time since seeing Johnnie come in, he was really scared of Johnnie and knew he would do it. They had hated each other and fought for so long, but now it was even more serious.

Johnnie had every intention on killing every last one of them if that was what he had to do. As he continued on down the steps, he noticed everyone was watching him. *Was there something going to happen? Or was it because he mainly stayed in his cell and kept to himself. Maybe people are curious.* He knew he was a target and was tired of feeling like he was hiding. If they wanted him, he was there. Nothing he could do about that. But he wasn't going to hide any longer.

The rest of the day, Johnnie just kind of sat and watched the others on the main floor. To the rest, Johnnie had made his statement. And some had gained a little respect for him. Every day that followed from that time on, Johnnie would be on the main floor and wait for them to bring it on. Johnnie and Vincent began to talk more and more every day and began to develop a friendship over the next few weeks.

As Johnnie sat on a bench, Richard, who was the one who ran the House temporarily, came and sat next to Johnnie. "You know you can't make it in here on your own. Everyone needs to have friends to watch each other's back. Personally, I don't care about Wayne or Ricco. But in here, there is a mutual respect that we have. But that doesn't matter for now. You're a loner, and loners don't last long in here," Richard said as he tried to explain to Johnnie.

"So let me guess. You will help me, but I will owe you, right?" Johnnie asked.

"Yeah, something like that. I will look out for you. Just come to my cell every so often," Richard said, as he put his hand on Johnnie's shoulder.

"I don't think so. And if you don't move your hand, I will remove it for you," Johnnie responded.

"Well, we will see if you change your mind after they come for you."

Johnnie just looked at him as he got up and walked away leaving Johnnie sitting there alone. Richard had grabbed Cobra, his number one

228

leader, that was in there with him. And they went to his cell to discuss business.

"I saw you talking to that Johnnie guy. What's up with that kid?" Cobra asked.

"He doesn't want protection. So I am going to put him on toilet duty next week," Richard responded.

"Toilet duty, huh? That will be the death of him for sure," said Cobra, being a bit shocked that Richard would do any kind of favors for Ricco and Wayne.

"The kid might surprise us. I got a feeling he is stronger than we think. Anyways for now, we keep this between us."

Cobra was not pleased with this decision but there was nothing he could say or do about it. The thought of helping Hells Sinners in any way, shape or form was not something he wanted to be a part of.

"Perhaps, Richard. But the odds aren't going to be in his favor, that's for sure."

Come Monday morning as everyone gathered together as it was custom at the beginning of each month to determine who gets what kind of work detail to do, Johnnie was of yet unaware that he would be receiving any kind of detail as he stood there wondering what all of this was about.

Richard began to speak, "Work detail goes as follows. Tim, this month, you will be responsible for keeping my cell kept up for me. Johnnie Steele, you will be responsible for toilet detail. Mark, you will be responsible for shower area. I want those toilets real clean too, Johnnie." As Richard made this announcement, Wayne and Ricco smiled as big as they could as they began to whisper to one another. Johnnie knew this wasn't going to be good for him. After the work detail meeting, Ricco and Wayne met up in Ricco's cell with a few other members to discuss the new opportunity that had presented itself to them.

"Since Rick has put Johnnie on work detail, we might as well go ahead and make our move," Ricco said to the other four that was in the cell with him that he was planning on using to get Johnnie.

"I think we should do it fast and get it over with. I am tired of looking at him," Wayne added. But he was only saying this because he was tired of being scared of Johnnie.

"Fast and hard. I'm good with it," said Sal who was always up for doing something to someone. He was a murderer that was convicted for killing his sister's boyfriend after he had raped her when she wouldn't give him what he wanted.

"No. We will get Johnnie, but I want to wait a few days and let him wait for it. I want him to suffer as much as possible. He knows its coming. Let's make him worry for a few days before we go in and get him," Ricco said as he was thinking about how much he was going to enjoy watching Johnnie have to look over his shoulder for the next few days.

Meanwhile, as Johnnie sat in his cell, Vincent came in and sat down on his own bunk and began to talk to Johnnie. "You know, you could put in for a transfer or ask to be put into protective custody.

But if you stay in here, one thing is for sure, Johnnie, they will get you. Especially now that you're on work detail. I don't know why Richard did that, but it wasn't an accident. He did that on purpose, which for me doesn't make sense because he hates Ricco. So I don't know why he would ever think to try and help him out," Vincent explained.

"Yeah, well, I'm not running or hiding from them. I know they will get me while I'm in there cleaning, but I'm not going to run from them," Johnnie responded as he was laying down on his bunk.

"You got guts, Johnnie. I respect that."

After their talk, Vincent got up and left the cell and went to see Richard. He didn't want to get involved in Johnnie's problem, but he had taking a liking to him and wanted to know exactly why Richard was setting him up.

"Hey, Richard, can I enter?" Vincent asked as it was their custom. For no one was allowed to enter someone else's cell without permission.

"Yeah, come in, Vincent. What can I do for you?"

After entering the cell, Vincent began to discuss the situation that Richard had placed Johnnie into. "Well, I was wondering about Johnnie. It's not like you to do anything for Ricco, and everyone knows they are after him. So I was wondering why you would put Johnnie on work detail?" Vincent asked.

"Everyone has to do work detail from time to time. And him being new, I thought it would be good to put him right in it, so he doesn't think he is exempt from it," Richard responded. However, this was not true, and Vincent knew it.

"I've been here a long time, Richard. I know how things work. There was a reason you did this," Vincent said as he continued to pry into the reason as to why Richard had done this.

"Do you have a problem with my decision, Vincent? I can always put you on work detail with him if you think he needs some help?" Richard said as his voice began to become sterner.

"No. I was just wondering is all."

Richard gave Vincent a cocky smile as he responded, "Are we done here, Vincent? Or do you have more questions that you feel I need to answer for you?"

Knowing he had possibly made things bad for himself now by coming here, Vincent thought it was best to just leave it alone.

"No, that was all. I am sorry I bothered you about this matter, Richard. I was just curious is all, Johnnie seems like a good kid."

Vincent hurried and left the cell after that and went back to his own cell in hopes Richard was not too upset with him for asking. He knew Richard could make things very bad for him if he was upset with him.

Johnnie was expecting them to come quickly, knowing how much they hated him. But the first three days he was on work detail, nothing happened. But he was still very conscious of the fact that it was coming. So every day, Johnnie kept his guard up, and was refusing to relax, while he waited for their attack on him. During the fourth day while Johnnie was on work detail, as he was all alone cleaning the restroom area, as he was scrubbing the toilets, he heard a noise that startled him. As he turned, he saw Sisko and Wayne standing there with Sal, Tye, and Jay.

"Jay, keep a look out for us," Sisko said as he walked toward Johnnie.

As Jay walked over to where the door area was and stood there to look out for any sign of anyone coming. Wayne began to mock Johnnie.

"Well, well, if it isn't toilet bowl boy. Looks like we interrupted your work there, Johnnie boy. I've been waiting a long time for this," Wayne said, as he was still standing back a bit.

"It's time, Johnnie. You have been a problem for me for a long time, and now, I am going to end it," Wayne said while Sisko had motioned for Sal and Wayne to move on both sides of Johnnie to circle in around behind him. Tye moved to close the gap between him, and Sisko which made it, so Johnnie could not pass in between the two of them. Johnnie tried to reposition himself to get a better stance as to be able to see all four of them, for Wayne and Sal had moved in behind him.

Johnnie stood tall and firm as he was waiting for one of them to make the first move. Finally, Sal tried to hit Johnnie, but he moved to the side and caught Sal with a right cross that knocked him down, for he was already off balance from trying to move in fast, and Johnnie connected hard. After that, Tye and Wayne came at the same time. Johnnie turned to make sure he got one good blow in on Wayne before they could grab him. Punching

Wayne right in the nose that made him double over as his eyes watered, and his nose began to bleed. As Johnnie turned, Tye caught him with a punch to his eye. By that time, Sal was back on his feet, and Ricco was trying to grab Johnnie only to be thrown to the ground. Before Sal could get to Johnnie, he met Tye with a punch to his mouth after receiving another blow himself from Tye. Sal rushed Johnnie and tried to tackle him, but Johnnie grabbed him and landed a knee to his face, just before Wayne hit him in the back of the head. Being relentless, Johnnie fought with all he had. Turning and landing a closed backhand to Wayne's cheek. As he turned back, he threw a kick that caught Ricco square in his stomach that knocked the breath out of him for a few minutes. Giving Johnnie a little bit of time to try to gain the upper hand. As Sal returned back to his feet, it was obvious that they were in for more than they had bargained for. Johnnie had hit Wayne and Tye several more times when Sal finally was able to grab Johnnie from behind. His right eye was already starting to swell for taking a knee to the face from Johnnie. By this time, Ricco was up, and he started punching Johnnie in his stomach as Sal held him. Johnnie threw Sal off him and hit Ricco back but was rushed and taken to the ground by Wayne and Tye at the same time. Johnnie hit the ground hard and was trying to get free before he was kicked in the face by Sal. Wayne and Tye both got up, and all four boys began to kick Johnnie and punch him all at the same time before finally leaving him there unconscious. There was a lot of blood on the floor.

Some of it was from Wayne's nose that had bled pretty good. Things hadn't gone as smoothly as they had planned. Wayne ended up going to the infirmary to get his broken nose fixed. And Sal's eye had almost swelled completely shut. All four had suffered bruises that was noticeable. There was no way to cover this up. Everyone would know it was them that had beaten Johnnie, not that the inmates wouldn't know anyways. But the guards didn't know anything about this rivalry and would not have known who did it if things had gone the way they had wanted them to. But there was no way to hide all the bruises, and Wayne had to go to the infirmary.

They were all sure to be in trouble now. Johnnie was much more than they thought he was. Every fight with him until this point had been fair fights. One on one. But now, they knew he was harder to handle then they had anticipated. When Johnnie didn't return to his cell, Vincent walked past one of the guards and whispered you might want to check the restroom area. When the guard came in and found Johnnie, he called for more guards to come and help as well as for a few of the nurses. After which they put the whole House on lock down to investigate the situation that had occurred. It was obvious at this point that Wayne was one of them, so they knew who to start with, and it didn't take long to find the other four. Their battle scares had given them away. The only one who hadn't been taken out of population for questioning was Jay who bore no sign of any fight whatsoever. There was no denying they were involved, but they all

235

remained silent, and Johnnie refused to say as to what had happened as well. He too kept his mouth shut.

After examining the other boys, they were all taking to the box with the exception of Johnnie and Wayne. They would not be able to be sent there until they were released from the infirmary. For Wayne, that would be the next day. But Johnnie was in bad shape and would remain in the infirmary for several days as he was in recovery.

After five days in the infirmary, Johnnie also was sent to the box. Still very sore from the beating he had taken, he would finish healing while in solitary confinement. Every so often a nurse would come and check on Johnnie to monitor his progress, as he was improving. They would not have released him if he hadn't been recovering as well as he did, and the checkups were routine to make sure that he was doing better every day.

Johnnie was in such great shape and had always took real good care of himself, that his recovery was faster then what it should have been. He had survived the first assault and was quite surprised at how well he had defended himself against all four of them. He was more confident now in his abilities to make them pay every time they would come after him.

CHAPTER 12

The Box

Once Johnnie had left the Juvenile Hospital two guards that had come to get him was Jeffery and Scott. As they had walked with him, they began to explain to him how it would be in there. Making sure he understood that he would not be allowed to have anything or do anything while he was in there. After reaching their destination, Jeffery opened the door and walked Johnnie in. After walking out the door echoed in Johnnie's box when it shut. It was terrifying to him and he felt as if the echo had shot through his whole body. Then it all faded into silence as Johnnie slid to the floor in the corner.

As Johnnie sat in the corner in the deep dark silence, there came a voice from the next box.

"Hey, what's your name?" The voice from the other box said to Johnnie.

"My name is Johnnie. Who are you?" he responded being surprised to even hear another voice.

"My name is Jason. So you're the new inmate the guards were talking about. I heard you put up a pretty good fight," Jason said as he was laying on the small cot they gave to them to sleep on.

"Yeah? I guess I did, but I don't think it's over with yet," Johnnie responded as he sat in the corner.

"You haven't been in here long, have you? I don't think I know you. I would have met you in population before. But I don't recognize your voice," Jason asked.

"No, I don't think so, just got here a few weeks ago," said Johnnie.

"Hmm, what was your beef with those guys? What happened that made them want to take you out?" Jason inquired out of curiosity.

"It goes back a long ways. We used to go to school together and have fought many times. But this time, they had the upper hand, as I don't know anyone in here except for them," Johnnie said as he began to think about his friends, which made him sorrowful. He had missed them all tremendously.

"That's a pretty big group to have against you if you're on your own. They belong to one of the biggest gangs in the city. How did you get tangled up with them?" Jason had asked.

"It's a very long story," responded Johnnie, as he didn't feel like going into all the details over the past few years.

"How long are you in here for? I mean in the box," Jason wondered as he asked Johnnie.

238

"One month is what they told me," Johnnie said to him.

"Then we have time for long stories. There isn't anything else for us to do in here, so we might as well talk as much as we can. I still have six weeks to go and have been without someone to talk to for two weeks," Jason told him, as he was wanting to hear more about this long standing feud between Johnnie and the other boys.

"Yeah, I suppose we do. But I don't know exactly where to begin," said Johnnie as he was thinking as to where to start at.

"At the beginning. Always start at the beginning," Jason said to him. "Well, it all started back in school. Wayne was a bully and liked to pick on the weaker kids. So one day, I said something to him about it, and ever since, we have been fighting. This has been going on for more than a few years. And my friends and his friends always fight. I don't like any of them, to be honest with you. They are all bullies, and I don't like to see kids pushed around. Especially kids who have done nothing wrong. So Wayne and I never got along," Johnnie said as he continued on and explained the whole story to Jason.

When Johnnie was finished telling Jason all that happened, how all of this started on the outside and had continued on the inside, it had become very clear to Jason that Johnnie was in real danger.

"So what are you going to do, Johnnie? I mean in here, you're all alone, and they have you greatly outnumbered," Jason asked as he was wondering just how long this kid was going to make it in here

239

under these circumstances.

No one made it in here on their own as it was, but it would be even harder having a rivalry with one of the top gangs. This would make it even harder for any of the other inmates to even want to friend him in fear of their own safety.

"Well, I suppose I will keep fighting until they get tired of it, or they kill me, whichever comes first I guess," Johnnie responded.

Hoping that it would be the first and not the latter. After Johnnie finished explaining the whole story which took some time, Jason became very sleepy and decided he was going to get some rest.

"Johnnie, I am tired now. I will rest for a while. When I wake, we will talk some more," Jason said as he closed his eyes while lying on the cot.

"Sure thing, Jason. I don't know if I will sleep at all. But I may try to rest myself as well," Johnnie replied as he laid there thinking about Tonya and the group.

He was supposed to have visitors next week and had been looking forward to it. But since he was in the box, he would not be allowed to have any visitors whatsoever. Johnnie's mind would not rest as he thought on many different things pertaining to his friends that he missed so much while he laid there thinking about Tonya and how she was doing. If she was going to wait on him or meet someone else. The thought of her being with someone while he was away made him sick to his stomach. *What would it do to him to get out of here and find her with another person other than himself? How would he handle it? Would she even be able to come visit him? How can he keep her for three years if he isn't even able to see her at all? Would she even be able to write him?* All of these questions raced through his mind as he laid there thinking about her. Missing her. Wondering how this would all end up once he made it out of here. Wondering how much everything will be different or how much this will cause things to change. After a long while as Johnnie was laying there awake, having only slept a little bit here and there, he was slightly startled when he heard his name called from the next box.

"Johnnie, are you awake?" Jason called from the next box.

"Yeah, I am awake, Jason," Johnnie responded as he laid on his cot.

"Did you get any sleep at all?" Jason asked as he was wiping the sleep from his eyes.

"Very little. I am tired though, but I cannot sleep. Just too much on my mind and so much to think about you know," Johnnie said as he sat up and hunched over as he sat on his cot and talked to Jason.

"Yeah, I understand that. Johnnie, may I ask you how did you end up in here? I mean what happened or what did you do to get locked up?" Jason inquired.

"Well, that's another long story, Jason, but as you have previously pointed out, I guess we have time. My father died quite a few years back, and my mom met someone later on. She fell in love with him. He talked so sweet to her and made her feel like he really loved her. Kind of swept her off

241

her feet kind of thing. My mom had been a widow for some time and was lonely, and he made her feel good, made her feel loved. So they got married. After a little while, he got laid off for the winter. He began drinking all the time and then started hitting my mother and I. He became very violent and mean to us. I thought eventually he was going to kill my mother. I have a great mom. She is very loving and kind and always sweet. She will do anything for you. She was always a good wife and mother. She never did anything to deserve to be hit. I had to protect my mother, so I got a gun. So one day, he comes home drunk and started trying to rape my mom and was beating her until she gave in and was going to let him have his way with her. I could hear it all happening. So I grabbed my gun and went into my mother's room and shouted at him as I lifted up the gun and was pointing it at him. When he heard me, he looked at me as I was pointing the gun at him. So he got off my mother and came at me. I pulled the trigger and shot him three times," Johnnie said as he could still see it all unfolding like it had just happened. The whole scene and every sound had been burned into his mind and had haunted him still to that day.

"Wow, Johnnie, that must have been crazy. How many times did you shoot him?" Jason had asked to test his story and see if it would change. Many times inmates would embellish their stories to make them seem as if they was worse then what they really was.

"I shot him three times. I kept shooting him until he fell to the floor. I wanted him to die. I wanted him out of our lives forever. So I made sure that I killed him, and he was never going to be here anymore," Johnnie said as he poured out his heart to Jason. He was still able to feel every emotion from the whole scene as he relived the event.

"I met a kid named Johnnie once," Jason explained as he was reminded of the kid who once stood by him on the playground. "I only met him once, but I always considered him to be my only real friend," Jason said as he sat against the wall in his box remembering every detail that had unfolded that day.

"Why would you consider him as your only real friend if you only met him once?" Johnnie questioned.

"Well, Johnnie, this is a very interesting story. See, I am an orphan. And I had no friends to be honest, and sometimes, I used to get bullied by these kids. Well, one day, I was at the park playing, which was unusual for me because I never really went there, but I wanted to play on the swings. Even if I just did it by myself with no one to play with. So I went and as I was playing on the swings by myself, this other kid showed up with his mom, and he was alone also with no one to play with as well. So, we started playing together. It was the first time in my life another kid took a real interest in me and wanted to play with me. I liked the kid he was fun to play with. So anyways as we were playing, these five kids that used to bully me came out of the woods, and when they came walking toward me, I knew there was going to be trouble. But that kid, he stood with me, even though it even wasn't his fight, and he didn't even really know me, he stood with me, Johnnie, and we fought those boys."

As Jason was telling this story to Johnnie, Johnnie had interrupted him. "Jason!" Johnnie said very excitedly in a loud voice.

"Yes, Johnnie?" Jason answered. "Jason, it's me, I am that Johnnie that you speak of." Johnnie told him as he was shocked the two had been talking to each other this whole time and did not recognize each other's voice, but it had been some time since that day when they had met each other.

"No, you can't be him. Are you serious?" Jason asked as he began to feel a sense of excitement come over him.

"Yes, I am very serious, Jason, it is really me. We played on the monkey bars after we jumped off the swings, and then later, my mom got us some ice cream just before I have to leave," Johnnie answered as he also had remembered that time with Jason.

"It really is you. I can't believe that it really is you, Johnnie. Johnnie, I had always wondered what had happened to you," Jason said being excited.

"Wow, this is very crazy, Jason. I never thought this is how we would meet again. If we ever did meet up again that is. But I have to tell you, my friend, that I am very happy to see you again, well sort of see you anyways. But at least I can hear you."

Johnnie felt anxious as well after all this time to be reunited with his friend who he had assumed that he would have never see again. "Jason, whatever happened to those bullies we fought? Did you ever see them again?"

Jason paused for a moment. "Yes, I did, Johnnie. I saw them a few times after that. No one will see them anymore though, Johnnie. I eliminated that problem," Jason said as he reflected on the situation.

"How so? I mean what did you do?" Johnnie asked.

"I killed them, Johnnie. All five of them," Jason responded as both boxes went silent for a few minutes.

Johnnie not quite sure how to take this all in asked, "How many people have you killed, Jason?"

As Jason went over and laid on the cot, he responded, "Nine in all, including the one I killed in here, that's what got me put in the box, Johnnie. I killed Paco. One of the members from the gang you're having problems with," Jason explained as he felt a little bit better about that kill, knowing that it also had helped out his friend Johnnie, which in turn gave him some satisfaction knowing that in some way, he had finally in part returned the favor to Johnnie for helping him out before at the park.

"Why did you kill Paco?" Johnnie curiously asked. Not that he cared, but he was curious nonetheless at what had happened between Jason and Paco to make him have to kill him.

"Paco had snitched me out, and that's what got me put in here in the first place. So when I found out it was him, I killed him," Jason explained hoping in some sense that Johnnie would feel grateful for what he had done.

"Do you also have a problem with that gang?" Johnnie questioned.

"No, not really. I mean I don't like them, but I don't have any problems with them either. For the rest of your time in here, Johnnie, you won't have any more problem with them either. From now on, no one will be able to touch you without my permission. I will put the word out that if anyone has any problems with you that they have to come to me first," Jason told Johnnie as they continued on with their conversation.

"What do you do in here, Jason?" Johnnie wondered. "I run this place. I run everything in here. Just like I do on the outside," Jason explained.

"I thought that Richard was running things in here?" Johnnie had further inquired.

"No, Johnnie. He is just overseeing things for me until I get out of the box. Then I will take it back over from him. And you will be at my side, my friend," Jason said as he felt good about being able to have Johnnie with him in population running things together.

"I just want to do my time and get out of here, Jason. I am sick of all of these problems. It's been one thing after another since before my father died. You know? All I want to do is to live a normal life, a good life, without having to fight all the time. I mean I don't mind having to defend others, but I am tired of fighting. I have been doing this ever since elementary school. Always some punk or bully or someone abusing someone. I'm sick of it, Jason. I just want a normal life where I can just do the things that I am supposed to do and make a life for me and Tonya. Three years are being taken from my life, and for what? Because some jerk couldn't stop hitting my mother? I have been fighting bullies since before my father died, then I lost him. After that, I watched my mother get beaten for months. So bad that sometimes she couldn't even leave the house for days, and I couldn't even have friends over because she looked so bad. I have lived in fear for most of my life. Oh sure, I can fight, and I can hold my own against just about anyone. But I hate it, Jason. Now I am sitting in here while my girlfriend is out there. I am supposed to be with her, Jason, not in here away from her. And my mother now is all alone with nobody to look after her. That is my responsibility, Jason, I am supposed to be looking after them and taking care of them both. It was self-defense what the heck was I supposed to do, Jason? Let him keep beating my mother until one day he killed her? Or killed me for that matter. It was no secret that he didn't like me. So I am sure at some point he was going to try to get rid of me. But I got rid of him instead. And the justice system should have protected us, not lock me up for three years. This isn't how my life is supposed to be, I am a good person I don't belong in here caged up like some kind of animal. They looked at my school record and saw the fights that I had been in and said I was already violent. The record didn't show how I was fighting bullies and sticking up for weaker kids who couldn't stand up for themselves. So they put me in here. I was taught that we get rewarded for doing good. What a lie that was. Isn't protecting and helping weaker people considered as doing good?"

"Don't worry about your time in here. You're on easy street now. I will make sure you get out of here and back to your life, bro. Just hang in there and do your time, I got you, my brother. No one in here can touch you now. I'm going to get some sleep, Johnnie, try to rest also, my brother," Jason said as he laid down on his cot and fell fast asleep.

In the box next to him, Johnnie was laying down also, but he found it very difficult to get any sleep after that conversation. For he could still feel the ever so present frustration and anger that was still within him. It would be a while before Johnnie would find himself calmed down enough to get any real rest. In the meantime, he just laid there thinking about his mother and Tonya as well as the rest of the group. He missed them all. He missed his best friend George who had always been there for him. He wondered how George felt about the whole situation and if he had regretted getting Johnnie that gun. He had hoped not. It was something that had to be done. And George, doing what he thought was right, did what he could for Johnnie. And Johnnie felt that by doing so that he once again showed himself to be a true friend and brother. After a few hours of laying there thinking in the silence of the lonely dark box, Johnnie finally fell asleep.

The next day, Johnnie was awakened by the guard opening up Jason's box to take him for his shower time.

"Get up, Jason, it's time for your shower," the guard said as he went in and brought Jason out of his box. As they walked down the hall and through the steel door and was in the clear, Jason began to speak to Guard Thompson.

"I need you to get a message to Guard Jeffery. When Johnnie goes back into population, he is not to be touched by anyone. Tell him to make sure that message finds its way to Richard," Jason said as he walked into the shower area.

"Okay, you got fifteen minutes, when I do my rounds, I will see Guard Jeffery," Guard Thompson said as he walked out to give Jason some privacy as he showered and brushed his teeth.

This was the only time they were able to get a fresh pair of clothes to wear. Afterwards, Guard Thompson took Jason back to his box. That meant it was Johnnie's turn.

"Let's go, Johnnie," Guard Thompson said as his box door opened. Time for your shower. Let's go."

Johnnie slowly got up and walked out of his box. "It feels good to be out of there for a few," Johnnie said to Guard Thompson as they walked down the hallway to the door.

As the others heard his voice, they all began to say foul things to him until they heard the main hallway door shut. "I wouldn't worry too much about that, Johnnie, it looks like you've made a good friend in here after all." Guard Thompson said as they walked into the shower area.

"Yeah? Oh, you mean Jason. Yeah, well, actually, we go back a few years," Johnnie responded.

"He's a good friend to have in here, you got fifteen minutes, Johnnie."

After Johnnie finished showering and putting on fresh clean clothes, he was taken back to his box. Guard Thompson continued down the line until they all had showered and was settled back into their boxes. But when he got to Ricco, he made sure that he knew of Johnnie and Jason's friendship.

"Looks like your fun time with Johnnie has come to an end," Guard Thompson said to Ricco.

"What are you talking about?" Ricco questioned.

"Yeah, it turns out Johnnie and Jason are friends. You might want to think about that while you take your shower. You got fifteen minutes." Guard Thompson said as he walked out leaving Ricco there to think about what he had just been told. Once Ricco had been brought back to his box, he began to send the message down the line that Johnnie was in with Jason. This news was the last thing that these boys wanted to hear. Now Johnnie and Jason were allies. And for the Hells Sinners members, this was not going to be good. But as of yet, they just weren't sure how much it was going to affect them.

"Jason, are you awake?" Johnnie asked.

"Yeah, bro, I am awake. Are you okay?" Jason answered.

"Yes, I'm okay. I was thinking about something last night. Can I ask you a question?" Jason sat up from laying down on his cot.

"Yeah, sure, man. What is it?" he responded.

"The five boys you killed that had been bullying you. You're okay with it? I mean it was revenge, right? And the other ones was the same?" Johnnie had asked.

"Yes and no. I mean yeah, it was revenge because they wouldn't leave me alone. But you have to understand. It was also business. Same with Paco too, it was also both. See, Johnnie, out there, I am a big deal. I work for the mob, you know? I run things. And like every gang has to pay tribute to the boss who I work for to be able to sell drugs and prostitute women. Well, it's my job to collect those ends and make sure that the boss gets his cut. I am very well respected as much as I am feared. I have to keep that respect and fear always, or people will start shorting the payment or stop paying altogether, and I could and probably would end up dead. So like Paco, he snitched me out, so I had to make an example out of him. The five boys? Well, I couldn't let no one push me around and do this job, so I had to get rid of them, so no one would ever find out that I too had been bullied before. I mean I have to protect my reputation, Johnnie. That is something that is very important in this life. You understand?" Jason answered as Johnnie sat up he began to question more.

"What about the others?" he asked. "That was all business. I was ordered to kill them," Jason answered. "So you didn't know them at all?" asked Johnnie as he sat listening.

"No, not really. I saw them around here and there a few times. But I never knew them personally."

251

"So it doesn't bother you that you kill for money?" Jason thought for a minute before responding.

"No, not really. I mean I came from nothing. No parents, no money, hardly any clothes. Barely any food to eat. I only was allowed to eat twice a day. I was hungry and poor. I had nothing, Johnnie. No one loves me or even wants to love me. I was never wanted by anyone to be honest. Most people don't even take the time to get to know me. You're the only person that ever did something for me and didn't expect anything in return. You just did it. You stood with me when you didn't have to. That meant the whole world to me. You're the only person who ever showed any sign of even caring about me other than the ladies at the first home I stayed at, but I barely remember them anymore. So for me to kill someone so I can eat or have a better life, that's nothing to me. All I have known is anger and hate. Not just in my own heart, but also from those around me who are supposed to take care of me. They treat me like I am nothing. Do you know what it's like to not be wanted? Do you know how it feels? No one has ever really wanted me or loved me."

As Johnnie sat there listening, he begin to realize how hard Jason's life really was. "What about your parents? What happened to them?" Johnnie asked.

"Shoot, man, I don't even know. They're not dead, I do know that much. But I don't know where they are or anything, or why they didn't want me. All I know is when I was born, I was born to the state, and been growing up in the system from my birth. It's hard growing up unwanted, never being loved or feeling loved. That's what hurts the most I guess," Jason explained as he sat on the edge of his cot almost in tears.

This was the first time he had ever reflected on this, and the pain was surreal. He had never allowed himself to feel these emotions before, and now, it was all pouring out to the one person who ever cared about him. It was like if a gate had been opened and for Jason this was the first time he had ever talked about this to anyone. Let alone the fact that he allowed himself to even go to the depth of pain to even think on these things. All of this had been buried deep within him until now.

"I'm sorry, my brother. I had no idea. Jason, you are family to me. Like real family. I care about you, man. And I will always be here for you," Johnnie said in a comforting voice with sincerity.

"Thank you, Johnnie. You're all the family that I have. I am sorry, my friend, that I dumped all of this on you. I have never even talked about this to anyone before."

Johnnie paused for a minute before responding. "Think nothing of it, Jason. I am here for you, and whatever we say to each other in private will never be talked about. This is between us only. This is our bond. We are brothers."

Jason, for the first time in his life finally feeling loved, broke down in tears. "I love you, Johnnie. We are brothers for life. There is nothing I won't do for you."

After this conversation, there was a long time of

silence as these two brothers sat and pondered all that had been said. Something had happened this day. Something that would take their friendship to a whole new level. A bond was formed that would never be broken. They had looked into the eyes of each other's weaknesses. Up until this point, they both had only known the strong side of each other. But today, they saw so much more. They had seen each other's brokenness and the hurts they both hid from their pains that they didn't allow others to see. This was all very new to Jason. For the first time in his life, he felt the pain and fears that he had always been hiding as he was extremely overwhelmed with emotions as he sat quietly in his box.

After several weeks went by, Johnnie and Jason continued to grow in their friendship as they discussed many things and gained a better understanding of who they were and what they believed in. In some ways, these two were right on point with what they believed, but in other points, they were not even close. But one thing that they both had was a mutual respect for one another.

Finally, Johnnie's time in the box had come to an end, and it was time for him to return back to population. As Johnnie's box door opened and Guard Thompson called Johnnie's name and motioned for him to come out.

"Let's go, Johnnie, your time here is served. I am taking you back to population."

As Johnnie got up and walked to the door, Jason spoke out one last time before he was gone.

"I will see you in a few weeks, my brother," said

Jason.

"I will be waiting for you," Johnnie responded as he walked out and was taking back to population.

CHAPTER 13

Population

YEAR ONE

As Johnnie stepped through the door and reentered back into population, he wasn't quite unsure of how things was going to be at first. Everyone was looking at him as he walked through the door and went up the stairs to his cell. It was a strange feeling to have the whole place focus all of their attention on him. He hadn't felt that since his first time entering into the facility. Only this time, he wasn't new to the House.

As Johnnie walked into his cell, he could feel that there was a change in Vincent's attitude toward him. There was a chair that was in the cell now, and Johnnie sat down on it and took a deep breath as he began to try to relax a bit as he was trying to once again readjust to this situation of being back in the House.

"Welcome back, Cypher," Vincent said to Johnnie as he sat there looking puzzled at the name Vincent was using to address him.

"What is this that you call me?" Johnnie responded. "That is what they call you now, Cypher. It means to calculate numerically. You are one who took on many. You were a nonentity with no importance, a mystery that needed to be coded. Now you are respected. You have risen to the top and have made your mark as one to be feared. They say you and Jason are friends? No one can touch you by Jason's decree, but no one would know anyways. You took on the top dogs of the Hells Sinners, and they could not erase you. They were supposed to take you out, but they couldn't. They thought they had left you for dead, and yet you are here. You have become their ghost. Your existence now haunts them. People will treat you differently now. You have gained respect in here now."

"I don't care about any of that, I just want to do my time and get back to my life. All of this in here to me is foolishness. You all make your time and life here much harder than it needs to be. Some even prolonging their stay here by their own actions. It makes no sense to me. Why not just do your time and then regain your life and freedom?" Cypher responded.

"These letters came for you while you were in the box. I kept them under your pillow as they would not get lost or taken."

Johnnie took the letters from Vincent. "Thank you for looking out for my stuff. I appreciate it," said Johnnie, as he began to open his letters that he had received.

He had more than a few from his mother Sara as well as Tonya. The rest of the group had also written him as well with George sending a few himself. Johnnie was excited to read all of his letters. It felt good to in some way be in touch with them, especially after all that he had been through already. It was refreshing to be able to read how everyone was doing and how they all had missed him. For a brief moment, Johnnie almost forgot that he was even in there as he began to think on the times that they all had together. Remembering the times at the camp and the river.

This was the first time that Vincent had seen Cypher smile at all since he was brought into the House. After a few days of being out of the box, Cypher was able to finally receive visitors. By this time, he had been away from his mother and friends for a long time and was needing to have a form of real contact with them. No doubt this was a moment that brought much excitement to Cypher when the guard came to get him for a visitation.

"Johnnie, let's go. You have a visitor," Guard Jeffery said to him as he walked him to the visitor area.

When Guard Jeffery opened the door and walked Cypher into the room, you could feel the excitement when Cypher and his mother saw each other. Cypher, not wanting to waste one single second of this visitation, hurried to the chair and sat down in front of his mother.

"Mom, I have missed you so much, tell me how you are and how is everyone else doing. How is Tonya doing, is she okay? Tell me everything that has been going on."

Sara wasn't quite sure where to start as she simply smiled and slowly began to talk. "Everyone is fine. Tonya is doing good, but she really misses

258

you so very much. George asks about you all the time. We all sent letters to you and have been awaiting your reply. I came to visit you a few times, and they said you weren't allowed to have any visitors since you were in confinement. What happened, are you alright? Why were you in solitary confinement? George said that some of the bullies that you were having trouble with are in here also. Are they giving you problems? Is that why you were in solitary confinement?" Sara said trying to cover everything as she spoke.

"Yes. I had a little bit of trouble in here with them, but that's all been settled for the time being. But everything is alright now, Mom, there won't be any more problems with them as long as I am in here. I am fine, and now, everything is okay. I didn't reply because I was in solitary confinement and didn't get the letters until I was back in my cell, but I am out now, and all of that is behind me. Now I am just doing my time and trying to get out of here as soon as possible. I need those letters to keep coming. That is all I have in here, and I need them so very much, especially from you and Tonya. Please, Mom, give her my love and tell her that I miss her so very much, and that I can't wait to see her. Tell everyone that I am sorry, and that I miss them all so much. And tell George all is well, and that everything is good. Make sure you tell him that okay?" Cypher said excitedly.

"We all miss you so much, Johnnie. I love you, and I am so sorry for all of this. This is all my fault, and I wish I had never met him. Please, Johnnie, stay safe in here. I could not bear it if anything ever happens to you. I can't lose you, Johnnie. I need you to come home as soon as you can, so please stay safe and stay out of trouble. I worry about you nonstop," Sara said as tears ran down her tired face.

"Don't worry, Mom, everything will be fine. This wasn't your fault, please don't feel responsible for this. Everything will be fine, I need you to not worry and just take good care of yourself. One of the top inmates in here is a good friend of mine, and he is helping me," Cypher explained.

"That's good. Christina and Thomas Hilton have been so very helpful. They are just the most wonderful people. They have been praying for you, Johnnie. And they have been such a great comfort to me. Christina comes by every day and spends time with me. We sit and talk and then she prays for us both, Johnnie. I always feel so good after my visit with her. As wonderful as those two are I have to wonder why Darrell and Randy get into so much trouble. Those two are something. But I will give them credit, they have also been by helping out. They even have mowed my lawn every week and made sure that I am okay as well. Randy even helps take in the groceries when he sees me come back from shopping. They always ask about you, Johnnie. We all miss you so much."

All of this made Cypher feel more relieved that they were making sure that Sara was being taken care of.

"That's great, Mom. The two brothers have been great friends to me from day one. Same with George."

Guard Jeffery came as they was talking to take Cypher back to his cell. "I am sorry, ma'am, I have to take him back to his cell now," Guard Jeffery said as he walked over to grab Cypher.

"I love you, Mom, I will write soon, I promise, and don't forget to give my love to Tonya."

Sara began to cry as Johnnie got up to go back to his cell. "I love you too, Johnnie. I will see you next week." Sara felt the time went by too fast as she watched Johnnie walk out of the visiting area and go back to population.

Cypher was finally getting used to being more secure now in this situation and began to warm up a bit and make some friends. Some of which were from a gang called the West Dragons, which was a rival gang to the Hells Sinners which was the gang that Cypher had been feuding with for some time now and was the gang that Ricco and Wayne was a part of, which was perfect for the West Dragons since Cypher had made a name for himself after the way he handled them. That fight had changed everything for him. The respect he received from that was tremendous, and with him being aligned with Jason made him even more popular as well as feared.

After a few weeks of being back in population, as Cypher was standing at the rail, Jason was released back into population. As he walked in, Jason and Cypher's eyes met as they gave each other a nod. After Jason went into his cell to get settled back in and to handle some business to see what's been going on since his absence he called for Cypher who had went back into his cell to relax for a bit to come and meet with him. As Cypher was on his way to meet with Jason, it was very clear that everyone was watching him. Cypher was not quite sure why, but all eyes seem to be on him.

"Jason, you wanted to see me?" Cypher asked as he stood at Jason's cell door. "Yes. Come in, Johnnie. Or should I say Cypher as it is now I hear. I sent for you because I want you to handle collections from now on. Which is to say that you will be collecting money from everyone in here who is earning. I get a percentage from all the top leaders who make money in here from drug sales to whatever else they get smuggled in. I know you don't deal with drugs, so Ricky will continue to handle that aspect of this business. All I need you to do is collect my ends at the end of the week. Every leader will report to you with some money, you just bring it to me. Simple enough for you, Johnnie. Just need you to handle that for me, and I will pay you a bit as well. Any questions?"

"No. No questions. I think I can do that for you, Jason." Cypher responded.

"Want to play some cards with us, Cypher?" Jason asked.

"Sure. What are we playing?" Cypher asked.

"Spades," Jason said as he pulled out the deck and got up to go to the main area where the tables were. That is where everyone would meet up for card games and dominoes.

There was a lot of tables set up in this area. Cypher and Ricky followed Jason as they went to sit at their own table. Jason's card games was invite only. If he didn't ask you to play, then you

262

weren't allowed to sit at his table.

"You ever play spades before, Cypher?" Richard had asked.

"No, never. You will have to explain to me the rules and teach me how to play," Cypher responded as he was watching Jason shuffle the deck.

"It's cool, Cypher. We will teach you as we go along," Jason said as he dealt the cards out.

As they played cards and talked, this was an opportunity for Cypher to get to know them a little bit better now that he was a part of this group and not off on his own any more. As time went on, Cypher finally was getting tired of playing cards and had removed himself from the game to go back to his cell and write to his mom and the rest of the group that he was missing very much, especially Tonya who was always on his mind. In his letters, he had expressed to each one of them that if they were able to come visit him, then he would work on getting them on the list, for he wanted to see them all.

While writing these letters which took a while to complete, Cypher began to feel quite homesick and wanted nothing more than to get out of this place and be back home with his family and friends. He had sat and thought of the time when he would be able to hold Tonya's hand again. He missed being able to hold her. He could even still remember how she smelled and what her favorite color was to wear.

As much as he felt homesick, he also couldn't help feeling the anger from all that has happened and the confusion as to why his life was turning out this way, when he was always trying to do what he felt was right. Seemed like every time he did something good, that something bad would happen to him. So many people get away with doing so much evil and harm, and yet here he was, a good person having to pay for everything he did even when it was to help others. The only thing that kept him was the things his father had taught him before he had died. This is what Cypher clung too many times when he was trying desperately to keep things together and keep his anger under control.

Toward the end of the week, Cypher began to get involved in some basketball games as a way of staying active physically and a means to keep from sitting around all the time. It was a game that he was unfamiliar with and had never really played before. He found it to be quite challenging to get in the flow and learn the game at first. However, he was quite fond of the fast pace of the game and rather enjoyed the game itself once he learned how to play. He was allowed to play at first mainly because of his status in the House, but after a while, he started becoming a much better basketball player and would often make shots and even get some rebounds from time to time.

Finally, Saturday had come. This was the big day for Cypher. It was visitation day. He was only allowed one visitor a week and had at this point only saw his mother, and that only a few times do to his time in the box. But today was a very special day for Cypher. Today, Tonya was coming to see him. Cypher never knew who was coming until he entered the room and saw them. As he walked to the room, he assumed he was going to see his mother again this week. But when he was brought into the room and saw Tonya, every part of his being was about to explode in great excitement. What an awesome surprise this was. He had missed her so very much and was so excited to see her. As he sat in front of her for a moment, he was almost unable to speak, for the feeling was overwhelming him to the point where he had to gather his thoughts.

"Hello, Johnnie," Tonya said as she sat gazing into his blue eyes as she was almost in tears herself.

"Tonya. Baby, I missed you so much. How are you doing? How is everything going? Have you been okay?" Johnnie asked as he spoke fast while trying hard to keep his composure.

"Yes, I am good, Johnnie. I have missed you as well. Everything is going good, but I hate us being apart like this. I wish you were with me and not in here. Are you okay, have you had any problems? We heard that Ricco and Wayne are also in here. Have you had any problems with them? There is a rumor that Paco died in here, Johnnie, is that true? Is it that dangerous in here? Johnnie, please be safe. I couldn't take it if something happened to you in here," Tonya said as she was scared for Johnnie's safety and was greatly concerned for his wellbeing.

"I am fine, honey. Everything is going good for me in here, so please don't worry. Yes, Paco did get killed in here, but it was a close friend of mine who did it. I am with a group that doesn't like them, and they don't want any trouble with me in here. Trust me, honey, I am very safe in here. I have made some good friends in here, and we watch each other's back. Really, there is nothing to worry about," Cypher explained as he tried to ease Tonya from her worries.

"We heard you were in solitary confinement? What happened?" Tonya had asked.

"Well, Ricco and Wayne had to find out that they couldn't take me out. We had a little altercation." Cypher downplaying the situation as to keep Tonya from worrying. "But it was no big deal really, and we all had to spend time in the box for it. But it's over with now, we all just want to do our time and get out of here," Cypher explained.

"I love you, Johnnie. I love you so much, and I miss you terribly. Please stay out of trouble in here, so we can be together sooner. We don't need you to get any more time added on," Tonya said to him.

"I won't, honey, everything will be okay. I will be out of here before you know it. Then we can get on with our lives and put all of this behind us," Cypher said as the guard came in.

"Johnnie, your time is up," the guard said as he walked over to him. "I will see you soon, Tonya. I love you so much. Write me. I need your letters while I'm in here," said Cypher as the guard let him hug her for a moment.

"I will, Johnnie. I love you too, and I will be waiting for you." Tonya stood there until Cypher was taken back out of the room and back into population.

"These hour visitations go so fast," Cypher said to the guard as they were walking back.

As the weeks went by, Cypher was more involved in cards and basketball than he figured he would be, but he liked being active. Jason always grabbed him up when they were going to play some spades. At first, Cypher wasn't too sure about the game, but as he learned and got better, he really started to enjoy the game as well as the conversations that took place during it. The respect that Cypher had now was growing as people got to know him more and more. His natural leadership began to come out and be more noticeable as everyone got to better know him. This was a quality that Jason was quite fond of.

For Jason, having someone like Cypher with him made him more at ease. And for once, he was with someone that he knew he could trust and didn't have to keep an eye on. However, with Jason having trust issues, there were still times that he would watch Cypher, but he mostly gave it no thought most of the time and just allowed him to handle his business without little involvement from him, just as long as the money kept coming without any hindrances.

The following few months went by with hardly any problems in the House. Cypher was able to get more visits from Tonya and even George was able to come up and see him. Sara came at least two times a month to see Cypher so that he could use the other two visits to see Tonya or one of the boys, but the two brothers hadn't come up to see

Cypher as of yet mainly because only one could see him. But Randy was really missing Cypher and wanted to come up and see him, so he was sure to make it up sooner or later after him, and Darrell worked out a time when they would each be able to make it up there. That is something they would have to work out with Sara.

Thomas Hilton was able to come twice a month with his Pastor from the Church. This was something that the State would encourage as they felt that having a Christian influence would keep the population violence to a minimum. Time went by slower than Cypher had hoped. He was really getting tired of being in here and wanted nothing more than to regain his freedom and get on with his life. Being away from everyone was becoming a real challenge for Cypher as his first year finally was coming to a close, and that meant one third of his time was finally about to be done.

The two brothers had both finally made their visits, and that helped to encourage Cypher to be able to see them both. The letters he received also was much needed and helped to pass the time as he would reread them just to feel like he was in touch with the group when he would go through the moments where he had missed them terribly.

During Christmas, every inmate was able to get a two hour extended visitation. Sara needed this time with Johnnie. This was her first Christmas completely alone. She had never had Johnnie being away for any holidays, and Thanksgiving was hard enough without him, as she felt there was nothing to be thankful for as she had spent Thanksgiving being terribly depressed. Christmas was even harder. But having an extra hour with Johnnie that at least gave her something to look forward to. Cypher was equally needing it as well. It was so hard for him to be away from everyone, especially during this time. This made it exceptionally hard for him during this part of the year.

YEAR TWO

Everything for a while had been smooth sailing. Not much of anything if at all had been happening, but then there arose some tension between the Hells Sinners and the the West Dragons. And now, there was a few of the Death Clicks in the House as well for some of their actions against the Hells Sinners on the outside that landed them in the House as well. This further added to the tension that had seemed to be growing. With all of the leaders from the Hells Sinners in the House, the Death Clicks decided it was a good time to take advantage of it and hit the Hells Sinners which started a war between the two rival gangs. Also sparking an altercation between Hells Sinners and the West Dragons because at first, it was supposed the West Dragons had made the move to do a hit on them, but later was found that it was the Death Clicks. As that issue had been somewhat resolved between the two rivals, or at least the Hells Sinners had thought it was, the Hells Sinners had turned their focus on the Death Clicks and made their own hit against them, sparking a war that left several dead between the two gangs.

Outside wars were supposed to stay outside, but with the addition of two major hitters from the Death Clicks in the House now, that had change things.

The Death Clicks was an up-and-coming gang that was started by two other gangs merging together that was not strong enough on their own as of yet. As a means to survive, the two gangs came together and formed a new click that could better hold their ground against the two major gangs that were mostly in control. As the tension between the rival gangs was unsettling to the whole House and created an uneasy atmosphere, things was greatly on the edge for the whole House. This kind of tension usually ended badly. The guards were keeping a close eye on things and monitoring all the gang members. Things could erupt at any time, and a riot was possible. To try to keep an awareness of the situation that was ready to explode at any moment the guards were watching, they also did a cell to cell search for any kind of paraphernalia such as weapons or drugs in the hopes to deter any issues from happening.

Rick was very nervous having drugs in his cell, but it was not found due to an empty radio that he used to hide the drugs in. The parts that was taken out and was used for other things like tattoo guns, etc. But it was still a huge risk for him and Jason, for if they get caught, some major time would have been added on to their time.

As the guards went through each cell, some

shanks was found hidden in some mats where they had made small holes to shove them in to hide them from the guards. Among them was two toothbrushes one had been filed down so the end had a sharp point to it, and one toothbrush had the end melted and a razor blade stuck in the end. One cell had some marijuana hidden in the tank of the toilet wrapped in zip lock baggies to keep them dry. All of these were confiscated, and all the cell occupants was put in solitary confinement for two weeks. After the search was done, everyone was busy putting their cells back together and reorganizing their things. It was a huge mess that was made by the guards. And everything in each cell was thrown about as the guards don't have time to be neat about their search.

After everything had calmed down after their things had been put back in place, the inmates went back to what they were doing. Only now there was a sense of awareness that the guards were watching every movement. For a time, it settled things down and brought a sense of order and calmness that eased things up for a bit and put a lid on anything that was about to explode.

During all of this Cypher focused on school which was going great for him. The way the system was set up, he could go at his own pace and was working very hard, which put him ahead of where he would have been in public school. Five days a week, he was in class working as much as he could. One thing that Cypher and Jason shared was their love for knowledge. They both worked very hard every day, and both was ahead of where they should have been. Being in here gave Cypher plenty of time to study and helped him to keep his mind occupied, so he wasn't constantly thinking about his Mother and Tonya. Writing letters to them was something he did often. It helped to keep the feeling of being connected to them while he was away from them. All the studying and writing helped to pass the time.

Wayne and Ricco hated what Cypher had become. His rise to power and the respect he had now was eating at them. Watching him become bigger than them was hard to swallow. But there was nothing they could do. Cypher had become so big that only Jason could bring him down. But the two of them were so close now as brothers that Cypher could do no wrong in Jason's eyes. His love for Cypher had grown over the past year, and his respect had grown also. Cypher had become the only real family that Jason had ever had. This made Wayne and Ricco to barely able to wait to get out of here where they could get to Cypher on the outside away from Jason's protection and their time in the House was coming to an end. They were only days away from being released, while Cypher was in his second year of a three-year sentence.

Time was going slow for Cypher, but his school and letters were helping him to get through it. While being out on the court playing a game of basketball, Wayne had walked past Cypher and purposely bumped into him. When Cypher turned around, Wayne began to speak to him.

"My time in here is about done. But I will be

waiting for you on the outside. Might even go visit your girl Tonya and see how she is doing when I get out of here. I bet she misses me after the way I gave it to her," Wayne said with a cocky smile.

"You leave her alone, Wayne. If you go there, when I get out of here, I will come after you with everything I have. And if you want some of me when I get out of here, then we can do that. But I will tell you this, Wayne, I'm about done with your crap for real. If I have to, I will kill you." Cypher warned him before Wayne walked off.

This feud between Wayne and Cypher was getting old, and Cypher was more than serious about killing Wayne, he had enough of this fighting between the two of them and was ready to end Wayne's life if that was what it was going to take. Cypher returned his attention back to the game with which he was playing. And after finishing, he returned back to his cell to do some writing to Tonya and his mother Sara as well as the rest of the group. Cypher spent the rest of night writing everyone before it was time for lights out.

The next day, Cypher took his letters to the guard to be sent out. After which he went to school for a few hours before taking his spot at the top by the rail where he would watch and monitor everything that was going on in the House, especially Wayne and Ricco who he kept a contestant eye on. As Cypher was standing there, out of nowhere came one of the Hells Sinners who was sent to try and shank Cypher. Seeing him coming out of the corner of his eye, he watched him approach and saw the shank in his hand. When he got close enough and went to stick Cypher, he moved to the side as he plunged the shank towards him, but when Cypher had moved it made him miss, as he turned Cypher threw him over the rail causing him to fall to his death.

As the guards rushed in, everyone had scattered, and the guards weren't quite sure who was there to witness this, let alone who actually threw him over the rail and nobody was talking either. But one thing was for sure, nobody was going to try it again. Cypher had become so powerful, and by this kill now no one wanted to try to get at him again in fear of what might happen to them.

Everyone was put in lock down after this incident as the guards sought to find out what happened and who was the culprit that had thrown him over the rail but to no avail as no one was willing to snitch out Cypher in fear of retaliation from Cypher and Jason. After the guards finished their questioning, everyone was free to enter back into the main area.

That night, as Cypher laid on his cot, he was restless and couldn't sleep. The event from the day was still replaying in his mind. Everything happened so fast that he didn't have time to think about it, as he had just responded by instinctive actions. The whole thing was waving heavy on his mind. Cypher couldn't help but think on if he was becoming a killer. *Had all of this changed who he was? Was he losing who he was? The struggle to try to not lose himself in here, was it becoming impossible? Had it all became about survival now? Who am I becoming? My life was never supposed to be like this. Can I ever recover who I am? I am losing myself day by day as I drift along trying to survive. My life used to have purpose, used to have meaning. Now what have I become? Why has my life turned out this way? I just want to go home. I hate who I am becoming in here. I feel so lost, I feel so alone. I have killed two people, and I can't change that. I have to live with this now for the rest of my life. I don't even know if there will be more. What will happen before I get out of here? Will I even get out of here? What if my life ends in here? What have I accomplished? What have I contributed to the lives around me? It's dark and it's cold in here.*

He finally started drifting off to sleep in the dark where he was he trying to hold back his tears. So many emotions had gripped him to the point of exhaustion.

A few days later, Wayne and Ricco was released, and things with Cypher seemed to have settled down, and there was less tension for him with those two gone. School and writing letters had become his main focus. Cypher hadn't spent as much time playing basketball these days. Having the ability to finish school early, he focused more on that.

As the days went on and Cypher walked through each day, the struggle of not losing himself became a constant battle. As he stood against the rail looking down into the main area, he was lost in his thoughts. Remembering his time with his father. A time that he had missed so much. As he walk back into his cell, he sat down and began to drift off deeper into his thoughts. Thinking about how his father would look at him and smile with love. Now wondering how he would look at him if he could see him now. Wondering what he would think of who he had become. How things have turned out for him. *What would my father think of me now? All he has taught me that I have tried to hold on to. I miss you, Father. I have failed you, failed what you have taught me. What I have become is not what you wanted me to be. Would you still love me? Could you love who I am now? I could never measure up to you, to who you were. I could never make you proud now. You gave your life to save another, and I have taken life to save my own. You had such great courage, and every day, I live in fear. You were my hero. You are who I wanted to be. Why were you taken from me, Father? I need you. Mom needed you. Why were you taken from us? I have become a prisoner, a prisoner to fear, and anger. Hate has filled my heart. In my grief, I have born many sorrows. I am no hero. I have forsaken the life you wanted for me. My heart fails me. All I tried to protect, but who was there to protect me?*

After a little while, Cypher went back out to the rail to watch the inmates as they interacted among themselves. As he was standing there, Vincent came and stood next to him.

"Are you okay, Cypher?" he asked as they stood at the rail.

"Yes, I am okay, but thank you for asking, Vincent."

"No problem, man, I just had noticed that lately,

you haven't been as talkative. Thought maybe something was wrong, and if so, I am here if you need to talk," said Vincent.

"No, I'm good but thank you," Cypher responded.

"Well, I am here anyways, man." Cypher looked at him responded.

"Yeah, I know. I remember when you weren't. But thanks for being there now."

Vincent felt the coldness in Cypher's tone when he said that. Feeling bad for how he treated Cypher when he had first came into the House, now he had great respect for him and really liked him as a person. If he could have went back and done things differently, surely he would.

The following week, Cypher got to visit with Tonya. It always made him feel better when he got to spend his time with her. The hour they give him with her always seemed to go so fast, and there always seemed to never be enough time to get caught up on everything that was going on. But even just an hour every so often was so much better than nothing at all. And Cypher was always so thankful when she would come and visit him. He knew it was hard for her to come up, but she knew he needed to see her. Their talks always left him relieved, but homesick at the same time.

After their time was up, Cypher always went straight back to his cell to think about Tonya and the conversation that had just had, and then he would usually write her a letter and say all the things that he didn't have time to say to her.

As this year came to a close, Cypher was feeling

a bit relieved to have the better part of his sentence behind him. His final year was about to begin, and he felt good about it as anxiousness filled his spirit. One more year and he could get back home to his family and friends. This left Cypher thinking about all the things that he wanted to do as soon as he got home. School was going so good also that this next year, if things stay on course, would see him graduating just before his release, and he was already thinking about what he wanted to do to make money once on the outside. His father was so very good at construction and Cypher felt that if he could do the same then in some way he could still honor his father with the rest of his life. Cypher was very good at fixing things and wanted to maybe even open his own business and work in the community helping out with repairs that people couldn't do on their own.

Johnnie had felt that that would have made his father proud of him if he could do that. At least in this aspect of his life he could still somewhat be like his father and fix things in the community like his father had done so many times when people needed his help.

As Cypher was about to end this year and begin his last year, he was going to focus on putting a plan together to launch his own business once he was out. His father had a good friend who owned a hardware store and maybe they could be of some help to each other. But for now all he had was ideas until he could get out of this place and finally get on with his life and make a new life for Tonya and himself.

YEAR THREE

This is it, one more year, and I get to go home. All I have to do is not get into any trouble and just do my time, and I am free. And with some of my haters gone, I am hoping that this year will go by fast with little to no incidents. I need to get out of here and get back home to my mom and Tonya. I am just going to focus on my school and writing letters. That's all I want to do. Twelve months and I am going home. Cypher laid on his cot in deep thought before getting up for the day.

Sliding down off the top bunk, he was hungry and ready to go to the cafeteria area for some breakfast. During breakfast, Cypher sat with Jason and the rest of the group that he stayed close to. As he looked around, he began to wonder how many of the inmates in here would get out of here and change the way they have been living. How many would use this as a turnaround or how many would keep ending up back in the system or even dead. It bothered Cypher to think on these things, but he was always quite aware of the reality that this place seemed to put in his face daily. There was no escaping the fact, some of these inmates would end up dead at some point, and others would remain in and out of the system their whole lives. It was sad to think of the countless potential that was being lost in here. Young boys who would never have any real kind of future. This wasn't the kind of life that would produce any real success in any shape or form. It was a dead end road for those who traveled it.

After breakfast, Cypher went back to his cell to write some letters to his mother and to Tonya. Just before he went into his cell, however, he stopped and stood at the rail to watch the inmates for a few, as was his custom. He always watched the other inmates and would wonder what they could accomplish or become if they would change their destiny and try to make something out of their lives instead of just trying to be a gang member.

After several minutes, Cypher returned back to his cell and started to write his letters. While Cypher was trying to write, he heard a huge commotion out in the main area. Getting up, he walked out to the rail to see what was taking place. Seeing his cell mate Vincent standing at the rail watching, he went over and stood next to him.

"What's going on, Vincent?" Cypher asked as they stood there together.

"I don't know for sure, those two just started fighting out of nowhere," he responded.

"Weren't those two just playing basketball together?"

Vincent watching on responded. "Yes, they were, and it looked like everything was okay, then they just started fighting."

Cypher scanned the main area until he pinpointed Jason. Jason made eye contact with Cypher and nodded to assure him it was all okay.

"Well, I guess it's their problem. Let me know what happens. I am going to go back to writing my letters."

By this time, the guards had finally responded and came in with great force to break it up. After sitting down for a minute, he heard the lock down siren go off. Shaking his head, he knew what that meant. No more playtime. This made everyone on edge having to be locked in their cells. But for Cypher, it meant time to focus on some writing with little interruptions.

Later that night as Cypher had laid down on his cot to get some sleep, it was time for lights out, and now, too dark to do anything else but rest or talk. He began to think about Tonya for a little while as well as his mother Sara. Now that he was into his last year here, every day that passed was a day closer to being home with them. Cypher hated that anxious feeling that it brought, but he couldn't keep his mind off it. Two years had gone by, and he had missed the group so very much. The two brothers had only came and visited a few times, but it was because he was only able to have one visitor a week, and Sara always got two of those visits, and she never missed her visitation time with Johnnie. As he thought on these things, he began to drift off to sleep.

Early the next morning at breakfast, Cypher and Jason was discussing the event of last night that landed two inmates in solitary confinement. Jason began to explain why the fight took place, and that it wasn't over with yet. There had been a problem brewing between the two inmates for some time, and it had escalated when they played basketball against each other, and one inmate kept running his mouth until finally, it exploded into a full blown

281

fight. This was common in a place like this for inmates to not get along. But usually, they respected each other's space, but when they are on the small court together, these things happen. The basketball court on the main floor wasn't very big. But it had to do since they only got one hour outside to play basketball on the big court. This small one was only good for three on three. Wasn't much, but it did help the inmates to pass the time.

Cypher had played some games but hadn't in a while now. He began to focus more on writing to Sara and Tonya and the rest of the group more and more. He began to write more and more about the things he wanted to do once he was released from here and able to be back home. George had wrote him about how he and Ann had really grown together, and their relationship together had become very serious. George always let Johnnie know how Tonya was doing and how she was with them a lot and how she always mentioned how much she was missing him. Randy and Darrell didn't write as much, but when they did, it was pretty detailed about how things were going and how they all missed Johnnie. They always let him know how they were looking out for Tonya and making sure she was okay while he was gone. These where the kind of letters that Johnnie loved to receive, they encouraged him greatly.

As the days passed by. Cypher's schooling was going great, and he was working very hard to graduate before he got out of here. It had become his goal. This was something that really helped him to focus on something that kept his mind off the time he was doing. It gave him something to keep him motivated and allowed him to do something positive to do in such a negative place and gave him a sense of accomplishment, which was very important to have in a place like this where it is so easy to be discouraged. If nothing else at least Cypher was getting his schooling done in here and would be able to graduate early and come out with his diploma and have something to show for.

Cypher and Jason depended on each other. They only trusted each other. They knew that neither of them would do anything to hurt the other. The trust between these two had grown and was proven many times while being in juvenile prison together. Cypher never worried about Jason. He knew he had a real friend in him and completely trusted him. They became like real brother in the previous two years that they had spent together. Cypher was the only family that Jason really ever had. And there was nothing that he wouldn't do for Johnnie. Cypher and Jason both excelled in their schooling together and would even sometimes compete to see who got better grades. Even making small wagers. Betting against each other made school more fun and interesting for them both. And the competition also fueled them to work harder. Jason was an excellent student, but Cypher was very smart as well and would slightly do a bit better. Usually, their grades were even, but both at times would win their bragging rights. Anything to make life a bit more fun in this place always made the time just a little bit easier.

As the week went by, Friday came, and it was time for Cypher to make his rounds and collect for Jason. This meant it was payday. And Cypher would get his cut as always. The money he got usually went on candy bars; that he would use to get other things from people. Candy in here was a big deal, and you could trade it off for whatever you needed. Candy bars and cigarettes, if you had these two things then you could make some good deals. For them, it was like currency.

Cypher was good at making deals, and he did what he had to so that Sara wouldn't have to put money in his account. She used to do that when she would come and visit him until he started stacking up on things and then told her that she didn't need to give him anything anymore. Cypher hated lying to his mother, but he did keep this from her. He never wanted her to know what he was doing in here to make money. He had told her that he was working in a program, and they gave him a little bit of money every week.

Cypher knew that Sara was on her own, and that money wasn't something she could afford to give to him all the time, so he wouldn't take anything from her. But he also didn't want her to worry or be upset or disappointed in him. So he kept what he did a secret from her. Cypher would use his money to buy his paper and pens for his letters that he wrote all the time. Envelope and stamps were expensive in here, and that would always cost him extra. But paper and pens came much cheaper. And he often would use the supplies they provided from the school. Even though he wasn't supposed to take anything out of the school area, he would often smuggle some paper and pens out or buy some from someone who did. Others knew how important Cypher's letters were to him, so some would even ask for their parents to send extra and would sell them to Cypher. Stamps and envelopes were the hardest to come by, but others would ask for them, so they could sell them to Cypher and get extra money or extra candy.

As much as Cypher tried to be as honest as he could, he found himself once again having to do things contrary to what he believed and how he felt. But life in here wasn't easy as the decisions you had to make in here was more for survival than comfort. Cypher hated not being honest. And sneaking things was something that he absolutely hated to do, but he wasn't about to let Sara spend any more money on him while he was stuck in this place and not able to do anything to help her out. His mother's welfare was still his first priority. He knew the money she had needed to be spent wisely. This was another reason that fueled Cypher to continue to work very hard at his schooling so when he got out, he would be able to do some work and make some money instead of having to go to school. One thing that he often thought about was something that Jason had said to him once about we all have to make choices that we don't want to and do things that we don't always agree with ourselves. But sometimes, corners have to be cut when your back's against the wall, and there is no other way out. Cypher hated that, but it did seem to appear to be right. Even though it was wrong. Cypher always tried to keep things black and white, but sometimes, he would have to walk in the gray area of life when he had to.

Cypher struggled with these things in life. Sometimes, there are no real answers, you just have to do what you have to do to survive even if that means taking a life when you don't agree with murder. Or taking things that you're not supposed to take even when you know it's wrong, but your situation requires you to do so. These were difficult decisions that he felt had to be made whether they were right or wrong. Nevertheless, he needed to stay in contact with Sara and Tonya. This was something he had to do no matter what. Even if it meant taking paper and pens from the school when he knew it was wrong.

Cypher was very thankful that he had Jason in here to help him and to keep him focused. It made it so much easier having a true friend that was looking out for him. Jason knew this side of life way better than Cypher did. Jason was from the streets and knew how to read people and situations better than anyone, and Cypher was learning a great deal from him. This was a life that Cypher was thrown into, but for Jason, it was his everyday reality. They both came from two different worlds and was learning from each other.

For Jason, he had grown to appreciate the innocence that Cypher had when he wasn't doing things that he was forced to do. A real honesty that you rarely found on the streets. He knew he could always sit down and talk to Cypher and get real honest answers or responses. This was a characteristic about Cypher that Jason loved and appreciated more than anything. Cypher was in it for the friendship, not for what he could get. And Jason knew that. Everyone else was in it to be close to Jason because of his power and his status in here and on the outside. But Jason knew that this wasn't the lifestyle that Cypher wanted at all, nor was he trying to pursue it. He knew Cypher was trying to get his time done and go home.

As the weeks went by, Cypher and Jason had many private talks in which they would discuss many things that would help each other to grow and learn. Jason was very much into philosophy as Cypher had pursued wisdom through many books that he had read while being in here. This was something that he wanted because of his father Mark. Johnnie loved the wisdom that his father had always shared with him when he wanted Johnnie to understand something, and this became a big part of his life. It was always interesting when these two would sit and talk about the many different things that they had both read and learned. Sharing with each other had become a huge part of their friendship as they both had a desire to learn. Their conversations sometimes would last for hours. This was a personal time between the two that no one else was able to be a part of. It was always just the two of them, and no one else. For everything that Jason had been through, he really did enjoy trying to learn more about life and the different beliefs that people had. He read various kinds of different proverbs. Everything from Chinese proverbs to Bible proverbs. All of these he would share with Cypher, and Cypher would read many books on leadership and wisdom as well.

Cypher had always admired his father and struggled immensely to become like him. This was his hope for one day. This he thought would make his mother proud of him as well as others. If he could only get things going in the right direction and finally be able to move on with his life and live without having to fight some battle.

Once Cypher was out, he wanted to learn how to do construction and be as good as his father was. Mark had a great reputation for being a great worker who always did it right the first time. He took his job very seriously and always wanted to give the customers what they paid for. For Mark, cutting corners was never an option, and this was a trait that Cypher had also picked up. Everything he did, he wanted it to be perfect. Even to the point of starting completely over until it was exactly the way he wanted it to be. All Johnnie thought about was making a good life for him and Tonya.

Cypher knew how happy his mother was and how Mark worked very hard to give him and Sara a good life. Johnnie admired how hard his dad worked and how the people in the community held his name up in high esteem. Cypher was hoping to one day build his name like that and have a good reputation in the community like his father had. He dreamed of a big house for him and Tonya, like the one that he grew up in with a huge backyard. Cypher wanted to give Tonya the life that Mark had given to Sara before he had died. Tonya was so good to Johnnie, and he wanted to spend the rest of his life with her.

During his letter writing time, he was suddenly distracted by some commotion. As Cypher walked out to the rail and looked over the main area, he saw most of the inmates down greeting a few new inmates in the usual way of pushing them and saying bad things to them. Cypher watched on from the rail. He remembered when he had to go through this. He hated it and would not participate in it. Being put in here was hard enough without being harassed as you walk in. It was a horrible experience for him, and he knew it was for all who came in here. To have to walk past people that you didn't know as they taunted you and tried to intimidate you. That was not his style, so he just watched as he looked on. Feeling sorry for them that was coming in to this environment. He looked at their faces as they walked through this mess of a greeting, one had his head down and was almost in tears. He felt bad. He knew they would prey on that kind of weakness.

After everything settled down, Cypher was going to go back into his cell until he saw Jason motioned for him to come down. When Cypher had come to Jason's cell, Ricky and Viper was both in there as well. *This is probably some kind of meeting.* He walked in and stood next to Viper.

"What's going on, Jason?" he asked. "You know there were a few new inmates that came in today," Jason said.

"Yes, I saw them. But I don't know them," Cypher answered just before Viper responded.

289

"I know one of them. There will be a problem, Jason, I'm pretty sure of that."

Cypher looked puzzled and not quite sure what all of this is about.

"Yes. I am anticipating that as well," Jason said.

"Well, I don't care, I'm ready for whatever. If there is going to be a problem, I just assume get it over with," Ricky added.

"Be cool for now and let's just see how things develop. We all want to do our time and get out of here. So let's not jump the gun, maybe he won't want any problems while he is in here either," said Jason as he was looking directly at Ricky.

"Who is he?" Cypher asked as he was wondering how this involved him. Other than the fact that he was Jason's right hand man.

"That's Miller. He isn't affiliated with any gangs at all, but make no mistake, this kid is as mean as they get," Jason explained.

"Yeah, and me and him hate each other. We used to hang out a while back. I've known him since the first grade. You talk about one bad dude. This guy is it. He really has no friends. And doesn't care to make any either. I think he hates everyone," Ricky said as he was remembering the fight that they had. Ricky is a real good fighter, but he couldn't handle Miller. That fight ended badly for him. Miller beat Ricky till he was lying unconscious.

"I also had a run in with him before. That kid ain't no joke, he can really fight. Most everyone is afraid of him. Gangs won't even try to recruit him because no one can control him, and he won't take orders from anyone. He goes by his own rules and that's it," Viper told them.

"I for one have never had any problems with him, but we have passed each other by a few times, and there was a bit of a stare down between us though. I think he kept his cool because of who I am though. Not that he is afraid of me, I just think he knows his limitations when it comes to living and dying. He knows I would kill him if he didn't kill me first," said Jason.

"Well, I don't know him at all. So as long as he doesn't start nothing, I'm good. But if he does, you know I am here with you, Jason," Cypher added just before this small meeting was to come to an end.

Jason gave one specific order before they all walked out of the cell. "No one move unless I say so or unless you have no choice. But you better have a good reason if you do anything."

After the meeting, Cypher returned back to his cell and continued his letters that he was writing. During his writing time, he found himself a little bit distracted about the meeting that took place concerning the new guy Miller. *He must be for real one tough character for them all to be concerned like that...all accept for Jason. I wonder if anything ever makes him nervous or scared. I wish I could be like that. Never be afraid. It gets hard to fight through the fear sometimes, but I have to if I want to survive.*

Off and on throughout the night, Cypher would find himself wondering about Miller and if he would become a serious problem to them while he was in here. They didn't even know as of yet as to why he is in here. *Had he killed anyone or was he just a bully who liked to beat up other kids? Maybe he is just in here for stealing something? I have no idea about this kid and really don't want to know either, but I am sure I will find out anyways as the next few days go by. But for now, I need to get some rest and try to keep my mind on more positive things.*

The very next morning, Cypher went to the cafeteria to have breakfast. After getting his food, he went over and sat down with the rest of the group that he was now connected to. Jason always had a seat saved for Cypher that was right next to him. As they were eating their breakfast, Miller came in and got in line. Everyone was watching him because his reputation had preceded him. Almost everyone knew who he was. As Miller made his way to a table, he made the ones that was sitting there get up and move to another table. This was seen by everyone, and it made a serious statement in the cafeteria this morning that he wasn't going to just do his time. He was sending a message that he was in control, and this was something that Jason took note of.

Everyone had seemed to glance over to Jason to see what his reaction would be. But as was Jason's custom, he almost appeared to not have even noticed. But one thing was for sure. He did notice, and everyone knew it because Jason never missed anything. This was his house, and he ran it. Now he had to make it clear that he was in charge. However, he was pretty sure that Miller already knew that. So for Jason, he took that very personal that Miller would make it a point to make a statement like that right off the bat. Everything in the House was taken seriously, every subtle move to major moves were all noticed.

Viper was sitting across from Jason and has asked. "What are you going to do?"

Jason looked straight into his eyes as he responded, "I'm going to run this House like I always have, and no one is going to take nothing from me. Miller will follow the rules just like everyone else in here does. And if he doesn't, then I will deal with him, just like I would if it was anyone else."

Jason went on with his normal conversations after that as if nothing had even happened. No one could tell if this had bothered Jason or not. Most people would have been scared to have to deal with Miller, but Jason didn't show the least bit of fear at all. He always kept his composure and stayed calm no matter what was going on. But everyone was starting to buzz about the possibility of Jason and Miller fighting. This would be epic. This was the kind of fight you would pay to see. The two most feared and respected fighters who commanded respect just by the mention of their names seemed to be possibly headed for a confrontation. And all of this over something as small as Miller making a few people get up and move just because he wanted to sit there. However, it was done on purpose, and everyone knew it. The only question was, how was Jason going to handle it, and what was he going to do about Miller if he wanted to take over the House as the one in charge? If anyone could take the top spot away from Jason, it would have to be Miller. No one else could do it. And no one was even sure if Miller could, but one thing was for sure. He had the best chance out of anyone else in there.

A few days later, as Cypher was walking through the main area out of nowhere, Miller came by and purposely bumped into him. Cypher knew what this meant, and he knew he couldn't back down. Even with Jason looking out for him in this world, you have to be able to hold your own at any given moment. As Miller bumped into him, he stopped and turned to him.

"What's the problem, Miller?" Cypher asked as he stepped to him.

"I heard you're a pretty tough kid. You think you can take me?"

Cypher, shaking his head, responded sharply. "Is this what you want, Miller? Are you wanting to find out?"

"I don't think you're as tough as they say you are. As a matter of fact, I think maybe you just got lucky."

By this time, everyone was watching, and Jason was on his way out of his cell to go confront Miller and get him off Cypher, but by the time he got there, it was too late, Cypher and Miller was in each other's face, and Miller took the first swing. Surprisingly, Cypher stayed on his feet and swung back. After that, it was a full on fight between the two. Jason knew that he couldn't jump in now, he had to let Cypher handle this.

Although he roughly expected Cypher to lose this one, he was actually holding his own pretty good and much better than anyone had expected him to be able to do against Miller. Cypher fought like a raging bull as he gave Miller everything he had. He just kept coming at Miller and was getting in some good shots until finally Miller was hurt, and then Cypher went to finish him off. This fight went on for several minutes before the guards could get in and try to stop it. By the time they had got there, it was basically already over with. Both were hurt and bleeding. As tough as Miller was, today he met his match and had lost. To everyone's surprise, Cypher came out on top of what should have been a win for Miller. Everyone knew that Cypher would give him a good fight, but no one expected him to actually win the fight. They fought like it was a war, and after today, Cypher would have a lot more respect in the House and even from Miller.

After everyone was separated and forced back into their cells, Miller and Cypher were taken first to the infirmary to get examined and taken care of before they were brought before Warden Tait, who would ultimately determine both of their punishments. After a day in the infirmary, they were both brought up to the office of the warden.

"Bring them two in here," said a voice from the office. "Well, Johnnie, haven't had you in here in a very long time, and you Alex Miller, I do believe that you just got here? Are you having a hard time getting settled in?" Warden Tait asked as he sat looking at both boys.

"No. I ain't having any problems getting settled in. Just a simple misunderstanding is all," Miller responded as he glanced at Cypher to see what his response would be to that statement.

"Is that right, Johnnie? Was it just a simple misunderstanding?" Warden Tait asked.

"Yeah, that's all it was. You know how things are sometimes. Just a simple misunderstanding is all." Cypher said as he looked back at Miller.

"Well, if you two promise to not have any more misunderstandings, maybe we can resolve this matter quickly and a lesser punishment."

Both Cypher and Miller agreed, and they were both given one week in the box instead of the two weeks that was usually the punishment for a situation like this.

"I don't want any more problems out of you two. Or next time, you both will get the full two weeks. Understood?"

"Yes, sir," they both responded as they were taken to their individual boxes.

"This sucks," Cypher said as he sat down against the wall. Seven days of this crap again. How awesome is that?" Sitting on the small mattress that was laying on the floor, Miller heard Cypher complaining.

"You been in here once already?"

"Yeah, I was in here a long time ago for fighting, last time it was much worse."

"Well, I hope you don't keep complaining the whole week we are in here."

"Shut up, Miller, you're the reason we are in here. What is your problem anyways? Thought you

296

would make a name for yourself? Well, I guess that didn't work out too good for you, did it?" Cypher said in an unusual cocky voice.

"You got some guts, kid. No one has ever fought me like that. I'm kind of impressed to be honest. Where did you learn to fight like that?" Miller asked as he began to take an interest in Cypher.

"Just been in a lot of them. You kind of get good at it after a while I guess."

Miller smiled in the other box. "Yeah, I guess you do. I love to fight. I don't know why, but I just love it you know. I always have. Maybe it's the thrill and excitement of it. But I don't know, I just always liked fighting."

Cypher shook his head. "Personally, I hate fighting. And I hate being in this stupid box. This sucks. Nothing to do in here but sit or sleep. Think and wait for them to bring you something to eat."

Miller laying on his mat, thinking about what Cypher was saying. "It wasn't personal. I heard others talking about you. They were saying that you fight like a beast. I just wanted to see for myself how good you really were."

Cypher sitting there was irritated at Miller's words. "Yeah, well, I hope you're satisfied with the results. You got seven days to think about whether or not it was worth it and whether or not you want to continue this." I'm going to get some sleep. I don't even know what time it is, but I'm tired," Cypher said as he laid down to get some rest.

Miller didn't respond, he just laid there and thought about Cypher's reaction to this whole thing. After a long week of being in solitary confinement, Cypher and Miller were both released back into population. Cypher had thought that it was strange that they both had only did a week, but nonetheless he was happy to be back in population. He and Miller didn't talk much while being in the box together, but they did form a mutual respect for one another.

After returning to population, they didn't talk much their either, but Miller was no longer a problem for him. He had actually liked what he saw in Johnnie and felt that he would just leave it alone after getting to know him a bit. It wasn't hard time for Miller because no one messed with him, which was just the way he liked it, and as long as people left him alone, then he could do his time and get back out, which is the very thing that Cypher was also trying to do as well.

After getting back into population, Cypher got back on his letter writing and his schoolwork and kept at it until he was all caught up again, which took a bit of work to get all of the stuff done that he had fell behind on for his schoolwork. Getting his letters caught back up was pretty easy though. That was just a matter of sitting down and writing them all out. Getting them mailed was always a hassle when he would do all at one time. The House only allowed you to be able to send out so many letters per week.

Cypher had to always hide his stamps. Stealing them was something that was always an issue, and everyone knew that he always had them. As the week went by, Cypher focused mainly on getting caught back up on his schoolwork and only interacted with Jason and a few others when needed until all of his school work was completed.

Everything in the House seemed quiet as of lately. All the hype had settled down now about Miller since he wasn't doing anything since his fight with Cypher. Miller had been sticking to himself for a bit after being released back into population, with the exception of a few conversations with Cypher, which always drew some attention because everyone thought that they might go at it again, but to be honest, Miller really just had taken to Cypher and gained a lot of respect for him. Cypher wasn't out much in the main area until he finally got all of his schoolwork all caught up, and then he decided to jump in on a quick game of basketball, which was something that he hadn't done in a long time.

As he was playing, he noticed that Miller began to talk to a few people that where known for causing problems, this was a bit of a concern for Cypher as he liked for things to be quiet with no problems. It really irritated him when things weren't calm like they should be. Every time things got hype, it always took a while for everything to calm back down. Every incident put everyone on edge, and it was easy for one thing to open up a door for something else to happen. And Cypher was always trying to keep a lid on things to make sure that that never happened. Someone had to keep control of this place. And Jason kept things under control for the most part, but he also would let people take care of their business when they needed to. Jason rarely involved himself in other people's matters whereas Cypher was more of a peacekeeper and would try to resolve an issues so that it wouldn't get out of hand. For Cypher, he just wanted to finally have some peace in his life without drama. But in here, that was never going to happen. Someone always had an issue with someone else.

The next week as Cypher was sitting in the main area on a bench reading, Miller came over and sat next to him as he wanted to talk which was unusual for Miller. He rarely liked talking to anyone.

"What are you reading?"

"Well, Miller, it's a book about two young people who fall in love and run away together."

Miller laughed. "That sounds like a girly book, man, I figured you to be more of an action kind of person."

"Yes, well, I seem to get enough action and excitement in real life so when I read, I like to have a bit of a different experience, you know kind of take a break from reality."

"Yeah, okay I can see that, but to read a girly book? That kind of weird, man."

"It's not really a girly book, Miller. It's just a book about two people who can't be together so they run away together, so they can have the life that they want without anyone interfering or trying to stop them. Anyways, what brings you over here today? Is there something you need?"

"Nah, man, I was just bored, so I thought I would come over and see what kind of book you were reading. But it's cool, man, enjoy your book," Miller said as he went to get up and walk away, but before he could, Cypher pulled him back down.

"You're okay, man, hang with me for a minute. Tell me what's been going on with you."

"Not much, man. Just been getting to know those two guys a bit. They seem okay. They like to get into trouble, so we have that in common." Miller laughed again. "You know how it is, man."

"Yeah, I know. I prefer things a bit more quiet though. Stay low key and just chill."

"Right, right. I hear ya, man. I don't know I love action and chaos. It's my thing I guess. Makes me feel alive. The more everything is out of control, the more I thrive off of it. Ya know?"

"Yeah sure. To each their own, Miller. We all have our own thing that we do or need. I just like things relaxed and calm. But excitement is fun sometimes also."

"Yeah, I don't know how to relax and stay calm. It's just not me, man. Anyways, talk to you later, man, I'm going to go see what's going on with some cards or something see if I can get into a game and pass some time."

"Okay, Miller. I will talk to you later. Thanks for coming over, man."

"Yeah, sure thing, man."

As Miller went to walk away, Cypher got his attention one more time. "Hey, Miller."

"Yeah, man?"

"You can come talk to me any time, man. I mean if you just want to sit and talk, it's cool, you know?"

"Yeah sure, man. See ya later then, huh?"

"Yeah, of course. Have fun with your card game."

After Miller had walked away, Cypher returned his attention back to his book and read a few more chapters before returning back to his cell to write a few letters to Sara and Tonya.

As the weeks went by, Cypher and Miller talk more and more. Cypher was probably the only person that Miller actually liked in this place other then the two trouble makers that seemed to peek Millers interest. Cypher was still iffy about Miller, but as long as they were good, he felt more at ease that there would remain some peace in this place between him and Jason. At times, things got a little edgy between the two, but for now, Cypher was able to keep the two from going at it. Nevertheless, the tension between Miller and Jason remained. The only real problem was that Miller just didn't like people and hated being told what to do. That is why he ended up in here in the first place because of his constant defying of authority.

Jason knew this was the problem, but because of that, he couldn't cut Miller any slack even if it meant having a fight with him. Jason for sure couldn't let Miller slide at all, knowing that if he did, it would be considered as a sign of weakness, and Jason could not and would not risk it. Miller knew that Jason wasn't afraid of him. That was something that he wasn't used to at all. He thrived on the fact that people feared him. He rather enjoyed bullying people as a way of pleasure. As time went by, Cypher was getting anxious as the year was going by pretty good and his release date was getting closer.

School was almost done, and soon, he would graduate, which he was looking forward to, especially since his release date was shortly afterwards. Keeping up on his schoolwork really helped to keep the time moving. It was good to be able at least get this accomplished while he was in here. As hard as it was being in here, Cypher learned a lot, in school and out of school. He saw how corrupt the system was and how the guards would allow certain things to go on. He saw the payoffs that the guards took so that inmates could get things in that was illegal. Being in here opened his eyes to a lot of things and how things worked. Nevertheless, for Cypher, being honest and straight with people was what he was taught, and nothing was going to change that. He knew in his heart that was how his father wanted him to be. And no place or no one was going to change that. Not even the House.

Life here sucked, but he knew there was a life waiting for him when he got out of here. As time continued on, Cypher kept his focus and continued to move forward with his schooling, and then the day finally arrived. It was graduation time. Cypher had finally finished his schooling and was about to graduate. The time had come, and everyone who graduated was able to invite two people. For Cypher, that was simple. Sara and Tonya were the two he had chosen. It brought great joy for Johnnie that he was able to graduate with Jason who had also worked extremely hard to get his schooling done. This was one of the rare times that Cypher really got to interact with his mother and Tonya. They would not be confined to just sitting across from each other at a table. But there was an auditorium set up and everything was just like a real graduation, and then afterward, they were all able to spend a little bit of time together.

The ceremony didn't last as long as Sara and Tonya had expected, because there was only a handful of students actually graduated. Each one received their diploma. Cypher was so excited to be able to get this accomplished and also be able to see his mother and Tonya. Once everything was done and they were able to go spend a little bit of time with the people that they had invited, Cypher immediately gave his mother his diploma so that she could take it home. After today, Cypher would be going home soon, which was good since he was done with school and had very little now to occupy his time now. For this brief time, it was an amazing feeling to be able to be with Sara and Tonya at the same time. Cypher hadn't felt this good since his arrival. Feeling like a normal family for a few hours before it was time to say goodbye.

Cypher introduced Jason to his mother and Tonya. Sara hadn't remembered him at first until Cypher had mentioned the day at the park. Then Sara remembered the fight and buying them both ice cream. Jason was very pleased to finally meet them. He had heard Cypher talk so much about them that he felt as if he had already knew them. And they were also feeling the same way for Cypher had talked often about Jason in his letters, and now, they were all able to finally meet each other.

After it was all done, Cypher and the rest of the graduates had to return back to population. Cypher immediately went to his cell to relax and think. He didn't want to be bothered by anyone as he felt a sense of calmness and didn't want to be distracted from it with the daily drama that comes with being in this place. He just wanted some alone time to think and get mentally prepared for the daily grind now without the distraction of schoolwork. He wondered how he would fill in the empty space that he would have now. Maybe some reading. Jason had a ton of books that he could borrow, and that would be the ideal thing for Cypher to do.

Focusing on his upcoming release date was making him anxious, and time had gone so slow over the past three years, and his time in the box had made it even worse. It's as if time stands still when you're in there. Staying out of trouble now was highly important. After being in the box twice already, he was afraid that he could get some extra time added to his sentence if he got into any more trouble. Having Jason and now Miller on his side helped out a bit to keep people off of him, all he had to do was keep his cool and not do anything that would cause a situation to happen. The next few months went by with Cypher staying in his cell mostly, while doing his letter writing, and reading a few books that he had borrowed from Jason. Everything was quiet, just the way Cypher liked it. Time went by with hardly any problems at all in the House. Even Miller wasn't being very active. However, the tension between him and Jason continued to remain. But Cypher had done good at keeping the peace between the two.

Finally, the day came. Cypher was being released. Sara and Tonya came together to pick Johnnie up. They waited just outside the gate for him. This was it. Cypher was finally going home. He was in his cell when they came to get him. It was Guard Jeffrey who came and got him for his release. Johnnie was so excited to finally be going home. He had took some time to say goodbye to Jason that morning and a few others who he had become close to him as well. He even took some time to sit and talk with Miller for a few minutes. Cypher had everything packed and was ready when Guard Jeffery came for him. Everyone was applauding as Cypher walked out and headed down the stairs to the main floor.
Jason stood at the end of the steps and gave his brother a hug. He was going to miss Johnnie.

"I will see you when you get out of here, my brother," Cypher said as Jason let him go.

"You will for sure, bro. Stay out of trouble."

As Cypher was walking to the door, Miller gave him a friendly nod as if to say bye, my friend. Cypher nodded back and then walked out of the main area to go to processing so he could be released. After changing back into his real clothes and getting the rest of his belongings, he was escorted out to the main gate where Sara and Tonya was waiting for him.

Cypher took a deep breath as he walked through the gate and into Sara and Tonya's arms as they hugged him. Sara and Tonya both were crying as they held Johnnie. He was finally free and back with them where he belonged. It was a long drive home, and Johnnie took it all in as he enjoyed the ride home. How he had missed the beauty and scenery that this place had outside of those cold walls that once contained him. Sara was going to stop off for some ice cream, but Johnnie just wanted to get home and see everyone. He had missed everyone so much and just wanted to get back to his life now and spend the rest of the day visiting with everyone that he had missed.

CHAPTER 14

Homecoming

As Sara was on her way home with Johnnie, everyone was out back setting up for Johnnie's surprise, welcome home party. They had supposed that they had more time but Johnnie didn't want to stop for ice cream. That was part of the plan to give them a little extra time to get everything set up. Thomas Hilton and Tim Read was setting up all the tables and chairs with the help of their sons, George, Darrell, and Randy. While the ladies Monica and Christina were preparing the food as they waited for the Flowers family to show up who was on their way, Tammy Flowers had made a cake and some brownies, and Tony Flowers was bringing his utensils for cooking out on the grill.

Steve was itching to get there and see the group. He knew they would have to work a little, and then it was playtime. This was the day for which they had been waiting the last three years. Now, it had finally arrived, and everyone was hurrying to get everything set as they excitedly was waiting for when Johnnie was to arrive.

Everyone had pitched in on the food. Sara made sure that there was a variety of drinks which included juice, coffee, and punch, also she had made a macaroni salad. Thomas had brought hamburgers and hot dogs, Tim brought the buns and chips, which included pretzels and regular chips with dip. Monica had brought fruit and a potato salad. Everyone had worked fast and hard to get it all set, and now, it was ready. And in good time too, Johnnie had just arrived. Everyone was waiting out back while Sara was acting as if everything was normal after they had pulled up and got out of the car. Johnnie had stopped halfway to the house and grabbed Tonya and hugged her for a minute while Sara was unlocking the door.

After they were all inside, Sara asked Johnnie and Tonya if they wanted to go out back and sit while she made them some fresh tea. As they both went out back, Johnnie paused as he saw everyone there waiting for him. He was overwhelmed as he was filled with such great joy to see everyone. They all got up and went and greeted him each one hugging him as they welcomed him home. Shortly after they all had greeted Johnnie and welcomed him home, they all sat down and began to talk with him, Ann had finally arrived. George had been waiting for her all morning.

After a bit, Timothy and Nate also had arrived. Ann and Mike Johnson were late, but they had finally made it. Timothy and Nate couldn't wait to see Johnnie. Everyone was so excited. The boys and Ann and Tonya all had went over to play for a while until it was time to eat. While the adults were discussing how Johnnie had already graduated and how he had used that time to accomplish things, everyone was so proud of him for how he had not allowed this to keep him from doing the things that he needed to do.

Sara began to share with them all the plan that Johnnie had to start up a business in the community. As the group was off doing their own thing, the parents all sat around and was talking about how much Johnnie had grown. Everyone mentioned how good it was to have Johnnie back home. They all kept looking at him. You could tell that he had grown a lot in the past three years.

As Sara sat and watched him, she couldn't help but wonder how much of his childhood had been lost to everything that had happened. He definitely seemed different. He had a more serious look about him then what he used to have, and you could tell that his time in there had matured him quite a bit. It really bothered Sara knowing that most of his youth was wasted on having to deal with so much crap. She hated that it had changed him in some ways. She didn't want Johnnie to have to be this mature already, she wanted him to still be able to enjoy his youth and be playful.

As everyone sat talking, Thomas went over and got the grill started, so he could get the hamburgers and hot dogs going. Thomas was great at cooking on the grill and always enjoyed being able to cook at summer functions. Tim and Tony sat back and talked about sports as they both were drinking a cup of coffee that Sara had made for them. It was the perfect day for Johnnie to come home, the weather was so beautiful and perfect for a cookout and small celebration like this. The sky was clear and sunny, but still a bit cool, wasn't too hot to be outside enjoying the day.

As the group was off talking, they all decided that they wanted to have a camp night back at the club sight where they often used to hang out at. It had been a long time since they all had been able to hang out there all night. Later, Johnnie would talk to Sara about it and make sure she didn't have any extra plans for him and her before committing to have a group camp over. However, he was anxious to do so. He had so missed the times they all had shared together back there in the woods. Plus, he knew he would be able to be with Tonya, and that was the most important thing to him. He couldn't take his eyes off her as they all sat talking. She had stuck by him and had waited for him. He knew she had been faithful and loyal to him. She hadn't missed a chance to come visit him while he was away, and her letters never stopped coming. She wrote him every week for the past three years without fail. Johnnie loved her more now than when he had went in. Tonya had more than proven herself to Johnnie. And there wasn't anything that he wouldn't do for her. It was her devotion to him that helped get him through the past three years. He felt that he owed her everything.

As they all sat, they were laughing and telling

311

jokes as everyone was so excited. Thomas finally got the meat on the grill cooking as he watched everyone having a good time. Johnnie sat thinking how beautiful this day was and how beautiful Tonya was as well. She wore a beautiful yellow summer dress that highlighted her nice dark tan that she had gotten during the summer. Johnnie couldn't help but stare at her and when the sunlight would shine on her, she looked like a beautiful angel. She was so beautiful. Every time she would smile her whole face would light up. She had always been so pretty. And over the past three years, she had grown into a very beautiful young lady.

They all marveled at how much Johnnie had learned while he was in juvenile prison. He was sharing things from all the books that he had read over the past three years. He was sharing stories about him and Jason and how they met and how they both ended up in the box together. How they both would push each other to get their schoolwork done, with their challenges.

The one highlight in there was being able to graduate with Jason. He knew he would miss Jason. But being back home with his mother and Tonya and the rest of the group was much better than being in that horrible place. He knew Jason would find him when he got out. And he was looking forward to introducing him to the rest of the group.

The smell of the hamburgers and hot dogs filled the place, as everyone was getting hungry. Johnnie could hardly wait for them to get done. He loved hamburgers and hot dogs, especially off the grill, and he hadn't had real food in three years, and it smelled so good. Everything looked so amazing, and Johnnie couldn't wait to eat. It had been so long since he had good food like this. How he had missed the summer get-togethers and cookouts that they all used to have together the games, the fun, the swimming, the food; and it always ended up back at the camp for the night when they would have those functions together. They all were more than friends and neighbors. It was like a small little family.

It was this small group of friends that really helped Sara get through these hard times in her life, when Mark died and while Johnnie was away. From the loss of Mark to the abuse and death of Mike to losing Johnnie for three years. It had all been such a tough time for Sara and they had all been there for her and was a huge support group. She needed them.

As the food got done, Sara called everyone together. As they gathered together, she had asked Thomas to say a prayer of thanksgiving for the food and the time together. As they all held hands, Thomas began to pray, thanking God for the food and for this time together to celebrate Johnnie's safe return home. He then prayed that God would give Johnnie a great future and repay him for all of his lost time, and the hardships that he had suffered. Afterwards, they all got their food and sat down to eat together.

As they began to eat, Tammy and some of Johnnie's other family members came. It had been a long time since he had seen any of them. He was so excited when his grandmother came. He hadn't seen her in years and had missed her so very much. Johnnie didn't get to know his grandfather, he had passed away before Johnnie was born. However, he did have a great relationship with his grandmother, and seeing her brought him much joy.

Johnnie had always been a bit modest when it came to eating, he didn't like to pig out in front of people. But today, he couldn't resist the great food. He got a little bit of everything and ate it all until he was stuffed. As the party began to finally wind down, everyone pitched in to help clean up. The group had decided on a sleepover at the camp, and they couldn't wait for all of their parents to leave.

Sara was very well pleased how everyone came together to make this happen for her and Johnnie. Everyone had a great time, and the food was excellent. But it was now getting toward evening, and everyone started heading out. As they all got everything cleaned up, Johnnie went in and sat with Sara for a few minutes and had thanked her for putting all of this together for him. As Sara hugged Johnnie, she had told him how much she loves him and had missed him. It was so nice having him back at home with her. After they talked for a little bit, Johnnie went back out to his friends for the night, but not after promising his mother that they would have some time tomorrow for just the two of them.

When Johnnie returned back outside, he found that everyone had already went back to the camp area and was waiting for him. He had told them that he would be back out in a bit, and that he wanted to sit and talk to his mother for a little bit. By the time he had got back there, they had already had a nice fire going and had all of their sleeping bags rolled out that their parents had brought back for them, as they was now sitting on the logs that they always used for chairs. They were all talking about how great it was to be back at the camp again like they had used to do before Johnnie went away.

Tonya was sitting there waiting for Johnnie to come so that they could hold hands as they sat together on the log. That was something that she had missed so very much and was eagerly waiting for him to come back there. Smiling as he walked over to where Tonya was sitting, he took her hand as he sat down next to her. *It feels so good to be home. I've waited for this for three years, and it feels so good to be back.*

At first, the conversation focused on Johnnie as they all wanted to know things such as what it was like in there and did he have any problems other then with their rivals. As Johnnie was telling them everything that he had experienced and all that had happened, even about the fights and having to kill the boy that he threw over the rail when he had tried to stab him, he never once let go of Tonya's hand. He told them about solitary confinement and what it was like being in the box. They were all amazed at everything he had went through as they sat and listened. There were things that he had kept from everyone while he was in there so that they wouldn't worry so much about him. Almost in disbelief at everything that Johnnie had been through, it was hard to believe he would have had to kill someone to stay alive in there. But they all understood the survival part of being in a place like that. And they all got hyper when he was telling them about his fight with Wayne and some of their friends and how they had jumped him in the bathroom and tried to beat him to death and how he fought back. It all came to quite a shock to them as they all sat and listened. He had told them many stories that night about Jason and how they became like brothers; and that as soon as Jason was out, that they would all meet him.

The next morning as they all began to wake up, they all came to the house to use the bathroom and get something to drink. When Johnnie came into the house, he found Sara in the kitchen cooking everyone breakfast as was her custom to do so when they would all sleep over. Johnnie as usual started helping Sara get things ready.

"Johnnie, go be with your friends. I can do this," Sara had said to him, but Johnnie was not going to let her do all the work when there were so many people here to feed.

"It's okay, Mom, I can help out. I don't mind."

As Johnnie was getting plates out, Tonya also came in to the kitchen and started helping Sara with the cooking. After seeing Tonya pitch in, Johnnie decided to go ahead and go back to the group and sit and talk with them while the ladies cooked breakfast for everyone. Ann also was helping out in the kitchen by making all of the toast while Tonya was helping Sara cook some eggs and bacon as the boys sat outside at the big table and talked. This was the first time that Sara and Tonya had cooked together, and they both were enjoying it very much.

Once breakfast was done, they all sat together and ate breakfast as a family. *It's nice to have the group all together like this again.* Sara was smiling to herself as she sat and ate breakfast with them. She had missed having everyone over for a sleepover, and it was refreshing to not be alone like she had been while Johnnie was away. She always liked waking up to having the group here.

After everyone had finished eating, Sara and the two girls went back into the kitchen and cleaned everything up from breakfast. Sara was not wanting them to do any of the work, but she did enjoy the company. She had always liked Tonya and was so very happy that she and Johnnie were together. She loved how Tonya had stuck by Johnnie while he was away. She knew how much Tonya meant to Johnnie and took every opportunity to bond with Tonya. They had become closer during the rides out to see Johnnie when it was her turn to visit him. They would talk all the way out there and back and would always stop off and have dinner together. Tonya loved Sara and always felt so comfortable around her.

After everything was cleaned up, Tonya and Steve walked home. The two brothers Darrell and Randy had already left, and George was leaving as well. After which, Johnnie hurried into the shower to get ready for the day he was going to spend with his mother. After he was out of the shower, they sat down and talked for a bit. Everything was so busy yesterday and with all of the company that they never had a chance to just sit and talk.

"It's so good to have you home, Johnnie. I know this was my fault, and I am very sorry for all of this," Sara said as she became very emotional.

"No, Mom, he is responsible for all of this. Not you. I don't blame you at all. He did this to us, not you. You can't take his blame or his guilt, Mom. You were a victim just like I was. I did what I had to do, and I would do it again. I will do whatever I have to do to protect you. I didn't see any other way out of this, but to just eliminate him altogether," Johnnie explained.

"I should have never put you in this situation. I am supposed to take care of you and make sure you're okay and you're safe, and I didn't. I didn't do the things that I should have done as a parent. It's my responsibility to make sure that the decisions I make don't affect you in a negative way, and I failed," Sara said as she began to cry.

Johnnie, leaned over and hugged his mother, as he responded, "It's not your fault. I know that you were afraid and didn't know what to do. But it's over now. We are safe, and now, we can get on with our lives. I don't want you to feel like you did this because you didn't. I know you wouldn't ever do anything to hurt me or put me in a bad situation. These things happen because men like him are liars and fake. They prey on helpless women and take advantage of them and abuse them. He didn't deserve to live. A real man takes care of his wife, they don't abuse them or mistreat them. Men like that are nothing more than insecure scared little boys who are afraid that if they don't control you, then they may not be able to keep you. A real man knows how to take care of his wife and keep her. He protects her and doesn't hurt her. This was not your fault," Johnnie said as he held his mother as she cried in his arms.

Johnnie comforted her like he knew his father would have done. In his heart, he knew Sara was just a victim, and he refused to let her take the blame for the actions of a worthless man who couldn't treat a woman right. There was no way he was going to let his mother feel guilty over this piece of garbage that no longer existed. Johnnie was happy that he had killed him, knowing that Mike would never again hurt another woman or child.

"Anyways," Johnnie said with excitement in his voice as he was desperately trying to change this somber mood into the happy, joyful day that it was meant to be. "Today isn't about all of that past. Today is about new beginnings, and I am going to make the best of my life. There isn't going to be any more days like today. I need to look for some good work and get on with my future. But today, I want to enjoy my freedom as we celebrate it together. I have been gone three years, and there is so much that I have missed. I especially missed being out back at the camp with the trees all around me and the campfire lighting up the night as we all sit back and talk. It was a great feeling being able to be back there and sit and talk all night without the lights being turned off on me and being told to go to sleep, and then being able to wake up on my own without being told to wake up. What a wonderful feeling it is to be free to make my own choices and my own decisions again. I suppose I had never valued such things before until now."

"When you lose, something that you are accustomed to, I suppose it does make you appreciate them that much more," Sara injected as she briefly interrupted Johnnie's thoughts.

"Yes, you do, you really do. It was so refreshing to be able to be outside all day and then spend the night outside as well. Oh, how I had missed that. The fresh air surrounding you like that makes one feel so refreshed. When I was in there, we could only go outside for one hour a day, and I so missed being able to just sit and enjoy it without the thought of they will make us go back in soon. Often, I would take a deep breath yesterday just to take in the fresh air, it's so exhilarating. There is a calmness that comes with being able to get some fresh air that I don't think many people realize. But it does make one feel so much better when you're able to just take a deep breath of fresh air."

"Yes, I suppose it does. So I was thinking today, we could go to all the places that you love and maybe even take a short ride through the country. I know how much you love to go for a ride in the country and enjoy the scenery. Not much has changed since you've been gone. What kind of work were you thinking about looking for? I know you want to start up your own business. But you know the old man that owns the hardware store, Mr. Smith, he is looking for a good young man to help out around the store and do stock and things like that. Maybe that is something you would enjoy doing? He always seemed like a very friendly man, and I bet he is very easy to work for. If that was something that you were interested in while you get your own business going."

"Yeah, maybe. I will go and talk to him and see about it. I always remember how much respect dad had in the community because of the things he was able to do for people with his knowledge of fixing things. I remember when he had fixed the window at the hardware store free for Mr. Smith. Perhaps he will remember that and decide to give me a chance. But I would really like to try my hand at doing repairs like dad used to do. I will go to where Dad used to work and talk to Tom and see if he has any kind of advice for me. We don't have to do a whole lot today. I don't mind just spending the day talking or maybe watching a movie together. However, if we do go out to eat, I wouldn't mind going to the old diner that you used to take me to. They have the best hamburgers. Speaking of which, the hamburgers that Mr. Hilton cooked on the grill yesterday was so amazingly delicious. I have really missed his cookouts. All of the food was so good for that matter, especially the cake and brownies that you made for us. Everything was so good. The food that they feed us in there is less than one would expect. I don't know how they can even classify that as food to be honest. Pizza, that's what I have missed. Pizza and ice cream. There is so much I want to eat right now. But I suppose I better pace myself," Johnnie said laughingly as they both sat talking for a few more minutes before Sara decided she did want them to go out and do something today.

She missed their rides together and the things that they used to go do together. And Johnnie didn't really care what they did. He just knew that this was something that his mother needed, and he wanted to make sure that he spent time with her. He really missed her as much as she had missed him.

As they were driving, Johnnie was looking out the window as he always did, taking in all the beauty that South Bend Heights had to offer. There were a wide variety of trees and such an amazing assortment of flowers that made the whole scenery just breathtaking with the way the light blue sky blended into the background. The picturesque view was as if Johnnie was staring at a moving picture that had been painted. Every color was arrayed in such a splendid way that it was perfect. South Bend Heights was known for its woods and forest. There were many trails that one could enjoy getting lost in for days upon days as if it was never ending. There was no other place like it. It was mesmerizing to say the least.

Finally, they had reached downtown where everything was located. Everything was still the same with except for a few additions of course. While Johnnie was away, they had built a shopping mall. It was the first one ever in South Bend Heights. Johnnie was amazed at just how big it was.

"Can we go there? I would like to see what stores are inside of there if you don't mind. I didn't know that they had built this. It looks so big. I am sure they have so many different kind of stores inside."

"Yes, of course, we can go inside. This is one of the reasons I brought you into town as to show you all the new things that they have added. We can have lunch here also. Besides the many stores that they have built inside of here, there is also a huge food court with many different options. I know you wanted to go the diner, but perhaps you would like to try some of the food here instead." Sara explained as she and Johnnie had pulled in and was now walking into the huge building.

This was very exciting for Johnnie, he had no idea that South Bend Heights had grown this much in the past three years. There was a few other new places also that he had not yet seen. It was nice to come home to something fresh. Something new. It was good for Johnnie to be able to have a new experience that was positive. After looking through a few stores and just taking in the whole new experience, an excitement sprung up to Johnnie when he saw it.

"An arcade! Oh my goodness, look at how big it is and look at all the games and lights. We must go in and look around, Mom, can we please?" Johnnie asked as he had already started walking toward it.

"Yes, of course, we can. I knew you would want to check it out. This is one of the reasons why I brought you here," Sara explained as she walked faster to try to keep pace with Johnnie as he was already entering into the arcade. The sound of all the machines was very exciting to him.

"Finally, we have something like this here. I can't believe it. This is so amazing. I love it." Johnnie was wandering all over the place trying to look at every game, that he had not realized that Sara was no longer with him. She had gone to the counter to get some coins for him so he could play some games.

When she found him, he was standing in front of a racing game that you could sit in. Sara gave Johnnie a handful of coins, and as he put them in, the game began to move and shake. Johnnie had never seen anything like this before. As he played the game, it would rumble and vibrate with every crash and would move with every turn. Johnnie was so impressed with it that he played the game three times before Sara finally talked him into checking out some other games, and there were so many games that Johnnie had enjoyed that day before it was time to go and have lunch at the food court.

It was amazing to him that they had so many varieties of food choices in one place. He took his time and looked around seeing what he wanted to eat today, but it proved to be no easy task as there was so much to choose from. Being away for as long as he was and having to eat the kind of food that they served him there made making a choice even harder. Everything looked so good and smelled so delicious. Finally deciding on some Chinese food and some hot tea, Sara and Johnnie finally sat down to eat.

After a nice lunch together, Sara and Johnnie did some more looking around before finally heading out. She knew he was missing Tonya so rather than go see a movie at the theater, she had decided it would be nice to watch a movie at home with Johnnie and invite Tonya to come watch it with them. It was Johnnie's first full day at home, and Sara knew he would want to spend time with Tonya also, and she had no problem with that at all. It would be nice to finally do something with just the two of them.

Usually, Sara wasn't able to with all the others being around all the time. This was a good opportunity for them to enjoy a movie night just the three of them with some homemade popcorn and some candy that Sara had picked up on the way home from the gas station when they had stopped to get some gas. Sara wanted to make it a special time for the three of them, so she got a lot of different snacks.

After finally returning back home, Sara had asked Johnnie if he wanted to invite Tonya over for a movie, which he was more than eager to do. It was a nice evening that three of them had enjoyed together. Tonya stayed for a bit after the movie as the three of them sat and talked for a while. Rarely did the three of them ever get to just sit and talk without all the others around. But it was very nice, as the evening rolled into the night. After which Johnnie walked Tonya home and sat on the porch with her for a little while and talked. After some time, Steve came out and joined them.

"So much to get caught up on huh, bro?" Steve asked as he sat down with them on the porch.

"Yeah, there is, and I want to find some work soon. You all still have school, and I have nothing to do while I am waiting for you all to get home. So I am hoping to be able to work and make some money while you're at school, then we can all get together when we are all home. But I do want to get settled in first and get adjusted to being back home and all," Johnnie responded as Tonya sat smiling.

She knew Johnnie was thinking of their future and was wanting to get things settled soon, so he could start working. "Yeah, I understand that, bro, and it would be great to be able to make some money. I hope you find something good. Not much open right now I suppose, but I am confident that you will find some work somewhere, bro."

As they all sat talking about it, Johnnie couldn't help but think about his father and how it would be nice to be able to do what he did, but he associated construction work with his father's death so instead he wanted to do repairs in the community because he knew that had brought his father so much respect. But he kept that to himself for now. He wanted to first see if he could get some help from where his father used to work. Maybe they knew of some people who needed things done that they couldn't do or didn't have time to do. He didn't know much about it, but he still wanted to go talk to Tom and at least see if he would give him some guidance. He was also hoping that Mr. Smith could give him some direction as well. But that would be later, and for now, it was starting to get late, so Johnnie hugged and kissed Tonya good night before walking back home.

After coming back into the house, Johnnie found Sara still awake and waiting for him.

"Mom, you're still awake?" Sara turned off the television.

"Yes, I am, I didn't want to go to sleep without saying good night and thanking you for spending the day with me. I really needed that time with you, and I hope we can do it some more. It feels so good to have you back home and not have to be here all by myself."

Johnnie smiled. "It's so good to be home. I've missed everyone so much. It will take me a little bit of time to get settled in, but I am so happy to be home. The party was so nice also, Mom. Thank you so much for putting that together for me. I loved being able to see everyone and hang out with everyone; and the food was so good as well. Way better than the crap they give you in there, that's for sure. Anyways, I'm tired, and I think I'm going to go to bed. I love you, Mom," Johnnie said as he walked up the stairs and headed for his bedroom.

"I love you too," Sara responded before Johnnie got to the stairs. She was also tired and was ready to get some sleep. It had been a long eventful day for both of them.

Early the next morning as Johnnie arose from his sleep, it was different for him to wake up to such a quiet atmosphere. He laid there for a few minutes and just relaxed. Loving that he didn't have to get right up and get moving. He could take his time

327

and wake up a little bit before going downstairs to get some breakfast. As always, Sara was already awake and had breakfast going while she was letting Johnnie sleep a little longer. But he was soon up and on his way down to the kitchen to help make the toast as he had always done before. It was a great feeling for the two of them, just like old times. This is how it had always been, and it felt good to once again be able to help her with breakfast.

As breakfast was finally ready and they both sat down to eat, they began to discuss what exactly was the game plan for the day. Everyone was in school, and there was no one Johnnie could to hang out with. But he had given some thought to going down to Thomas Hiltons and spending some time talking to him if he was home. Thomas had wrote Johnnie letters while he was in the House and had often came and visited with him. Thomas was a huge encouragement to Johnnie when he was in there. He would often pull out some of the letters that he had received from Mr. Hilton when he needed to be encouraged during times when had he felt depressed or wanted to give up. Johnnie had written very little back to Thomas, but the few times he had, it was to thank him for the times of encouragement and express how he had needed that so much and was very thankful to receive such wonderful letters that helped to keep him focused. But that would have to wait. Thomas Hilton was gone to work, and Johnnie would have to find something else to do.

Sara was trying to think of things she could do to

help Johnnie during this time of adjustment. With all of his friends being at school, she feared that he would become lonely. But she did remember how he used to talk to her about the things he had read when she would come up and visit him. So she had decided that maybe a trip in town to the bookstore might be a good idea. Johnnie was all up for that. He had already been given some thought about getting some books to continue learning about wisdom and many other things.

Johnnie had become fascinated with things pertaining to the different wisdom and philosophies of other cultures since his time with Jason in the House. It was one of the greatest influences Jason had on him. When Sara had asked him if he wanted to go to the bookstore, Johnnie had perked right up and was very anxious to go.

Johnnie always loved the ride into town, it was always so beautiful no matter what time of the year it was. The scenery he had found to relax him and allowed him to drift off in his thoughts as Sara was driving. She never liked talking too much when she was driving, so it was perfect for Johnnie to enjoy the scenery as he sat and thought while enjoying the ride into town.

After arriving, they went into the bookstore and began to look around. So many books on so many topics. *There was so much one could learn from a bookstore.* As he looked around there were rows and aisles of different topics, and yet none of them argued about who was right or wrong. No books fought over another book being misplaced in their area. They all stayed quietly together, holding their knowledge for some suspecting reader to come and pursue what was inside. None yelling or shouting out, "Pick me! Pick me!" They all just sat there waiting.

Johnnie took his time looking through the many different sections before finally coming to the area that contained the books that he valued the most. Philosophy and wisdom, these were the books that he loved to read the most. He found himself intrigued by the thoughts and ideas of those who had been highly respected for their input into their own societies and cultures. He slowly walked down the aisle running his finger along the edge of every book, trying to find that one that would jump out at him catch his eye, or peak his interest. Till finally there it was. A book that he wanted to read. A book about the wisdom of past leaders, including such great men from past Presidents to former inventors. Men and women who had shaped the face of nations through the groundbreaking ideas that they had. This was the book that he wanted.

Sara knew he would read it, and then want some more, so she had encouraged him to pick out two or three books while they were there. After getting a few more books, they proceeded to the checkout area. Sara found his choices interesting. She knew this was a path that his father Mark had put him on when he was much younger, and after all he had been through, he was still pursuing it.

Mark was so full of wisdom, and was such a great thinker, and that was what made him so good at his job. He was always able to think outside the box and be very creative. Mark could have been anything that he had wanted to be, but he loved to build. It was what he loved to do. Mark always found that working with his hands brought more satisfaction to him than sitting at some desk or doing something else that was less physical. Mark loved hard work and loved the challenges that being in construction could bring. Many of the companies' projects was designed by Mark, and then he would be involved in the process of making it become a reality. For Mark, that was his greatest thrill. It was also why Mark had made so much money.

Johnnie was taking some time getting settled back in to being home. He had plans, but he wasn't rushing to jump into anything as of yet. He wanted to find some work to do, but for now, he just wanted to get readjusted to being home and spending time with his mom and friends. There were things around the house that needed to be done anyways, and so he began to work on things that needed to be fixed around the house, things that Sara was not able to do.

Sara had given Johnnie a list of things that needed to be done, and so he went around the house and checked everything out that was on the list and made a new list of all the things he would need from the hardware store. While he was there picking up supplies, this would be a great time to ask Mr. Smith if he needed any extra help. After he had made his list, Sara took him into town to the hardware store to get all the things that he needed. As he was looking around and getting everything, he saw Mr. Smith, the owner of the hardware store. So Johnnie went over to talk to him about a possible job there.

"Mr. Smith, hello, it's me Johnnie Steele. I do believe you used to know my father Mark Steele," Johnnie said as he shook Mr. Smith's hand.

"Yes, Johnnie, I know who you are, your father was a very good friend of mine. He was always so helpful when I needed something fixed, and he brought me a ton of business through the construction company. How have you been? It's good to see you back home now. I know you have been through a lot. I see you're picking up some supplies. Are you working on a project?" Mr. Smith responded.

"Yes, well, it's good to be home for sure, and yes, I am going to fix some things around the house. I was wondering, Mr. Smith, if by chance you had any work I could do for you? I am done with school and would like to earn some money. I don't know what all I can do, but I do know that I am a fast learner, and I do work very hard."

Mr. Smith paused for a few minutes as he was thinking if there was anything he could do to help Johnnie. "Well, Johnnie, I don't have any room here for you, I just hired a young man the other day, but I do have some things I haven't had time to get to, if you wouldn't mind doing some yard work or some painting for me?"

Johnnie was excited at the chance to make some money. "Yes, I sure would, Mr. Smith. Thank you very much. I really appreciate this. When can I start?" Johnnie asked.

"Well, just give me a call when you're all done fixing things for your mother, and we can set up a time for you to come. I mean it can be any time really. It's mostly outside work, and I can leave the garage door open for you."

Johnnie smiled. "That sounds great, Mr. Smith. I will call you tomorrow and work out all the details. Thank you again, Mr. Smith."

On the way home, Johnnie told Sara the good news about being able to make some extra money with Mr. Smith. Sara was very excited for Johnnie and was so very happy that he was able to at least get something that would help him out a little.

Once they had arrived back to the house, Johnnie wasted no time getting right on the chores that Sara had given to him. Johnnie found that he was a natural at fixing things as he began working around the house and doing little things that were just too hard or too complicated for Sara to do. There were a few screens that had holes in them that he was able to repair. And he fixed the leaky faucet by installing a new one. There were some old holes in the walls that needed to be patched and repainted from when Mike used to live there. He was very destructive and would often punch the walls when he was mad or upset, which was quite often. Johnnie took his time and fixed every one of them by patching them and sanding them before repainting it.

The next day, he got up early and took everything off the back deck and washed it down so that he could re-stain the whole deck. After it was dry and ready, he put a fresh coat of stain on it

333

and waited for it to dry as he called Mr. Smith like he had promised and worked out all the details for the work he had for him. After a few hours, Johnnie put another coat of stain on the back deck and then got cleaned up before Tonya and the group got out of school. Everything on the list was done, and the rest of the week he could focus on doing the yard work and the painting for Mr. Smith which was coming to a fast end.

It was Friday, and after a long week of working, the weekend was here, and Johnnie was excited to have some money for him and Tonya to be able to do something. Johnnie had worked late the past few days so that he could be done a bit early on Friday so he could get all cleaned up and collect his money before Tonya got home from school. So as he hurried home and got a shower and got ready for when Tonya would be home from school, he hurried over to the hardware store and collected his money from Mr. Smith. Johnnie wanted to surprise her with a date to the movies.

Once Tonya got home and did all of her homework, she called Johnnie who was anxiously waiting for her. They hadn't been on to many dates, and Johnnie was looking forward to it. When she called, Johnnie had asked her if she wanted to come over. After they talked for a few, he walked down to get her, and they walked back together, holding hands all the way back to Johnnie's house. When they got back, Sara was waiting for them, so she could drop them off at the theater.

Tonya was curious as to where they were going,

but Johnnie refused to tell her. Sara decided while she was there that she would take some time and go see a different movie and let Johnnie and Tonya have some alone time for their date. After both movies had finished, they all went back to Sara's where Johnnie and Tonya walked out back to the camp where they had found the rest of the gang hanging out. Being surprised, Johnnie asked what they all were doing there.

"Well, its Friday, Johnnie," responded George.

"Yeah, it's Friday, we are always here on Friday," added Darrell.

"Where are you two coming from?" asked Randy.

"Well, Tonya and I went to see a movie together," Johnnie said as he and Tonya sat down together in their usual spot on the log by the warm fire.

"How exciting. A date," Randy said as they all began to talk about the movie and other things.

Johnnie was happy to see the group, but at the same time, he was hoping for a nice quiet night with Tonya. Tonya, however, wasn't as pleased to see everyone. It wasn't often that she and Johnnie was able to spend any real alone time together, especially when it was unexpected. It was weird that they all just showed up when nobody was even home. Tonya had wanted what could have been a great romantic time for the two of them.

In the morning after a long night of talking and laughing, the boys all went home, while Johnnie walked Tonya home. After returning back to the house, he got cleaned up and ate breakfast.

Usually, Sara would have made breakfast for them all, but everyone left early. When Mr. Smith had paid Johnnie, he had asked him to let him know if he needed any more work done or if he knew of anyone who might need some things done to please let him know. Mr. Smith was always talking to his customers. He had a great relationship with everyone in town. So he had put Johnnie's name out there that he was looking for some work.

Mr. Smith was very well pleased with the job that Johnnie had done for him and was letting people know that he does good work. After a few days, some people came in and was talking about wanting someone to help out with some yard work and odd jobs around the house and yard. Mr. Smith was happy to recommend Johnnie for the work. He took everything that came his way no matter what it was, painting, yard work, or fixing things around the house. The more jobs that Johnnie received to fix things, the more he realized that he enjoyed doing that. No matter what it was, he always found a way to fix it.

Fixing and repairing things was so natural to him. There was a white picket fence that he had fixed and repainted and made it look like new, and everyone was very well pleased with his work and enjoyed his pleasant attitude. Johnnie was always so easy to talk to and very easy to work with. He enjoyed what he was doing and did it with a very positive attitude.

Johnnie was always so thankful for every job that came his way as he expressed his gratitude to his customers. This made everyone recommend him to where staying busy working became no problem at all. In fact, during the week, Johnnie was swamped with so much work that he had little time for anything else. Monday through Thursday, he worked long hours so that when Friday came, he wouldn't have to work late at all. He did this every week so that he could be ready for when Tonya got home from school.

When the weekends came, Johnnie was getting into the habit of buying them all pizza on Saturday nights when they all sat and ate back at the camp area. They had started calling it pizza and pop night. Johnnie was making good money working for everyone. During this time, he was really connecting with the people of the town and building a strong relationship with them. He was earning their trust very quickly. It was easy to see that he had the same characteristics that his father had, and many noticed it as they took a liking to him.

Many remembered Mark and how he always took time to lend a helping hand when he could. Johnnie was always going the extra mile and doing a little more than what his customers had asked him to do. His reputation continued to grow the more he worked and the more he took time to talk to the people he was working for.

Friday was always about taking Tonya out somewhere. It was important to make time for her. And she loved every minute of it. Johnnie would spoil her, and she ate it up. She loved that Johnnie liked to take her out every Friday. He had become so very much like Mark when it came to being romantic.

As the winter month came to a close and another summer was upon him. Johnnie was settled in to working for his customers, he knew that summer would be the busiest, time of the year and he wondered how he would balance it all out with Tonya not having school anymore. For now, he had been working late during the week until Fridays. He had given thought to seeing if Randy wanted to help him during the summer. Randy was always trying to stay busy, while Darrell was a bit more preoccupied with playing video games. Johnnie knew that work would be a lot busier during this summer, especially now that his reputation was growing. He could maybe work Randy a few days a week to keep from getting behind. George was too busy with Ann to want to do anything else right now, so Randy would be his first choice, and he was sure that he would take the job if asked, and the work orders was coming in fast and getting good help now was a priority.

Randy was eager to work for Johnnie and took the job immediately. Randy was proving to be a great worker and the two of them worked great together. Johnnie was happy that he had hired Randy and was even considering hiring Darryl at some point when the business grew a little more. But for now he only had enough work for him and Randy. This allowed Johnnie more time to spend with Tonya and less time working long hours. Randy was enjoying the opportunity being able to make money, and worked very hard for Johnnie.

The both of them had a lot of fun working

together. It was good having someone to spend the day with and having someone to talk to while they worked together. Johnnie loved not being alone all day working by himself, he would often feel a little lonely at times, but now he had Randy with him and it was working out great.

CHAPTER 15

The Park

School was finally out, and summer was here. Work was steady and going great. Randy was helping out every chance he got, and Johnnie tried to use him as much as he could without hurting his own income. They worked great together. Randy was as hard working as Johnnie had expected him to be. He was letting Randy do all the easy stuff like mowing and painting, while he was focusing more on fixing things, but he also would help Randy with the other things when it was a really big job. It was working out great. Randy was never any problem at all and did all that Johnnie had asked him to do. They were able to keep from having to work late and still got things done early on Fridays as Johnnie had hoped.

There was so much work for them because of the reputation that Johnnie had built up over the winter, and Mr. Smith had recommended him to so many people. And some of his other customers had done the same. He was able to get fifteen mowing jobs that was weekly whereas the painting was only once in a while. Fixing things was pretty steady for now though. Seems like something was always needing to be fixed. Landscaping side of things began to grow also, now that it was summer, there were weeds that needed to be taken care of and flowers needed to be planted as well. They even began to get some gardening jobs from a few of their customers that they mowed for, which was also needing to be done weekly.

Coming into the summer, Johnnie wanted to make some plans for him and Tonya. He was making pretty good money now and had been able to save quite a bit. Even with paying Randy pretty good, Johnnie was still making a lot of money. Tonya didn't care what they did just as long as they were together. It was nice being able to go out though. She especially loved being alone with Johnnie and not having the group with them everywhere they went. Now that they could go and have dates, they were spending more and more time alone together. Johnnie loved it too, there were things that he couldn't say to Tonya in front of everyone, and now, they were able to have private conversations. This alone time helped them to grow closer together and fall deeper in love with one another.

Johnnie was working hard to save up as much money as he could. It was his plan to ask Tonya to marry him after summer. He wanted to see how the work was going to hold up before he asked her to marry him. It was something that he had been thinking about while he was in the House and even more since he got these jobs.

As Johnnie awakened early the next day, it was a nice summer morning, the ski was clear, and the sun was shining. A perfect day to go for a stroll through the park. Something Johnnie and Tonya hadn't done before just the two of them. Many times, they went to the park with the group, but this time, it was just the two of them. Tonya came over, and Johnnie told her his plans for the day for the both of them. There was a nice small place right by the park that had great food. They could spend the whole morning together at the park and then grab some lunch together.

Once they got their plans set, Sara took and dropped them off at the park and then went back to the house to do some light cleaning. Sara loved to clean when no one was home. It allowed her to do stuff that normally she wasn't able to do.

While she was cleaning, Johnnie and Tonya was at the park enjoying their time together as they walked for a while before sitting on a nice bench and just holding hands and talking. There was a nice wooded area with several paths you could walk that they was going to do together after they sat for a bit and talked. It was so nice being alone together at the park.

After a little while, Johnnie took both of her hands and pulled her up as they walked toward the woods. This early in the day, there wasn't much going on in the park, so it seemed a bit secluded with the exception of a few families that were there together. The kids where playing on the playground area which was huge and had many different things for them to do. One family was set up in the picnic area while the other was over at the pavilion area with the grills. It was common to see people riding their bikes there on the bike trails. But today, it seemed a bit quiet. Usually by now, the park would have had many people in it. It was sure to fill up before lunchtime though.

Johnnie and Tonya walked slowly through the wooded area as they held hands and talked. There were so many trails to go down. Each branching off into a different area. As they took a long winding trail, they came to a small bridge that stretched out over a small pond that was full of fish and turtles. As they walked over the bridge when they got to the middle, Johnnie stopped and stood behind Tonya holding her as they looked over the side. He leaned in and brushed her hair back away from her neck as he kissed her cheek. Tonya turned around as they held each other and kissed. It was a very romantic spot where the two could take in the beauty of the secluded area and love on each other. The whole scene was so beautiful. The sounds of the running water mixed with the wind blowing through the trees. In this moment, they were lost in each other until the sound of a fish splashing out of the water caught their attention.

After a bit, they finished crossing the bridge. As they wandered along, coming to a quiet spot they stopped and paused as a few deer was standing just a bit off in the distance. They had not noticed them at first and had walked pretty close to them before stopping. Johnnie put his arm around Tonya as they stood there and watched the deer for a moment. As the deer took notice of them they ran off deeper into the woods as Johnnie and Tonya watched them while they began to walk again. There was so much life in these woods. It was common to see so many different kinds of animals as you walked the trails. Mostly small animals like chipmunks and rabbits, black squirrels, and different kinds of snakes. Most of the snakes here were small and harmless, not many venomous snakes here at all. It was pretty common to see a few while walking the trail. There were lots of small ponds and rivers that ran through the woods connecting them all together. Several miles away was a huge lake that the rivers ran off from.

After a long walk through some of the trails, they decided to go back and get some lunch. Across from the park were several stores and restaurants. The park was a busy place and businesses had built up all around it. Some of the best shopping and eating was along this road that stretched around the park. Many kids would go there to fly their kites and play sports. This massive park had everything from baseball diamonds to volleyball nets with a huge outdoor swimming pool. The play area was huge, having all kinds of swings and slides and monkey bars as well as forts with tunnels made out of plastic and wood. Johnnie always wanted to ride the bike trails, but never brought his bike here to do so. But the wood trails was his favorite. It was quiet and peaceful. Johnnie always enjoyed it by the water, that is where he found it the easiest for him to just relax.

At the restaurant, Johnnie and Tonya sat and talked as they both enjoyed a nice Italian meal. Both of them had ordered spaghetti with a meat sauce. Johnnie loved the bread sticks there, they were always soft and warm when they brought them to you. While they were eating, they discussed what else they wanted to do while they were in town.

There were so many little shops to go to and look around. There was everything from toy stores to clothing stores. It was a little too easy to spend money there. Johnnie loved the ice cream shop and the fudge shop that was right next to each other. It was a long walk if you wanted to go into every place and look around. There were benches all along the way, so one could sit down for a few minutes and relax during the long walk around the park way. The ice cream shop had a few benches, and some small tables and chairs set up outside. There was a small soda pop shop there that had many different kinds of flavors. Johnnie loved to go in there and get a soda pop, every time getting a different flavor. It was an old style shop with new machines, so you could get a fountain drink instead of a bottle.

Down along the way, there was a candy store with many unique kinds of candies as well as some regular kinds that most people was accustomed to. When you got to the clothing section, there was everything from a jean shop to a shoe store, including a shop of just hats.

Tonya was wanting to go into the dress shop. There was a very nice black dress that hung in the window that had caught her eye. She and Johnnie both went in to look around to see how much it was. After finally getting some assistance, the price was reasonable, so Johnnie bought it for her. After which they strolled on down to the T-shirt shop, where they had so many different kinds of shirts and even had shirts that you could customize if one wanted to.

Johnnie and Tonya had spent all afternoon looking in the shops after lunch until evening had come. They wanted to walk through the trails one more time before heading home. They had never walked through there during the evening time. It was beginning to get a little dark out as the sun was starting to go down. They both wanted to see what it looked like at night as the trail was lit up with small lamps. The lights on the bridges lit up the water just enough to make it look real pretty. Tonya had almost wished that she had waited to buy the dress so that she wouldn't have had to carry it with her along the trail.

As they were walking and talking, Tonya had asked when Sara was coming to pick them up. But Johnnie had told his mother that they would have a ride back home. Johnnie was planning on staying out late with Tonya and didn't want his mom to have to come out late to get them. Before they had left, Johnnie had already called a cab service and made sure that they would be able to assist him when he was ready to go home. After writing the number down, he made sure that he had change for the pay phone that was still in the park. This way, they could stay as long as they wanted without having to be on a time frame. There was no work to get up to and no school for Tonya to get up to, and no reason to hurry home tonight. So far, everything had gone according to plan, but all of this walking through the day had left them a little tired. Johnnie had begun to think that maybe they shouldn't have come here so early and was thinking that next time, they won't come until a little before dinnertime.

As they both continued to walk and talk together, they both began to feel hungry again. They had not eaten dinner, but they did have a big lunch and dessert as well as lots of snacks from some of the shops that they had went to.

By now, it was starting to get real dark, and Johnnie felt that it was time to start heading back. On their way back to the main park area, Johnnie and Tonya heard a noise off in the distance. It sounded like other people, which was common for this trail, so they both blew it off. As they kept walking, the sounds not only got closer but seemed to be scattered all around them. This began to make both of them a bit nervous. There was never any reports of anything ever happening to anyone out here, so Johnnie played it cool as they kept walking, not letting on to the fact that he was a bit nervous. The sounds didn't seem right to Johnnie, there was something going on, and he could feel it. Something about the way the sounds were just didn't seem or feel right to him or Tonya. They were pretty deep into the trail and had a long way to go before they would be back in the main area. Johnnie had learned to trust his instincts, and he could feel that something was about to happen.

As they walked over the bridge and was heading down the trail to the main trail that would lead them back to the main park area, Ricco and Wayne stepped out in front of them. When Johnnie turned to look behind him, he saw Sal and Tye coming across the bridge to where they were. *Crap!* Johnnie knew they were trapped in between the two.

As they slowly walked down the trail, Johnnie's mind was racing as he was trying to figure a way out of this. As they got closer to where Ricco and Wayne were, Sal and Tye had closed the gap that was between them. Then Jay and Martin stepped out on one side as Matias and Alejandro stepped out from the right side. Johnnie knew he was boxed in with no way of escape. He was more concerned with Tonya than his own self. He wasn't quite sure what these guys would do to her. Tonya could handle herself, but there were eight guys and only her and Johnnie. There was no way he would be able to hold them all off while she got away.

As they got closer, Johnnie begin to talk to Tonya. "As soon as this starts, just take off running. I will do what I can to hold them off."

Tonya squeezed Johnnie's hand tight. "I'm not leaving you. I didn't take years of martial arts to run from these low life losers," Tonya responded.

As they were about to meet, Ricco and Wayne stopped and waited for Johnnie and Tonya to get to them.

"Well, look what we have here. If it isn't our old friend Johnnie. How are you, Johnnie? I was

348

thinking about you the other day and here you are. How amazing is that. And look, you even brought your plaything with you," Ricco said.

"Our new plaything you mean, Ricco. I've been wanting her for a while. I think it's time to take her for a spin, don't you think?" Wayne added.

"You here that, Johnnie? I think Wayne and the boys want to have some fun with your plaything? How do you feel about sharing her with us?"

Johnnie took a deep breath. "You touch her, and I will never stop coming for you until you're dead."

Tonya began to get even more nervous when she realized what they were planning on doing to her. "You touch me, and you will regret it."

Ricco and Wayne both chuckled as Sal and Tye both grabbed Tonya from behind. Johnnie tried to help Tonya fight them off her when he was hit by Jay and Martin. Tonya wasn't able to fight them off because they had grabbed her from behind. Sal had grabbed her legs while Tye had his arms around her. At the same time, the other four guys began to beat Johnnie down until he could no longer fight back.

While Matias and Alejandro held Johnnie down, the others took Tonya down to the ground, and Ricco and Wayne began to rip her clothes off while Jay and Martin held her down. Tonya was trying to fight them off while Matias and Alejandro held Johnnie's head up as they made him watch what they were doing to Tonya. Johnnie struggled to try to get free but was not able to fight any longer as his strength had left him from the beating he had taken.

349

Johnnie looked on with tears streaming down his face as he watched each one take a turn on Tonya as they all raped her. It was more than Johnnie could bear to hear Tonya screaming as she begged them to stop.

"Look at her, Johnnie, I think she likes it. I knew she wanted it," Wayne mockingly said to Johnnie. After a while, Wayne and Ricco came over and grabbed Johnnie so that Matias and Alejandro could take their turn on Tonya as well. Ricco made sure that everyone raped her. Johnnie's heart sunk as he watched them all laugh and spit on her as they were all having their way with her. An hour went by before they were finally done raping Tonya. During the whole time, they would occasionally hit Johnnie some more just for fun.

When they were done with her, they all walked off laughing and joking about it. Ricco yelled back to Johnnie as they were walking off, "You can have her back now, Johnnie, she wasn't that good after all."

Tonya laid there crying, and she was curled up on her side as Johnnie fell to the ground when they had let him go. He crawled his way over to Tonya and tried to cover her as she told him not to touch her. After what seemed like forever, Tonya was able to get back to her feet and put her clothes back on. Her shirt was ripped, and there were no buttons left to keep it closed. Johnnie was trying to help her, but she kept pulling away from him.

"I will call an ambulance for you," Johnnie said.

"No! I just want to go home, take me home!" Tonya responded.

"I will call a cab for us when we get back to the main area." Tonya was being very harsh with Johnnie.

"I don't want you to call a cab for us. Just walk me home, Johnnie."

Johnnie wasn't sure what to do at this point. It was a long walk home and would take a few hours to get there if they walked.

"Baby, it will take us forever to get back if we walk," Johnnie explained to her.

"I don't care, Johnnie, I said I'm walking." Tonya refused to do anything other than walk.

Johnnie had no other choice but to walk her home, which took two and half hours. At first, Johnnie tried to talk to Tonya, but she was clear that she did not want to talk to him at all. So the rest of the way home, it was a very silent walk home. Johnnie didn't know what to say or do. His body hurt so badly from the beating he had taken. But he stayed with Tonya until he got her home.

Once they reached Tonya's home, she went straight in and went to her room and cried herself to sleep. She was so exhausted just from all the walking they had done today, let alone all she had to endure as she was repeatedly raped by the gang.

Johnnie walked home and cleaned himself up before going to his room as he laid there all night thinking about how he was going to kill each one of them for what they had done to Tonya. All night, Johnnie laid there without a trace of sleep as he was crying and thinking about how he would get his revenge for what they had done.

The next day as Johnnie decided to get up and

take a shower, when he came down, Sara panicked as she saw that Johnnie was a mess. "Johnnie, what happened to you? Are you okay?" Sara said as she grabbed Johnnie and was trying to look him over.

"I'm fine, Mom," Johnnie said as he pulled away from her.

"Tell me what happened, who did this to you?" Sara asked.

Johnnie sat down on the couch as Sara sat next to him and began to explain the whole situation to Sara about how they had beat him up and raped Tonya. Sara began to cry as Johnnie told her everything.

Afterwards, Johnnie walked down to see if Tonya was okay. When he got there and knocked on the door, Tonya's mother, Tammy, answered the door.

"Johnnie, she doesn't want to see you," Tammy said to him.

"Please, Mrs. Flowers, I just need to see her and know that she is okay," Johnnie said as he was almost ready to start crying again.

Tammy could see his eyes tearing up. "Please, Johnnie, just go home. She doesn't want to see you," Tammy said as she shut the door.

As Johnnie began to walk home, Steve came out and chased after him. "Johnnie, wait. I know what happened last night. Are we going after them?" Steve asked him.

"Yes. I am going after all of them. And this time, I'm not stopping until every last one of them are dead. I am done playing with them. They will all pay for what they did to Tonya," Johnnie explained as he was fighting back tears.

"I am with you, my brother. All the way. We will make them pay for this," Steve said as he hugged Johnnie.

"Thank you, Steve. I have to go away for a few weeks. I will be back, and when I do, we will get together and discuss how we are going to handle this."

Steve looked confused. "What do you mean, Johnnie? Going where?" Steve questioned.

"I am going to go see some friends that can maybe help us. I will explain everything when I get back."

Steve nodded in agreement. "Okay, my brother, be careful. I will be waiting for you to get back."

Johnnie walked back home as they both parted for now. Shortly after Johnnie walked in the door, Sara heard him on the phone with someone. The rest of the day, Johnnie stayed in his room and didn't talk to anyone.

The next day, Johnnie was up early and getting himself together. After breakfast, he grabbed a bag with some clothes in it as he told Sara that he would be back in a few days or so.

"Wait, Johnnie. Where are you going?" As Johnnie turned around and answered his mother. "I have to go meet some people, and I don't really know when I will be back. I will see you as soon as I can, Mom."

Sara was not pleased with his answer. She wanted to know where he was going and who he was meeting. But Johnnie was not giving her very much information. Sara was very worried. She knew that Johnnie might be going to do something that wasn't good. She was afraid of what he might be doing after what had happened to Tonya. Sara knew that it was very unlikely that Johnnie would let this go. She knew her son all too well. She knew it was only a matter of time before he went after them.

Sara sat down on the couch worrying as she watched Johnnie walk out of the door. Johnnie hurried down to where the bus stop was. He had to time it right, it only came through here every few hours, and he didn't want to be sitting there that long waiting for the next one to come. After getting on the bus, Johnnie found an empty seat toward the back where he could sit alone and just stare out of the window. The ride seemed like it took forever. This was a ride that Johnnie didn't want to take, but here he was in a place where he felt he had to. Johnnie was heading to West Bend Heights to meet up with Ricky Mack, the leader of the West Dragons. This meeting was to get help on fighting against Sisko and the Hells Sinners. If anyone would be willing to help out in this situation, it would be the West Dragons. Johnnie knew all too well how much they hated the Hells Sinners. Perhaps they could benefit from each other.

Johnnie was quite aware of the fact that the West Dragons wanted the territory that the Hells Sinners was occupying. Johnnie and Ricky became good friends while being in the House together. Ricky had asked Johnnie before about joining them, but Johnnie knew he wasn't a gang member, and even though he was on his way to meet them, he still didn't want to join them. But he was hoping to work out some kind of partnership.

After finally arriving, Johnnie had set up a meeting place at the park, so it would be less complicated for him to find them. Viper was already there waiting for him. He was Johnnie's contact man. It was his job to meet up with Johnnie and bring him back to the club house.

"Hey, Cypher, how are you doing? I was surprised when I was told that I would be meeting you here. I wasn't expecting to ever be bringing you back to the club house. So what brings you here?" Viper asked as he was very curious as to why Johnnie was here.

"I came to talk some business with Ricky. I think maybe we can help each other out," Cypher responded as they began their walk to the club house, talking all the way as they went.

Johnnie didn't say much to Viper about exactly why he was here. Although Viper was quite curious and full of questions, Cypher didn't say much about it, as he kept trying to change the subject with his own set of questions. But it was all too obvious that someone had beaten him up pretty bad. He was curious about how the gang was doing and if they had any problems with the Hells Sinners.

"Oh, well, you know, Cypher, that's always a problem. The feud between us will never end until one of us is completely wiped out altogether, which might be real soon to be honest with you, Cypher. Ricky is growing tired of them, and the territory they cover is good ground for us. We can make a ton of money once we eliminate them and gain that ground for ourselves. This long standing feud has gone on for so long that fighting between us just seems all too natural. But it is our plan to one day be on the top and see them no longer existing. The day is coming, Cypher, I can feel it getting closer."

Cypher smiled as he listened to Viper talk. "That day may be closer than you think, Viper. And the sooner we get to the club house, the sooner we can discuss some things that just might make your day a little better."

"Sounds good, Cypher. I'm guessing now I know why you're here. We are almost there, just across the way a bit, and we are at the club house."

Cypher nodded. "Not a bad little walk was much closer than I had expected to be honest. Ricky said it was a short walk, but I did expected it to be a bit longer than it was."

"No, bro, this park is our territory. We make a lot of money in here. The park is good business for us. Anyway, there's the club house, Cypher."

As they got to the club house and walked in, Cypher was taken by surprise at how many people were there. He was expected a meeting with just Ricky, but the place was packed with members.

"Cypher, my brother. Come in and meet everyone. This is my core group right here. My leaders, the one who make sure things get done. You know Viper and Cobra from your time with us in the House with us. This is Snake, he infiltrates places where we need an inside man. This is

Mainframe, he can do wonders with a computer, especially with a credit card. But he can hack anything. This is Killswitch, he can shut down any system, no matter what kind of alarm it has. This is Auto, there isn't any car in America that he can't steal. He's fast too. This is Newsfeed, he monitors everything, from rival gangs, places and people and tracks people's movements and everything concerning buildings that we just happen to be watching. This is Joe the Pimp, we call him Pimp for short. He handles all the ladies. And this is Trailblazer, this guy right here is one of our main soldiers. He leads the way every time we go out on a hit or go to war. You will meet everyone else as we go along, but this is the main core group."

"Well, it's nice to meet everyone, I guess you all know who I am already."

"Yeah, they do, Cypher, the real question is why are you here?"

"Okay, Ricky, can we maybe take a walk and talk for a bit while I explain this whole thing to you?"

"Yeah sure, Cypher. Cobra, you got the house while I am gone."

As Cypher and Ricky Mac went to talk alone in private, Johnnie explained everything to him.

"Cypher, they have done so much to you and your friends. You want revenge I understand that, but how can we help you in this matter? I mean what exactly are you looking to do? You have made it clear many times that you would never join any gang."

"Yes, Ricky, that is very true, and that still stands

357

to this day. But I was wondering if you would be willing to form a temporary partnership? Just until this is done."

"Very interesting, Cypher. Are we talking with just you or are there others coming with you?"

"There will be others coming with me. There will be at least five of us all together."

"Five extra people to help us knock of the Hells Sinners? Are they cool? I mean you would have to bring them here for us all to meet them. They would have to be around us for a bit, so we can all get to know each other."

"Yes, I do understand that, and that is why I am here. I need to feel everyone out and get to know them as much as they need to get to know me as well."

"Yes, you had mentioned that on the phone, how long were you wanting to stay for?"

"Maybe two weeks to a month."

"Yeah, okay, we can do that, and then you go back and bring them to us, so we can all get acquainted."

"That was my exact plan."

"Okay, Cypher, we do this, and when it's over, you all go back to your own place, and we take over their territory and add it to ours."

"What you do with their territory is completely up to you, I just want them gone once and for all."

"Sounds good to me, Cypher. We have a deal."

Cypher and Ricky shook hands to signify their agreement. Cypher was now a temporary West Dragon. As the week went on, Cypher went on a few rides with some of the gang to get a good look at how they do things before making a move to hit rival gang. Trailblazer took Cypher with him on a few hits to make sure he was really ready for this war they were about to engage into. Smooth J and HK (Hit Killer) rode with them as they popped some shots off at some rivals who had crossed over into their territory. This was a little more than Cypher had expected, but he was willing to do whatever he had to do at this point to end this feud once and for all, even if it meant having to kill whoever to get the job done. This time, it was serious, and there would be an end to Wayne and Sisko even if it meant killing the whole group.

These hit rides left Cypher feeling exhausted from the stress it caused him each time he went out. He hated all of this and couldn't wait till this was done. Every day, he was spending more time with the core group talking about what they wanted to do to hit the Hells Sinners so hard that they wouldn't be able to recover.

Afterwards, he would go off with other members and do different things to get to better acquainted with them and what they do on a daily basis. Cypher wanted to know everything, all the ins and outs of what it took to make a gang successful so that he would have a better idea of how to bring a successful gang down.

At night, when Cypher was alone in the bedroom that he was staying at is when he would lay and think about everything from the day and would go over everything in his head and try to figure out how he wanted to handle these things and mentally prepare himself for what laid ahead for him. He had so many ideas that he went and got a few notebooks and some pens and began making notes of what he learned and how he was going to use this knowledge to his advantage. Documenting everything from every day helped Cypher to better process his thoughts.

Cypher was learning everything from the top to the bottom, even spending time with foot soldiers learning their daily routine as well. After the first week was over, he had a better understanding of how everything ran and operated. It was much more than he had thought. It was more complicated how the structure was built than he had expected.

At first, coming into this, he thought it was just one boss at the top telling the rest what to do. But it wasn't anything like that at all, it was built like a business. Everyone had a job and responsibilities. Everyone was responsible for making sure they did their jobs right. And if they didn't, the consequences was served because the whole organization depended on it; and if one person slipped up, it could bring the whole group down. Everyday lives in the group was at stake. And Cypher was in the middle of everything, learning every piece of the puzzle as to what it takes to maintain and keep things running smooth on a daily basis. He would go out every evening on patrol with a few hitters that made sure no other rival gang was in their territory.

The next week came with a little more of proving time for Cypher. It was time for them to see if he could handle what it was going to take by sending him out on a hit where he would be the shooter. It was late at night and very dark. The car lights were off as they crept through the hood of a rival gang. Riding in a car that Auto had stolen earlier that morning. Slow riding as they crept up on a set where the Mob Killas hung out. That was MKs for short. It wasn't a very strong gang, but they were growing, so Ricky felt it might be good to take out some of their members to keep the gang from growing in the hopes of also keeping others from wanting to join. This was common for the bigger gangs to do this to the smaller gangs as to keep from allowing the smaller gangs to become a serious threat.

The next morning as Cypher was meeting with the main core group as he did every morning, he had a few things that he wanted to say to Ricky.

"Good morning, Cypher. How did you sleep after last night?" Ricky asked him as he walked into the room and sat down.

"I slept good. Thank you for asking. Before we start, if you don't mind, Rick, I have a few things I want to say this morning."

"Yeah, sure, Cypher go ahead."

Cypher began to speak as he looked around the table at the rest of the leaders. "I have more than proven myself over the past week and especially last night. But I have no problems or issues with any other gang. My issues is with the Hells Sinners only. I have done all that you have asked of me, but now, I am only going to focus on getting the Hells Sinners. These other gangs I have no problem with, they have done nothing to me. I know you wanted to see if I could do it. Well, I can. All I want now is the Hells Sinners."

"Fair enough, Cypher. You have proven yourself. When are you going back to talk to the rest of the group that you are wanting to bring along with you?" Ricky asked him.

"Well, I was thinking maybe going back next week, and sit down with my group and go over some things and then bring them to meet everyone. When do you plan on putting all of this into action?"

"As soon as you are comfortable enough to go back and bring your people here. Then we will go over everything and make the first hit."

"Okay. I will stay here for the rest of the week and get more acquainted with everyone then go back home and get them ready."

"Are you sure they will want to do this?" Ricky asked.

"Yes, I am. They are tired of this almost as much as I am. We all want them gone. This has gone on long enough, and what they did, they must pay for it. They have taken it too far now, and we are going to make them answer for it."

"Sounds good, Cypher. Now let's get down to business. We need to address some other concerns."

As Cypher sat there listening, he felt in his heart that he needed to prepare the rest of the group quickly for what they were about to do. He didn't feel right about all of this, but at this point, he didn't see any other option. He missed everyone. He knew his mother was home worrying about him, and he wanted to get back to her and make sure she was okay.

In the meantime, his business was being taken care of by the two brothers. He had instructed them to split the money and only set aside fifty percent for him, which was pretty good money for the two brothers. They were working hard trying to keep up because Cypher was a good worker, and he worked fast; and the two brothers weren't able to work as fast as Cypher did.

After the finish of the second week, Cypher packed his things and was getting ready to go back home. Ricky had offered to get Cypher a ride back home, but he wanted to take the bus so that he could have time to sit and think as he rode back home. On his way to the bus stop, as Johnnie had just crossed a street in front of an ally, he heard a voice come from behind him saying his name.

"Hey, Johnnie." Johnnie startled as he turned around to see who had called his name. "I thought you would come to see me while you were in town."

"I wanted to, my friend, but I just didn't have time. I was here trying to get some things together," Johnnie responded, thinking how he had really wanted to see him.

"Are you heading back home now?" he asked him.

"Yes, I am, but I will be back soon, and with some of my friends. I needed Ricky's help with the Hell's Sinners."

"Yeah, I know, Johnnie. I know everything. My hands are tied as far as what I can do, but I am here, my brother, and I will be watching everything that goes on."

Johnnie felt a bit more relieved. "Thank you, my brother. I always appreciate your help. I have to go, but I will stay in touch for sure. I promise. Besides the fact that, I didn't know you were out yet."

"I just got out a little while ago and already back to handling my business. But I will be watching, Johnnie. You can bet on that. Anything I can do, I will."

"Yes, thank you, my friend. I know I can trust you. I have to go, or I will miss this bus, see you later though."

"Okay, Johnnie, see you soon."

Johnnie just made it to the bus stop as the bus was arriving. A minute or two later and he would have missed it altogether. Johnnie sat down and was staring out the window as his mind drifted off all the way back home. He didn't even notice any of the other passengers as he just stared out, looking through the trees as the bus was passing by them. He was oblivious to anything that was going on around him as he sat looking out the window and thinking, looking at the forest as they passed by it until finally reaching his destination. It was a short walk home, and Johnnie was happy to be making it. After a few weeks of being gone, he was ready to get back home and get everyone else caught up to speed. After arriving back home, Johnnie had called the group to let them all know that he wanted to meet with everyone tonight back at the camp.

After he got off the phone, Sara made him something to eat. While he sat eating with Sara, they were talking about his future. Sara wanted to help put thing into perspective so that Johnnie wouldn't lose his focus on his goals. After finishing eating, Johnnie went to the camp area and then walked back to the water pond and sat to think while he waited for the rest to show up. He sat there for a few hours and went over in his head everything that he wanted to say. He loved these guys, and he struggled with bringing them into this war. But he knew they would have it no other way. Not after everything that has happened over the years.

Finally, it was time as Johnnie got up and walked back to the camp area. As he got closer, he could hear everyone there talking. He paused for a minute and just listened. Hearing them talk about it reassured him that there was no way they were going to stay out of it. Finally taking a deep breath, he stepped out into the camp area. Everyone stopped talking and looked up at him.

"So what are we going to do, Johnnie?" Darrell had asked.

"Yeah, Johnnie, what are we doing bro? Are we going after them, did you get help from those other guys?" Steve asked as they all sat looking at Johnnie.

Johnnie took a long look around the camp at everyone, looking into their eyes. Seeing that they were all ready for this. "We are going to end this once and for all," Johnnie responded.

Everyone stood and cheered as they were all

wanting revenge for this. "We have a great group backing us. They want it also."

"Man, that's great, Johnnie, when do we go?" Randy asked as the rest quieted down to hear Johnnie's response.

"I am going to go back one more time and make sure they are ready. Then we are all going there to meet them," Johnnie said to them and then explained all that he had learned while he was there.

After they all had talked about it Johnnie said, "We will end this once and for all."

The rest of the night was spent talking about what was going to happen. Before ending the night, the last thing Johnnie said was, "Well, this is it. We are going to war.

Robert Thomas would like to thank the following:

I would like to thank the following...God for giving me the talent and creativity to be a writer. I like to thank God for the completion of this book. All my family members and friends who believe in me and support my work
My wonderful Mother Martha Thomas
My brothers Eugene, John and Matt
My wonderful Sister Stacey Staimpel - for encouraging me and pushing me to get this book completed - I love you very much Sis
My amazing nephew Zach
My niece Christan Thomas
My sister in law Crystal
My best friend David Manning
Racquel Reid Grandison - without you this series and future books would not have been possible. Thank You Rac, love you always my friend
Cynthia Hatcher and everyone at Hatchback Publishing LLC
My uncle Bob and Aunt Cheryl, Kevin and Lisa
The rest of my nephews and cousins
Everyone who has encouraged me:
Ashley Morris (Thank you for your love and support. I love you so much)
Eddie and Bertha Vikolin, Stacey Staimpel
Lester Haynes Jr. (Slimwonderdarainman),
Shannon Smithman, Bobby Dansby, Robert Latson (The Car Guy),
Reginald Upshaw, Jake and Joey
My Sister Kristy and all of those in the U.K.

Everyone in Jamaica and all my Family and friends in Malaysia
All my fans in Canada and across North America
All of Asia especially Taiwan, the Philippines and Thailand.

Thank you to everyone who purchased this book. God bless you all. Thank you so much for all of your love and support.

ABOUT THE AUTHOR

Robert Thomas is an aspiring writer who was born and raised in Flint Michigan. Robert has a background in leadership and mentorship. Robert is an Author, Poet and Song Writer. He is also an art enthusiast who loves Art Galleries, Museums as well as Nature walks, fishing and camping. He has worked in various manufacturing plants as well as becoming a floor care specialist before pursuing his writing career.

You can find Robert on Facebook @ Robert Thomas Authors Page, where he posts upcoming projects as well as links to other things pertaining to reading and inspiring videos.
You can also follow him on Twitter Robert Thomas @ camarothomas